SLEIGHT OF HAND

Laura Resnick

A KISMET® Romance

METEOR PUBLISHING CORPORATION

Bensalem, Pennsylvania

KISMET® is a registered trademark of Meteor Publishing Corporation

First Printing July 1993.

ISBN: 1-56597-075-6

Printed in the United States of America.

To Grandma Cain, because no one
has ever been kinder.

LAURA RESNICK

Bestselling, award-winning author Laura Resnick has
published ten contemporary romance novels under a
pseudonym. She loves to travel and, shortly after
completing **Sleight of Hand,** she left for a seven
month overland trip across the African continent. She
hopes to return alive and well, in order to write more
books for Meteor.

ONE

There was no mistaking the woman's profession. She wasn't any ordinary streetwalker though. He was sure of that.

He spotted her on Broadway as he walked up the west side of the avenue and she walked up the east side. She chose to window-shop for a moment as he waited for the light at Broadway and Forty-second Street to change, and that was how he caught up with her. She glanced at her slim wristwatch as he crossed the noisy street.

She set off at a more hurried pace then. She must be late for a . . . a client? An appointment? A customer? He wondered what she would call it.

He walked at a more idle pace than she, since he was early for his own appointment. But his legs were long, and her heels were high and narrow, so he always seemed to stay within a few yards of her on the crowded street.

He didn't mind having found something beautiful to look at. New York City had always struck him as distinctly unappealing. No matter how many times he came here, a country boy like him would always find it stifling, filthy, gray, and unfriendly.

He wondered if she was a native. She looked slightly foreign, a little exotic, but he knew that New Yorkers often did. She was petite, perhaps five three. In those

7

perilous heels, she would come a little closer to his height of six feet. She walked on them with care, setting each foot down firmly, toes pointed straight ahead, but she was extremely graceful and didn't appear to be in danger of toppling off them.

After several blocks, she turned and entered an office building. He glanced up at the address, and his brows rose in surprise. This was also his destination.

He followed her through the lobby and slipped into her elevator just before the doors swished shut, locking the two of them in together.

"What floor?" she asked. Her voice was low and melodic, smooth and pleasant.

"Twenty-five," he answered.

Her brows arched slightly as she pressed a button for the twenty-fifth floor. He noticed it was the only one she pressed. Were they actually visiting the same offices? His curiosity about her expanded.

Thick, rich, glowing, red hair tumbled smoothly around her face and shoulders. Her skin was pale and creamy and absolutely flawless. Her eyes were wide and slanted slightly upwards at the corners. They were a stunning, vivid blue color, shot through with sparks of emerald green. He had never seen such beautiful eyes. They were without a doubt the most lovely feature of a very lovely woman.

She was perfectly proportioned everywhere, slim without being skinny, voluptuous without being plump. And her dress emphasized everything about her that was female and mysterious. A delicate concoction of black silk and lace, it snuggled tightly over her full breasts, hugged her narrow waist, and slid intimately around the smooth curve of her hips. The slits in the material, which exposed one shapely thigh and a considerable amount of midriff, were positively indecent.

He loved her dress.

He was about to tell her so when it occurred to him that she would think he was coming on to her. Did he want to come on to her? As beautiful as she was, he gave it some thought before deciding against it.

The elevator came to a jarring halt on the fifteenth floor. The woman jiggled slightly when she fell against the wall, and the sight nearly banished his resolve to stay silent around her.

Two elderly women looked into the elevator, did a double take when they saw her, and then mumbled something about waiting for the next elevator.

The doors swished shut again. He saw her mouth curve slightly, and he wondered if she often endured that kind of insult. She looked more amused than embittered.

All the same, if he tried to compliment her, even flirt with her a little, she would probably become business-like—either name a price or tell him she was booked for the day. And that would destroy the love-goddess aura that seemed to surround her. Besides, she would resent his wasting her time. He had never paid for a woman's company and certainly didn't intend to start now, not even for her.

The doors opened on the twenty-fifth floor. Remembering the manners his grandfather had drilled into him, he gestured for the lady to go first.

Alicia Cannon looked at the man from under her thick lashes for just a moment. He must be a nice guy, she thought, because he had managed to study her—surreptitiously, but unmistakably—all the way up to the twenty-fifth floor without making her feel embarrassed or uncomfortable. This was the first time she had ever left the theatre dressed like this, and she had found men's stares either lustful or contemptuous as she walked along. This man's gaze was flattering and curious, but also polite and respectful. A nice combination, she admitted to herself.

She walked past him, and then some devil inside, perhaps a residual characteristic of the role she was currently playing, made her turn to face him. Surprised at herself, she touched him lightly under the chin with one forefinger, and then winked coyly at him as she pivoted to walk away.

Out of the corner of her eye, she could see his dumbfounded expression change to a broad grin which swept slowly across his face. He shook his head and then followed after her.

Much to her surprise, he wasn't going to one of the other two offices on the same floor, but to her destination: Slade and Jackson Associates, Talent Agents. He opened the door for her and followed her inside.

"A bit overdressed today, aren't we?" said the receptionist dryly.

Ally Cannon propped her leg up on the desk, leaned forward, arched her back, and said in a low, seductive voice, "Tell Monty I'm here. He'll want to see me."

It had been a running gag between her and the staff of the talent agency during the six months she had been playing a prostitute in an off-Broadway production.

Playing along, the secretary said, "Monty said you're to go right in. I'll hold all calls."

Hips swaying beneath her uncomfortably tight dress, Ally started down the hallway.

Behind her, she heard the secretary say, "Can I help you, sir?"

"What? Oh . . . I have an appointment. I'm a little early."

His voice was gorgeous, like the rest of him. Ally wondered if he was an actor. He looked more California than New York. He was tall, slim, well muscled beneath his blue jeans and cambric shirt, with thick, curly, honey blond hair and warm, dark brown eyes. If she had been dressed like a normal person, she might have tried to be a little friendlier. However, dressed as she was, he would have probably jumped to erroneous conclusions.

"Well, if it isn't my favorite little tramp," said Monty Jackson wryly as she sat down before him. Her squirming made him frown. "What's wrong, Ally?"

"It's so hard to find a comfortable position in this dress," she said. "And this wig itches."

"Yes, I can imagine."

"I dashed over right after the matinee—the wardrobe

mistress will kill me when she finds out—and I have to eat and be back for the evening performance in an hour," Ally said hurriedly. "You wanted to see me?"

Monty nodded.

"Is it about Roland Houston?" she asked eagerly.

Monty nodded again. For three months they had known that Roland Houston, the writer-director, was preparing to make a film out of the novel *Grass in Heaven*. It was a strong, uncompromising story of inner-city poverty. One of the supporting roles in the movie would be the part of Rainy, the tough young woman who died trying to help the hero realize his dream of finding a place where they could live in peace and safety, a place with plenty of green grass to walk on.

Ally had dreamed of playing that part ever since she had first read the book. When she heard that Roland Houston was turning it into a movie, she was determined to seize her chance. When she learned that her agent, Monty, had dealt with Houston several times before, it seemed that everything was going her way. All she needed now was to meet the man, talk to him, read for him. She wanted the part so badly, she would willingly blow what was left of her meager savings on a plane ticket to Los Angeles to meet with him if necessary.

Ally frowned suddenly, aware that Monty did not look like a man about to deliver good news.

"Does he want to see me?" she asked hopefully.

"I hate this," Monty said, and stood up abruptly. He turned away and looked out the window. "No, Ally. He doesn't."

The words fell like stones. The room seemed to echo the rejection in mockery of all Ally's hopes and plans.

"He doesn't?" she repeated, her voice barely a whisper. "Why not?"

"He . . . took one look at your picture and said no."

"What?"

"He said you were too fresh and sweet, too delicate-looking. He said Rainy is a tough, wisecracking, hardened woman who's been through everything by the age of twenty-four. He said a face like yours could never pull it off on-screen.''

"But right now I'm playing a prostitute who kills her own pimp! And I do it eight times a week," Ally sputtered. "To rave reviews, I might add.''

"I know, Ally. But when he looked at your resume, all he saw were—''

"Underwear parts," Ally finished bleakly. The words "underwear parts" were Ally's euphemism for the plethora of roles she had played that required nothing except that she run around scantily clad, looking pretty and uttering straight lines. Although dissatisfied with the roles, Ally had been grateful to at least get work more often than many of her talented friends. What's more, her first two agents and numerous producers had insisted again and again that a young woman with her sexy looks was *only* going to get "underwear parts.''

Montgomery Jackson was the first agent who had ever told her she was strong, talented, and impressive, and should be doing more important work. When he had left the huge agency he had originally worked in to form his own agency with a partner, Ally had gone with him as a client, flattered to be asked since Monty's client list was extremely impressive. She had never regretted it. He had gotten her a whole season with an excellent Shakespeare company in Oregon, and three challenging roles since then. Monty had kept his promise to help Ally build an impressive repertoire of roles she could grow in and recall with dignity.

As she approached thirty, Ally was determined to continue growing. She resented the implication that her pretty face made her incapable of playing Rainy in *Grass in Heaven*.

"Didn't he see the more recent listings on my resume?'' she demanded. *"Pray for Us, The Seagull, Much Ado About Nothing*—''

"Of course he saw, Ally. But he's not convinced. He said that he can tell by looking at your face that you're not right for the part, and there's not enough evidence on your resume to make him think otherwise.''

"Then why doesn't he come to see me in the play I'm doing now? I'm tough enough in this play to scare a roomful of linebackers.''

"He's not planning a trip to New York right now, and your play closes next week. He's not going to make a special trip out here just to see you in *Northern Comfort*. He's not interested, Ally. I'm sorry.''

Ally bowed her head, feeling defeat hit her with merciless force. She had wanted this so badly. The part itself would have meant everything to her, and the chance to work in a Roland Houston film could have skyrocketed her career. She ran a hand through the illusionary red tresses that spilled over her shoulders.

"Okay," she said at last. "Thank you for trying, Monty.''

"I think he's wrong, Ally, and we'll find a part for you that will make him eat his hat. But for now . . .''

"If only I could meet him, just talk to him. No one will play that part like I could. . . .'' She sighed heavily. They were both silent for several long moments. She was grateful to Monty for telling her this in person; telephones were so impersonal. Finally she said, "Since *Comfort* closes next week, I'd better ask. Has anything else turned up yet?''

He shook his head. "Things are very slow right now. How are you fixed for cash?''

"Not good," she admitted. "My free animal-shelter cat just required some surgery that nearly cleaned me out. And my rent is going up.''

"Well, there might be a breakfast drink commercial coming up, if you're interested.'' He looked doubtful.

"Beggars can't be choosers," Ally said glumly. "What about that woman who was thinking of me for that play about Emily Dickinson?''

"She called last week. Can't get enough backers.''

"Well, keep me posted, Monty. As of next week, I'm unemployed." She rose to leave.

Monty opened the door. "Don't worry, Ally. I'll find something for you."

She smiled fondly at him as she stepped out into the hall. "I know. You always do." She really was very lucky to have such a dedicated agent. Many of her friends were not so fortunate. "I need a hug," she said.

Monty gave her an affectionate squeeze. He pulled back and looked into her face. "Look at you," he said wryly. "It's a good thing my wife's not the jealous type."

"Ahhh, it's a good thing you're not the philandering type," Ally answered.

She touched his cheek lightly and turned to leave. As soon as she turned away from Monty, her eyes locked with those of the blond stranger who had entered the office with her. She heard Monty's door close behind her.

The stranger's eyes were warm and curious. Not judgmental, but certainly speculative as he looked at her. A suggestively dressed woman being physically affectionate with a talent agent had all sorts of possible implications.

"Do it again!" cried the receptionist, distracting Ally and the blond man.

He grinned at the receptionist. He had a devastating smile, Ally noticed, sunny and sexy at the same time.

"No, I'd better not. I might get hurt this time."

"Oh, come on!" Seeing Ally, the receptionist gestured to her to come nearer. "You've got to see this!"

Ally stepped closer and looked at the stranger from under her thick lashes. "See what?"

The receptionist pulled a cigarette out of her purse and put it to her lips. The man glanced at Ally for a moment, shrugged good-naturedly, and snapped his fingers.

Ally gasped and stepped back as his fingers caught fire.

He leaned gracefully across the desk to light the woman's cigarette. He turned to Ally. "Want a light?" he asked with the endearing tone and expression of a teenager trying to impress an older woman.

"I . . . No, thanks." Ally was definitely impressed.

He waved his hand with a quick flourish, and the flame disappeared. His dark eyes were soulful and laughing at the same time, his face was intelligent and handsome, and his voice was husky and deep.

"Look! He's not even burned!" exclaimed the receptionist.

"That's amazing," Ally said politely.

As the receptionist purred with admiration, a thought occurred to Ally. Actors needed all sorts of bizarre skills. A friend of hers had spent eight weeks in roller-skating lessons to get her role in *Starlight Express*. Another non-smoking friend had spent many hours learning to roll her own cigarettes for a scene in *Plenty*. Ally's last boyfriend had learned to use a lasso for his role in *Oklahoma*. Perhaps, Ally thought, she could someday profit from knowing a trick like this. It was a good one, after all. Like many people in her profession, he might be willing to share his secrets.

"Do you give your tricks away?" she asked suddenly.

"No." The man's soft brown eyes glinted and traveled down her body with subtle implication. "Do *you*?"

Ally felt blood rush to her face as she realized the implication of his words. This was the last straw. She should have realized what people would think if she walked around in the real world like this, but she had just suffered a crushing disappointment in Monty's office, and felt neither tolerant nor humorous at this particular moment.

She gave the stranger her most withering look, her eyes telling him that she thought he was loathsome and vulgar. Then, without another word, she turned on her heel and left.

Chance watched the redhead stalk out of the talent agency without a backward glance. A puzzled smile played around his mouth. He still wasn't sure what her profession was—or what her connection to Montgomery Jackson was. He was tempted to follow her and apologize.

"I'll tell Monty you're here, Mr. Weal."

"Call me Chance," he said. He was rewarded by an adoring flutter of eyelashes before the receptionist picked up the phone to buzz her employer. He grinned, then thought about the redhead again. Her eyes were amazing. He would have liked to see her laugh or smile.

"Chance, good to see you again." Monty came down the hallway and clasped Chance's hand in a firm handshake. Monty didn't greet him with the exaggerated joviality Chance had come to detest in some show-business people. In fact, Monty's sincerity and genuine concern for his clients was one of the main reasons that Chance, having fired his last agent, had decided to sign with Slade and Jackson Associates.

Monty's reputation was another reason Chance had chosen him. At fifty-six, Monty had handled a wide variety of talent, had boosted numerous careers to stardom, had obtained and cultivated excellent connections, and maintained a reputation for fairness. And Chance had worked too hard all these years to settle for less anymore.

They had shaken hands on their agreement in Los Angeles two months ago. Chance had finished out a contract at one of the big Las Vegas Hotels, and now he was in New York for some more television appearances Monty had booked.

"Have you found a place to stay?" Monty asked as they sat down in his office.

"I'm subletting a place from a friend of mine. It's comfortable."

"To get right down to business," Monty said, "I got a call from Los Angeles today. It's a go."

"The one-hour special we discussed with that producer we met with? Ambrose Kettering?"

Monty nodded. "One hour, prime time, network television. Of course, there are still contractual details to work out."

"Monty, I don't know what to say. For two years I badgered my last agent about a television special. And you've done it in two months!" Chance grinned. "And now I guess it's up to me to make sure they sign me for another special after this one is over."

"Exactly," said Monty. "To that end, I count on you to make magic onstage while I stir up excitement about you offstage. If we both play our cards right, you could be doing as well as David Copperfield and Doug Henning before long.''

"And if I mess it up, it's back to Ghirardelli Square for me,'' Chance said wryly, naming the colorful square in San Francisco where he had started his career more than a dozen years ago by performing for pedestrians and passing the hat.

"As I said, there are a number of contractual questions,'' Monty began.

Chance had an unlimited attention span when it came to perfecting his craft, but business bored him quickly. He was aware that, as a responsible adult and professional, he needed to know the business details of his career. He was, however, shifting restlessly in his chair and eager to leave after a half hour of concentrating on Monty's conversation.

The phone intercom buzzed. Monty picked it up. "Yes? Tell her I'm with a client now. . . .'' Monty frowned. After a moment, he glanced up at Chance. "It's another client. She says it's urgent. Do you mind if I—''

"No, of course not.''

"All right, put her on.'' He waited a moment. "Yes, Ally, what is it? Slow down, I can't understand you.'' He frowned again. "Atlantic City? Ally, it's *not* right around the corner. . . . Well, *I* didn't know he would be there. How did you— Oh, I see. But I don't think . . . He won't . . . You're not . . .'' Monty gave a sigh. He smiled ruefully. "All right, Ally. I will. . . . Yes, I'll think of something. I promise.''

After a few more moments, Monty said good-bye and hung up. He smiled at Chance. "Ambition must be a terrible burden. I thank God I'm just a businessman. Now, where were we?''

"Publicity.''

"Oh, yes, that call reminded me. There's going to be a benefit in Atlantic City in a few weeks. A fund for homeless children, I believe. It's a big weekend shebang that'll take place at the Wilson Palace Hotel and Casino.

Ambrose Kettering is producing the show, and he's suggested you give a brief performance."

"What do you think?" Chance asked.

"I think it's a good cause, it'll get a lot of coverage, and there will be a lot of important people there. If we can fit it in, I think you should go." Chance nodded affably, and Monty added, "I'll find out more about it for you."

They wrapped up their conversation quickly, since Monty was expecting another appointment momentarily.

As Chance left Monty's office and rode the elevator down to the first floor, he knew he had been right to sign with Monty.

In the past, Chance had suffered a number of setbacks, both professional and personal, regarding his career. Conjurers were still often poorly regarded by talent agencies and by other performers. Often by their loved ones, too, Chance thought with a faint twinge of unpleasant emotion. After all these years, he had almost forgotten the woman— but he had never forgotten the feeling of betrayal.

Monty didn't strike Chance as the type to steal a little afternoon delight with a call girl, so he assumed the redhead was really an actress. He wondered if she dressed like that all the time, or if it was part of some work she was doing. He was sorry he had let the opportunity to meet her slip by. But then, he thought with a smile, the venomous look she had given him when she left proved she had quite a temper. Perhaps it was just as well he had let her go.

He sauntered down the street, hands in his pockets, and wondered what to do until he met a friend at the cinema later. He could do some work, but he was feeling suddenly nostalgic. On a whim, he decided to go to Central Park and see if he could find a street magician or two.

Chance loved the spectacle of legerdemain, the awe, wonder, and suspicion on the audience's faces, and the triumphant surprises offered by the magician. He especially loved the impromptu aspect of conjuring right in the middle of a throng of people. Anything could, and frequently did, happen.

He checked his pockets to make sure he had something to put in the hat, then he set off for the park with a smile on his face.

After leaving Monty's office, Ally had decided to grab a bite to eat on the same street. Her outfit made it necessary for her to sharply rebuke would-be companions several times after she sat down at a window table in a shabby pasta bar. However, once she tucked four napkins around her costume to prevent it from getting inadvertently stained, she must have looked considerably less alluring, since no one else approached her.

She was glad she was performing tonight. Otherwise, she was so depressed, she would just go home and feel disgustingly sorry for herself. It was times like this that she sincerely envied fictional women—some of whom she had played—who had a loving, supportive man to go home to and share their troubles with. She'd never had a relationship like that. In fact, for the past couple of years, she hadn't had a relationship at *all*. Too many bad experiences had made her choose peaceful solitude in the end. However, on days like this, solitude wasn't all it was cracked up to be.

Ally sighed and pushed her pasta around on her plate. She tried to chide herself out of this uncharacteristically low mood. She had maintained her stamina because she was an essentially cheerful and optimistic person, but sometimes the setbacks really got her down. Monty was right, she reminded herself; there would be other roles.

But she had wanted *this* one so badly. She loved the character, understood her, could give so much to the role and learn so much from it. If only there were some way of convincing Roland Houston to at least meet her.

Realizing she wasn't going to finish her pasta, Ally pushed her plate away, asked for a cup of coffee, and picked up her newspaper. After several minutes, she found an article that captured her attention.

Helmut Wilson, the fabulously rich entrepreneur, was hosting a gala weekend charity event in Atlantic City at his Wilson Palace Hotel and Casino. The entertainment included nationally and internationally known singers, dancers, comics, actors, and radio personalities. The cause was worthy, the price astronomical, and the guest list absolutely stellar.

The name Roland Houston jumped out at Ally. He would be attending! Within two minutes she was on the phone to Monty.

"Atlantic City, Monty! It's just around the corner! Why didn't you tell me he would be so near?" she demanded. "Oh . . . it's in the paper today. . . . Well, maybe he'd want to come up to New York afterwards? Before? But I— Well, in that case, I'll go to Atlantic City." She frowned. "Yes, the paper says it's five thousand dollars or something per person. But can't you get me in? *I* don't know how. Please, think of something, Monty. *Something*. Just get me there. I'll change his mind once I find him."

Satisfied that the karmic pendulum was once again swinging her way, Ally hung up the phone and sat back down at her table. She paid her check and finished her coffee, staring out the window.

She felt some misgivings when she considered how pushy Roland Houston might consider her if she tracked him down in Atlantic City after he had already said he didn't want to see her. However, this was the toughest, most competitive profession in the world. Her teachers, her directors, her peers, and even her agent had all always advised her to pursue work with the tenacity of a terrier.

"It's got to be the right thing to do," she murmured to herself. "I wouldn't want this so badly if it weren't right."

Suddenly a familiar face appeared in the crowd that rushed past the window. He was tall, blond, well built, slightly tanned, dressed in denim and cotton. His fingers, she noticed, did not appear to be on fire this time.

He was smiling, and his expression made him look very

appealing. He stopped to pull a few dollars out of his pocket, then tossed them into the violin case of a hapless young musician who was being ignored by the New Yorkers rushing by.

The blond man said something to the violinist that made him laugh, then he sauntered away.

Ally watched with interest. There was an animal grace about the man that was irresistible. He exuded an air of charisma and confidence that couldn't be ignored.

He'd been smiling beatifically, Ally mused. And he was being rather free with his dollar bills. Monty Jackson must have given him good news.

Seeing him again like this seemed to be an omen. Whether it was good or bad remained to be seen.

TWO

A shark walked into the room.

Actually, the shark shuffled into the room. Chance could see little feet peeping out at the very bottom of the shark. They moved along a bare inch at a time, their motion restricted by the tight costume.

Chance sat in Monty Jackson's office, in the same chair he had used on his first visit here a month ago, and stared in amazement. He glanced at Monty, who also seemed flabbergasted by the unheralded arrival of a walking shark.

"How could you!" cried the shark in a throaty female voice.

Monty's jaw dropped. "Ally?" he said incredulously.

"I've never been so humiliated in my life! So abused, so *demeaned*—"

"Ally, calm down," said Monty. Then, not too surprisingly, he burst out laughing.

This went on for quite some time, with Ally the shark berating Monty, and Monty trying to stifle his laughter long enough to take control of the conversation.

From his chair in the corner, on the shark's right side, Chance studied the costume. It was so awful, it was wonderful. The woman's body was encased in an absurdly snug gray sheath that was decorated and textured to bear striking resemblance to a shark's body. The tightness of

22

the costume must be unbearably uncomfortable; but, being a healthy, red-blooded male, he couldn't help noticing that it showed off every line and curve of Ally's admirable shape.

The top of the costume was the shark's head, covering all of Ally's head. The snout pointed straight up, with beady black eyes on either side of it. In front, where Ally's face should be, was the shark's gaping, toothy mouth. He wondered what the teeth were made of. They looked rather sharp. Ally's eyes and nose were hidden in the shark's mouth behind a gauzy material that matched the color of its gums.

Chance doubted she could see him. He doubted she could see much of anything, with her peripheral vision completely cut off and her eyes hidden behind a web of material.

The costume tapered down to the shark's tail, sewn so realistically narrow that Ally could barely move her legs as she shuffled closer to Monty's desk, still raging at him. Her arms were plastered to her side. She appeared to be quite helpless.

"What," Monty gasped, "are you doing in that ridiculous costume?"

"*This* is what I'm wearing at that cockamamie deep-sea fishing convention!"

"Oh, Ally, I had no *idea*." Monty tried unsuccessfully to still his quivering mouth.

"A hundred dollars a day, you said! Just stand around in a wet suit and hand out leaflets about deep-sea fishing companies, you said!" the shark cried accusingly.

"That's what I assumed—"

"Well, you *assumed* wrong! How do you find these people?"

"You said you needed to make a quick few hundred this week, so I called a friend who knew about—"

"Wait till I get my hands on you! They zipped me into this thing as soon as I arrived this morning. Since then, I have been pawed, mauled, molested, harassed, and pestered by drunken men who kill big fish with their bare hands for fun.''

"Surely they're not—''

"My butt has been pinched so many times, I may have to eat standing up for the next two weeks!'' the shark shouted.

"Perhaps if you—''

"Not to mention what has been done to other portions of my anatomy,'' snarled the shark. "Portions which no one but my most intimate acquaintances had ever touched until today!''

"Maybe—'' Monty began, but he was cut off again.

"This damned costume is so hot, I think I've sweated two gallons of essential body fluids already! And the wardrobe mistress had the utter unmitigated *gall* to tell me my pay would be garnered to cover the cost of dry cleaning if I couldn't arrange to perspire a little less!'' The shark quivered with rage. "I thought Eva Braun was supposed to be dead!''

"I'll see what I—''

"And the *only* reason I'm staying at the convention for a full day is because I can't get out of this hideous thing without experienced help, and Eva Braun refuses to help me until my shift is over. I get one hour for lunch, and I've used up most of it shuffling over here—since I can't hail a cab or sit down in one—to tell you that I will never forgive you for this!''

There was blessed silence following this announcement. Chance looked over to Monty, waiting for his reaction.

"Finished?'' Monty said quietly.

"Yes,'' said Ally the shark.

"Feel better?'' said Monty.

"A little.'' She didn't sound better, though. Chance thought she sounded exhausted and demoralized.

"Ready for two pieces of good news?''

"Yes.'' Breathless, too, Chance noticed.

"You're slated to film the breakfast drink commercial next week. They agreed to our fee.''

"Oh, good!" The voice had perked up, though it still sounded faint.

"And . . ." Monty permitted himself a little dramatic pause. "I've found a way to get you into the Wilson Palace Hotel the weekend that Roland Houston is there."

Chance glanced at Monty in sharp surprise and then looked back at the shark. *This* was Alicia Cannon, the woman they had just been discussing? Her timing was extraordinary.

"You can get me a meeting with Roland Houston?" The shark swayed alarmingly for a moment. "How?"

"Well, I called Ambrose Kettering's staff. Unfortunately, they primarily want variety acts. The only actresses they want there are celebrities. However," Monty continued, "I have a client who accepted their invitation to perform there and discovered, only this morning, that none of his regular staff can be there. So if you're interested in stepping into his act for an evening, you can go. The only other way, Ally, is to buy a five-thousand-dollar ticket or get hired as a chambermaid at the Wilson Palace."

"Oh, Monty, I love you!" As if to express satisfaction, the shark gave a little vertical hop. Chance grinned. Alicia Cannon was kind of cute, despite her temper. He wondered what she would be like without the fangs. "Who am I going with?"

"A new client," Monty answered. "He's a magician."

"A magician?" The shark swayed again.

"Yes, in fact . . ." Monty stood up, obviously preparing to introduce them. Chance rose to his feet, aware that Ally still hadn't noticed him.

"Wait a minute. A *magician*? Monty, you can't be serious!"

The contempt in Ally's voice froze Chance. Monty glanced his way uneasily.

"Now, Ally—"

"Monty, Roland Houston took one look at my picture and decided he couldn't take me seriously. Do you honestly think it's going to do me any good at all if he sees me wearing a skimpy costume and getting sawed in half by some guy in a red satin cape?''

"That's not—'' Monty began.

"I do not need the burden of meeting this man under those circumstances,'' Ally insisted. "Appearing onstage with someone pulling rabbits out of a hat and making bad jokes . . . Oh, Monty. Please.''

"I thought you said you wanted to go, no matter what,'' Monty said irritably. He cast Chance an apologetic glance.

"I do! But first the shark outfit, and now this?'' Ally sounded despairing. "I've spent the last five hours being mauled by every red-faced drunk in the English-speaking world. This costume is so tight, I suspect it's damaged several of my internal organs. And my name—*my name*—is printed in the convention's brochures for all the world to see.'' She sighed and swayed again. "Monty, I've taken all the humiliation I can stand for the moment. Couldn't you find me something with a little more dignity? I mean—a *magic* act?''

She pronounced the words with such distaste that Chance felt his gut tighten. "I think I've heard enough,'' he said suddenly, burning with resentment.

The shark hopped around so that its gaping mouth faced him. He heard a soft gasp come from within its depths, and then it started to fall backwards. Chance jumped forward reflexively to keep Alicia Cannon from falling. He grabbed whatever he could reach as he lunged for her, and his right hand closed over a plump breast. His brows rose in surprise as he righted her. She hadn't been exaggerating; she was packed into that thing tighter than a sardine, and he could tell she was perspiring heavily and breathing with difficulty.

"Get your hands off me!'' Ally snapped.

"Maybe I should have let you crack your head open,'' he said unpleasantly, backing away from her.

"I've seen you before,'' she said suddenly.

"If you've seen my act, then maybe you know I don't—''

"No, it wasn't your act. It was—'' She shuffled around

a little to look at Monty. *"He's . . ."* She sputtered incoherently.

"Ally," said Monty wearily, "meet Chance Weal."

"My pleasure," said Chance sardonically.

"Oh, brother," said Ally.

"I wish I'd stayed in bed today," said Monty.

There was a long, uncomfortable silence. No one seemed to know how to rescue them all from this embarrassing scene. Finally Ally said, "I really have to be getting back. I . . . I'll call you Monday. Okay, Monty?"

"Okay, Ally."

Ally shuffled laboriously out the door. Chance closed it behind her. He sat back down. His eyes met Monty's.

"I'm so sorry about that, Chance," Monty said. "I had no idea . . ."

"Actors are sometimes contemptuous of magicians. I'm used to it." Actually, he thought he would never get used to it. It was doubly annoying that someone dressed as a shark thought she had too much professional dignity to appear with him.

"It was inexcusable," Monty said. "Of course, she didn't realize you were in the room. Even so, she's not normally like that. She's quick-tempered, but she's a regular trooper. I guess she's just not herself today."

"It's all right, Monty. You didn't realize she would be so . . . opposed to the idea."

"I'll talk to her when she's calmer and—"

"No."

"You still need someone to accompany you."

"I'll go alone. I won't be doing a whole show, after all. Just ten minutes or so. I've worked alone many times. I can either do illusions that require no help or ones that need only an audience member to assist me."

"I still think—"

"No," said Chance again, more emphatically this time. "I don't need someone with her attitude around me. Forget it, Monty."

They had concluded all their business for the moment, and neither man was in a particularly good mood at that point, so Chance left. Once alone inside the elevator, he released the tight hold he had been keeping on himself. He was far more insulted than he had let on.

He left the building and stepped out into the street. A lovely early September day seemed wasted in New York City, he thought, his mood darkening. He started walking up the street.

Not far ahead of him, a shark shuffled along.

She was drawing a lot of attention. Even jaded New Yorkers couldn't help looking twice at a shark on Broadway. She moved so slowly that he caught up with her in just moments.

He fell into step beside her. ''Nice outfit,'' he said blandly.

''Buzz off,'' the shark muttered.

''Careful, I might make you disappear if you're rude to me.''

The shark stopped suddenly and shuffled around to face him. The gaping mouth tilted up slightly to allow Ally to look at his face. ''It's you,'' she groaned. ''Are you following me?''

''No. I didn't need to. You're slow as molasses, and you're pretty easy to spot.''

''Go away.''

''Won't you let me tag along for a little bit? I'm fascinated by you serious actress types, me being just a low-brow magician and all.''

''Look, I'm sorry I insulted you. Everybody has to make a living, after all.'' She didn't sound particularly apologetic, though.

''But walking around in a shark suit and selling breakfast drinks on TV is just such a cut above what I do, is that it?'' he prodded, letting some of his anger come through in his voice.

The shark practically vibrated with outrage. ''The breakfast drink commercial is to pay my rent. And the shark suit is . . . is . . . an aberration.''

''Just something to keep you occupied in between

Brecht, Shakespeare, and Chekov, is that it?'' His voice was dripping with sarcasm.

"Look, I've apologized for insulting you, but I didn't know you were in the room. What more do you want, Mr. Weal?'' She snorted suddenly. "Chance Weal. You've got to be kidding! What kind of a name is that? Couldn't you at least have thought of something a little more believable?''

"That's my real name,'' he snapped.

Ally burst out laughing. "Really? How could your parents have done that to you?''

"Leave my parents out of this, Miss Cannon.''

"Mommy, look, there's a man shouting at a shark!'' cried a small child.

"Don't go near them, dear,'' said the mother, protectively drawing the child away from Chance and Ally.

Chance looked around and realized that several people were staring at them unabashedly.

"What time is it?'' Ally asked suddenly.

"A quarter to one.''

"Oh, no! I'll never get back in time. They'll dock an hour's pay,'' she moaned.

"Where are you going?''

"West Fifty-third Street.''

Chance regarded the shark for a moment. A slight smile played around his mouth as the idea in his mind took root and began to please him. "Miss Cannon,'' he said silkily, "I want you to know, before I do this—''

"Before you do what?''

"—that my grandfather taught me to treat every woman like a lady. And though you don't deserve it, I'm going to see you back to work—whether you like it or not.''

"I don't— Yahh!'' Ally yelped as she felt two strong arms slide around her and lift her effortlessly off the ground. The world swirled crazily for a moment as Chance Weal tossed her into the air. In a split second, her stomach connected harshly with a hard shoulder and her breath flew out of her lungs with a *whoosh*. Her costume was so tight, she couldn't bend all the way, so her head and legs stuck out at a peculiar angle.

"Comfortable?" Chance asked innocently.

"Put me down!"

"When we get there," Chance assured her sweetly. He had one arm hooked loosely over her legs. The other hand, he planted insolently on her round bottom. She gasped in outrage. "Got to keep you balanced, Miss Cannon."

"Let go of me, you lowlife scoundrel! You dirty, rotten, stinking son of a—"

"Ah-ah, language," he chided.

"I'm going to be sick," she threatened.

He ignored her. Ally tried to kick her legs. That threw him off balance for a moment, and she swallowed a scream as he nearly dropped her.

"Do that again and you'll land on your head," he warned. "Which might not be such a bad thing," he added nastily.

"Help! I'm being kidnapped!" Ally cried. This drew an inappropriate roar of laughter from nearby pedestrians. Ally seethed with rage. She had never felt so helpless, or ridiculous, in her whole life.

She nagged and cursed and shouted at Chance Weal halfway to Fifty-third Street. She finally gave up only because she could tell by the laughter in his voice that her outrage only made his revenge all the more enjoyable. By the time they entered the convention hotel on West Fifty-third Street, she was ready to kill him.

Ally could hear tittering in the background. Finally a female voice said, "Can I help you, sir?"

"I'm returning this shark. I found it wandering around on Broadway," Chance said pleasantly. Without warning, he shifted and let Ally slide to the ground. Her legs gave way, and he slid an arm around her to hold her upright till the room stopped spinning.

"Don't touch me!" she snapped. She heard more giggling.

"Who is it?" asked the woman's voice.

Ally shuffled around until she could see the woman's

face. It was the same security officer she had checked in with that morning. "I'm Alicia Cannon," she said, struggling against a parched throat and increasingly thick tongue, "and I want this man thrown out of here. Immediately!"

"Alicia Cannon," said the woman, glancing down at her security roster. "Ah, yes. Here we are. You're thirty seconds late, Alicia. You know the rules. We'll let it pass this time, but don't let it happen again."

"Don't be too hard on her," said Chance. "Miss Cannon is a *serious actress*, you know, and very sensitive."

"Really?" said the security woman blandly as she looked at the shark. She was clearly unimpressed.

"If I ever get out of this costume alive," Ally growled, dark spots swimming through her vision, "I will kill you for this."

"I doubt it. I doubt we'll ever meet again." He tilted his head sideways. "But I would have loved to have seen your face."

With that parting shot, he sauntered out the door, leaving Ally fuming behind him as the security woman suggested she go back to amusing the deep-sea fisherman.

"Monty? I'm sorry about Friday," said Ally humbly as she spoke to her agent on the telephone on Monday.

"What the hell got into you?" Monty demanded.

"That costume. It was so humiliating in the first place. And incredibly uncomfortable. And hot. I keeled over an hour after I returned to work. Dehydration."

"Ally!"

"I just . . . wasn't quite myself when I came to see you. I'd had no food or water for six hours. Low blood sugar, heat exhaustion, and all that pinching and pawing and fondling I endured . . ." Her voice trailed off miserably. "Anyhow, I was in no fit state to be sensible when I saw you Friday."

"I'm sorry, too. If I had known it would be like that—"

"Never mind. Let's chalk it up to experience." There

was a heavy pause. "And, well, to be honest, Monty, I would still rather not go down to Atlantic City as a magician's assistant. However, I realize that if I want to meet Roland Houston, it's probably my only chance."

"That's the problem. Chance," said Monty.

Ally recalled their scene in the street with mortification. She wondered if Monty knew. "Have you talked to him since he left your office?"

"No. But I think you alienated him completely when you were both here. He was adamant about not having you in his act. He's a fine performer, and you offended him deeply with your comments." Monty sighed. "You both have tempers that give me a nervous rash."

Ally puzzled over her situation. She had to get to Atlantic City to meet Roland Houston, and Chance Weal was her ticket. She wondered if publicly humiliating her on Friday had cooled some of his rage. Perhaps she could reason with him. "Monty, I want to talk to him. To apologize. Maybe I can get him to change his mind."

"I doubt it."

"Can't you at least set something up?"

Monty was silent for a long moment. "Tell you what. You start filming the TV commercial tomorrow, right? He'll be appearing on a talk show just a block away from you. I'll see if he's willing to stop by the studio on his way. How's that?"

"Thank you," said Ally sincerely.

"I can't guarantee he'll show up," Monty warned.

"Tell him . . . tell him I said to thank him for helping me get back to work safely," Ally said impulsively. That should get Chance's attention.

"What?"

"Talk to you later, Monty." She hung up the phone.

"All right, everybody, lunch break! We start again in exactly one hour," called out a production assistant.

"In the nick of time," said Ally wryly. Standing under hot lights, she was dressed like Little Bo-Peep and surrounded by a dozen sheep. Two of them looked like they felt the call of nature and would give in at any moment.

"Ally, dear," said the wardrobe man, "if you're going to eat, I'll need to cover you with a big bib."

"No, thanks. The smell has spoiled my appetite."

"Ally? Someone here to see you," called the production assistant.

It must be Chance Weal! She squinted but couldn't see into the blackness beyond the bright lights. She picked up her wide, heavy skirts with one hand and her pink Little Bo-Peep walking stick with the other. Rows and rows of platinum blond sausage curls tumbled around her face as she picked her way through the sheep, who bleated as their trainer organized them for feeding.

She kept her eyes lowered so she wouldn't trip on any of the dozens of electrical cords covering the floor as she stepped out of the bucolic set and entered the darkness beyond.

She suddenly heard Chance's voice say uncertainly, "Ally?"

She looked up and their eyes met. He looked vastly amused. She felt strangely glad to see him, despite their raging fight on Friday. He was dressed in denim, as usual, and his dark eyes sparkled with curiosity and humor, just as she remembered. His buttery-colored hair, his handsome face, and his leanly muscled body stopped her breath for a moment. He really was gorgeous.

"Well, I—" she began.

He put a hand to her face, touching her very lightly. "Wait a minute." He looked deeply into her eyes. "Blue," he murmured, "shot through with emerald . . . My God, it's you." His expression mirrored his surprise.

"What?"

"The prostitute. Uh, I mean . . ." He grinned and shrugged, letting his hand drop back to his side.

"Oh." She smiled self-consciously.

His eyes raked her fairy-tale costume, red Kewpie doll lips, and phony platinum blond curls. "I'm almost afraid to ask," he said.

"It's a breakfast drink made with powdered sheep's milk. This—" she plucked at her bell-shaped skirt "—was the bright idea of someone in advertising."

"Words fail me," he murmured.

"Me, too," she said bleakly.

"But it pays the rent."

She looked away, remembering their argument and feeling embarrassed. "Look, let's step through here and sit down where we can talk."

Ally led Chance through the door and down the hallway to a canteen. They chose a table away from the production crew and sat down opposite each other.

"I'm sorry about Friday," Ally said. "I wasn't myself."

"Since you said what you did before you realized I was in the office," Chance said slowly, "I assume that you were being honest with Monty and really meant what you said."

"I don't know how much Monty told you—"

"He said you're after a part in *Grass in Heaven*, and since I need someone to accompany me to Atlantic City, why not you? He said you want to talk to Roland Houston."

She nodded. She explained her situation. "I know it's a little irregular."

He shrugged. "It's a tough business. If you really believe you can change Houston's mind about you when you meet him in person, then, from your point of view, it's worth a shot." But her gamble wasn't Chance's concern.

"So I can go with you?"

Her incredible eyes were filled with hope, and Chance felt himself weakening. He fought it. "Ally, I don't want someone onstage with me, even for ten minutes, who has your attitude about my work."

"I admit that my limited experience with magicians has not impressed me favorably," she said carefully. "Maybe you could change my mind."

"I'm too busy to reeducate you," he said flatly.

"Who will you take if you don't take me?" she challenged.

"I'll go alone."

"But it would be easier to have someone with you, wouldn't it?"

"I don't think it would be easier to have *you* with me."

He could see the determination in her expression. "All right, so I have a bad attitude toward you. Wouldn't you love to see me grovel in mortification when I find out I'm wrong?"

He grinned slowly. "It's tempting."

"Look, I promise I'll behave. I'll be cooperative, respectful, amiable—"

"I don't believe any of that for a moment."

They looked at each other in mutual consternation. He could see she was going to take another stab at it. Chance wondered if she knew how close he already was to giving in. She fascinated him. How many women was she?

"Why can't any of your regular people go?" she asked suddenly.

"One quit and another one's injured. The others are in L.A., getting ready for the TV special Monty got us."

"Chance." She reached across the table and laid her hand over his. Surprising himself, he responded and folded his fingers around it. She was so petite, pale, fine-boned—and strong-willed. A dozen sensations ran through him at once.

"A TV special must be a big dream of yours. A long-sought goal."

"It is," he admitted quietly.

"Then you know what it's like to want something that badly, something that seems so unobtainable." Her voice was low and intense.

"I know." He remembered years of hard work, burning ambition, tough breaks, and seemingly insurmountable obstacles.

"And you know what it's like when you finally have your hands on it." Her fingers tightened around his. "I want this so badly, so much. *Northern Comfort* has closed, and my life right now is shark suits and breakfast commercials. I want more, and I've worked hard enough to deserve more."

"Even if I take you, there's no guarantee he'll talk to you," Chance warned. "Even if he talks to you, there's no guarantee he'll consider you for the part."

"I know that. I'll take it one step at a time."

Her eyes searched his face. She had laid all her cards on the table. She had let him see how badly she wanted this, how disappointed she was with her career at the moment. He wished he knew her well enough to know whether she had the guts to be this honest with him, or whether she was turning on a performance and using him to get what she was after.

Her eyes, set in an over-made-up face and surrounded by that ridiculous hair, burned through him.

"What do you really look like?" he murmured.

"Take me to Atlantic City and find out," she said.

And that's when he knew he would do it. And not for professional reasons, either.

THREE

"No! I can't do it! I *won't* do it! No!"

"Ally, calm down," said Chance, trying to be patient. "If you'll just—"

"Yahhh!" She backed away as he tried to convince her to turn on the circular, jagged-toothed blade suspended high over the table upon which he lay in chains.

"Ally, trust me," he urged from his vulnerable position. "I've done this a hundred—"

"No!"

They were in a rented rehearsal room in New York. They had spent most of the weekend in this room. Chance had hoped, with Ally's help, to perform a couple of really impressive illusions for the stellar audience in Atlantic City the following weekend. He was running out of options, however. She had already refused to crush him or set him on fire, and now she wouldn't saw him in half.

"I thought you didn't like me," he said plaintively.

"I don't want to spend the rest of my life in jail because of you," she snapped.

"There's no point in taking you to Atlantic City if all you're going to do is stand around and act hysterical."

"Aye," said Angus.

"Yup," said Zeke.

Ally glared at the two technicians who had been their

37

constant companions all weekend. They had patiently set up two complicated illusions—while she waited elsewhere so she couldn't see what they were doing—which she had then refused to participate in. Now they watched glumly as she rejected a third possibility. She had to admit that Chance had good cause to be testy. They had accomplished relatively little this weekend. It was Sunday evening, and they had to leave for Atlantic City on Friday.

She walked back over to where Chance lay chained and padlocked to a table, sixteen feet beneath the threatening blade of the saw. She tested the chains.

"These are real chains," she said weakly.

"Aye," said Angus.

"Yup," said Zeke.

"And real locks," said Ally.

"Yes," said Chance tiredly.

"I don't care how slowly the blade comes down. You'll never get out of there before it cuts you in half."

Chance sighed in defeat. "All right, Ally. I didn't want to tell you, because you're not the most even-tempered person I've ever worked with."

"Tell me what?"

"That's the whole point. It adds a little spice to the sawing-in-half routine."

"*What?*"

"I struggle with my bonds while the blade comes lower and lower. I nearly escape, and just when the audience thinks I might make it—the blade cuts me in half."

Ally looked at him in horror. "You're out of your mind!"

"Then you pull the two halves of me a few feet apart so everyone can see—"

"Over my dead body! That's the most disgusting thing I've ever heard!"

"And then you push them back together, and we do a reverse. You turn the saw on again—"

"No!"

"And as the blade rises, I go back together. Then I finish escaping and stand up in one piece. And we need to do it in time to the music," he added. "Angus, can you turn the tape back? We're going to need to start over."

"Aye."

"No! I will *not* saw you in half in time to Kenny G. It's absolutely out of the question. Personal animosity does not enter into it. It's a matter of principle. I don't even squash spiders."

"Ally, will you just trust me? This is my job. I know what I'm doing."

She slumped against the table he lay chained to. "I just need to be convinced you're going to live through this before I actually do it to you. Maybe if you could tell me how it works—"

"No. We've already been through this, Ally. I can't give away trade secrets I've spent thousands of hours practicing. Especially not to *you*."

"What's that supposed to mean?"

"Personal animosity doesn't enter into it. You're just someone filling in for ten minutes onstage. I can't let you have access to secrets that many professionals don't even know."

"I don't want to expose your precious trade secrets," she snapped. "I just want to make sure I won't kill you."

They remained silent for several moments. They had reached an impasse. Again.

"You're a stubborn wench," Chance said at last.

"And you're just plain weird," Ally said critically. "I mean, look at you. When I was ten years old I saw *Macbeth* and knew what I wanted to do with my life. *You* saw some guy getting sawed in half, set on fire, and locked in a safe that got thrown into shark-infested waters, and then you knew what you wanted to do with *your* life."

"I think we've accomplished all we're going to today," said Chance diplomatically. "Get the keys."

"No. You're so clever—get yourself out of there." Ally hopped up and went to gather her belongings, relieved they were calling it quits. It had been a trying day.

Angus and Zeke went about disassembling the overhead saw while Chance squirmed and contorted in his chains.

Ally finished her coffee, brushed her hair, and closed her tired eyes. Chance joined her a few moments later. He was awfully limber, she admitted, resisting the urge to surreptitiously admire his body as he approached her.

"Hungry?" he asked.

"Is that a trick question?"

"No. I thought we could eat something together."

"Why?" she asked suspiciously. They had scarcely exchanged a civil word since she had refused to set him on fire. His sudden overture of goodwill made her wary.

"Because we're working together, if only briefly, unwillingly, and temporarily. And we have to drive down to Atlantic City and spend next weekend together."

She relented. Maybe he really was just trying to be nice. "Okay. Sure. Pizza?"

"Sounds fine." He turned around. "Guys, we won't be needing that setup again. We'll work out something new tomorrow. Lock up before you leave, and be here at ten sharp tomorrow, okay?"

"Aye."

"Yup."

"They don't like me," said Ally as she and Chance left the building.

"They don't *dis*like you," Chance assured her. "They're just used to my regular staff. We've never had a day quite like today. Or yesterday."

"I'm sorry. I don't mean to get so temperamental. But you can't expect someone like me, who raises money for baby seals, to willingly maul and mutilate you when all I have for proof is your word that I won't really hurt you."

"My word is worth something, Ally. But I suppose you have a point," Chance conceded. "How about right here?"

"Looks fine to me," she said as he gestured toward a pizzeria they were approaching. "Want to sit outside?" It was a comfortably cool September evening.

"Sure."

They got a table for two and looked over the menu.

"What do you like on your pizza?" Chance asked.

"You choose. I eat everything."

"It's nice to find something you're easy about." He ordered them a pizza for two and a pitcher of beer. A few minutes later, he and Ally clinked their beer mugs together. "To Atlantic City."

He sipped his beer and regarded his companion. He finally knew what she looked like, devoid of bizarre costumes, distracting wigs, and heavy makeup. And he was far from disappointed.

Ally's real hair was a glossy chestnut color, cut in a simple style that let it fall to her shoulders in thick waves. The finely sculpted bones of her face and the naturally creamy tone of her skin were more readily apparent since, like many actresses, she wore very little makeup when she wasn't performing. Her eyes were subtly highlighted, and they looked even lovelier tonight as she sipped her beer and toyed with her fork.

"Chance . . ."

"Hmmm?"

She frowned and looked down at her hands. "This weekend has been so far outside of my experience, I know I haven't been a help to you. I guess I've even been a hindrance. But I am trying hard, and I promise you I'll make sure you're not sorry you brought me along." Her eyes flashed up to his face. She looked uncharacteristically humble. "I haven't thanked you properly for giving me this opportunity, and I want you to know that I'm very grateful, even if I haven't behaved that way."

She had been so assertive up until now, he was moved by her softly spoken words of apology and thanks. "It's been different, that's for sure. But I have to admit that in a peculiar way, I've had fun so far, Ally." He was surprised at his own words, and even more surprised to realize they were true. As aggravating as she was, she was fun.

"Fun?" She smiled at him. "Really?"

"Really."

She shrugged. "Well, I guess we *have* had fun. In an offbeat kind of way."

"And it's heartening to know that after all the times we've argued, you still didn't want to cut me in half with a buzz saw. It gives me hope for our relationship. We might even approach civility if you continue to care that much," he teased.

"I told you: I don't want to get twenty to life just because you overestimated your skills," she said tartly.

"Well, maybe I'll still get to see you eat crow."

She raised her brows inquisitively.

"Maybe, by the time this is all over, you'll have learned that I'm not just some jerk in a satin cape pulling rabbits out of a hat and making bad jokes," he said.

"Do you wear a satin cape?" she asked weakly. Her expressive eyes told him how much she still dreaded appearing in public with him.

Chance considered stringing her along for a while, but he decided they already had enough problems. "No. Of course not. Can you honestly imagine me that way?"

"Then what do you wear?" Ally asked as their pizza was placed in front of them.

He shrugged. "Usually my jeans." He grimaced. "This TV producer told Monty he wants me to wear black leather pants and boots and a matching jacket with lots of silver zippers."

"Why?" Chance had such a warm, wide-eyed, country-boy look, combined with such obvious physical prowess and naturally blatant sexuality, that it gave him an irresistible appeal. Ally felt the pull of it herself—though she hoped she was finally too mature to fall for such shallow attractions. His allure was powerful enough, however, that she couldn't imagine why a television producer would want to tamper with it.

"We've been arguing about it. He thinks it will make me look sexier." Chance almost looked embarrassed. "Do you agree?"

"Ah-ah, now you're fishing for compliments," Ally chided. "Another slice?"

"Thanks." He watched her put more pizza onto his plate.

SLEIGHT OF HAND / 43

"Who is this producer?"

"Ambrose Kettering. Heard of him?"

"Yes." She frowned. "Didn't he lose a bundle of money on that dreadful miniseries that was such a flop last year?"

Chance shrugged. "Monty would know about that. I don't pay much attention to business."

"I think he's the one. I've heard he tends to overproduce. You know, bigger, better, more lavish, more spectacular." She made a face that told him what she thought of that.

"Then maybe he's just the right sort of producer for a lowbrow act like me," Chance said, feeling annoyed again.

Ally slapped her fork down. "I don't understand what you're so offended about. Do you honestly think that getting sawed in half and escaping from a locked safe in shark-infested waters is on an artistic par with Shakespeare's tragedies and Sheridan's comedies, which have endured for centuries? With plays by Harvey Fierstein, Edward Bond, David Mamet, Sam Shepard, and Beth Henley? With television productions like *Hill Street Blues*, *MASH* and *Roots*? With movies like *Stalag 17*, *Lawrence of Arabia*, and *Friendly Persuasion*?"

"Yes, I do," he said heatedly. "Magic is older than Shakespeare, older than Aristophanes. It's even older than Thespis himself, the first actor. You see, I'm not totally ignorant, Ally."

"I never said you were. Why do you have to take everything so personally?"

"Because when you look down your theatrical nose at conjuring as just a bag full of cheap tricks that mean nothing to anyone, as a vulgar variety act with no dignity, value, or substance, then you're insulting my profession, my livelihood, and my overriding passion in life. I've dedicated myself to this art ever since I dropped out of college. I've spent years on the road; I gave up having a personal life; I've worked twelve, fourteen, sixteen hours a day, studying the masters, perfecting my style, training my body, focusing my mind. When you dismiss my work with a sneer, you dismiss my life.''

She shifted uncomfortably and looked away, feeling guilty and embarrassed. He definitely had a point.

"Magic was the first form of theatre, Ally. Hunters enacted the hunt around the campfire to magically ensure a successful kill the following day. Witch doctors invoked spirits, mixed potions, and maintained their influence over the tribe with sorcery and unusual abilities. Magic knows no age or language barriers. It challenges and suspends belief systems. It creates wonder in everyone, from the most innocent child to the most jaded sophisticate.''

He spread his hands, and his dark eyes melted her. "As a magician, a conjurer, a sorcerer, I create that sense of wonder. I know secrets that baffle and intrigue millions, but don't harm a single person. I participate in a profession older than recorded history. It's like . . . being a modern day Merlin.''

Ally stared at him, already feeling some of that sense of wonder he was talking about. His enthusiasm and passion were contagious. She knew she would come to her senses once she got away from him, but for the moment she was completely wrapped up in the low intensity of his voice, the magic web of his words, the sheer wonder he himself felt and communicated to her when he spoke of his work.

Chance waited for her reaction. Would she laugh at him, sneer, or remain unmoved by his words? She said nothing, just sat there looking at him thoughtfully with those wide, blue-green eyes. Finally she lowered her head.

"Could you at least find some magic,'' she said softly, "that doesn't require me to maim you physically?''

He felt faintly disappointed. Well, what had he expected after his outburst? That she would throw away a lifetime of prejudice and be awed by the wonder of illusion?

"All right, Ally,'' he said with a rueful smile. "I'll think of something that won't go against your principles.''

They finished their pizza quietly. He offered to see her home. She refused. He insisted.

"My grandfather taught me to—"

"Treat every woman like a lady. Yes, I know."

"And always to see a lady to her door."

"I can find it without your help."

"Chivalry really is dead in New York," Chance said sadly. "The one place it's most needed, too."

She rolled her eyes. "All right, if you insist, you can take me home. But I'm too broke to get a cab. We're going by subway. No arguments."

"Would *I* argue with *you*?" His look of wide-eyed innocence made her smile reluctantly.

As they walked down into the smelly, dank, graffiti-ridden cement hole that characterized New York subway stations, Ally dug into her purse for a couple of subway tokens. "Here," she said, handing him one. "You can have my last token. So don't say I never gave you anything."

They went through the turnstiles simultaneously. Chance turned around for a moment. Ally looked back over her shoulder at him.

"Chance, come on." He kept his back to her and didn't respond. "Chance, I think I hear the train coming."

"Okay." He turned around and caught up to her. "Here."

She stared as he dropped a subway token into her palm. "What's this?" she asked stupidly.

"Your last token. I don't want my seeing you home to cost you even a dollar," he said gallantly. "Come on." He took her arm and propelled her toward the stairway leading down to the tracks.

"But—how'd you get through the turnstile?"

"I put the token in, of course."

"But how'd you get it back out?"

"Ahhh, trade secret," he said with mischief in his eyes.

She stopped halfway down the grimy stairs. People brushed past her irritably as she gaped at him. "You mean to say you actually know how to get your tokens back from the turnstiles once you've passed through?" she demanded.

"Of course. Actually, it's so easy, I'm surprised more people don't do it."

"Chance!"

"Hey, lady, you gonna stand here blocking traffic all night?" muttered someone trying to push his way past Ally.

"This is amazing," Ally said.

"Oh, come on, Ally. You weren't nearly this impressed when I lit that cigarette with my bare hands in Monty's office, and that was a lot more difficult. Shall we get out of everyone's way now?"

Ally was nonplussed when he refused to discuss his trick or share his secret. They boarded a crowded train. There were no seats available, so they stood together near the door and held onto railings for support. The train jolted alarmingly every time it stopped and started, so Chance put his arm around Ally to steady her.

The roar of the train speeding through its tunnel was far too loud to permit conversation, so Ally leaned against Chance silently, and surreptitiously studied the angle of his strong jaw and the sheen of his wavy blond hair as they rode along.

She felt incredibly aware of the strong arm he curved around her back and used to hold her loosely, casually, against him. An unexpected excitement stirred inside of her. He was so obviously just being considerate, so obviously not making a pass, that she felt perturbed with her uninvited reaction to him.

Who was he, she wondered, this magician with whom she had nothing in common, this gorgeous man who felt faintly embarrassed by his producer's heavy-handed attempts to make him look sexier, this irreverent and mischievous country boy who was committed, eloquent, and dedicated?

He was full of surprises, in more ways than one. Did the women in his life wake up to find him conjuring breakfast out of thin air? Was there a special woman in his life? When he said good-bye, did he vanish with a puff of smoke?

"What are you laughing at?" Chance asked suspiciously.

"Oh, idle thoughts. Come on, we get off here," Ally added as the train drew to a jerky halt.

They left the subway and walked outside. Ally turned and led him down a street.

"Where are we?" he asked in confusion.

"West Ninety-third Street."

After another block, Chance said, "I can't believe you were actually going to walk through this neighborhood alone at this time of night." His eyes narrowed threateningly as several tough-looking teenage boys ambled by.

"I'm used to it. It's not bad. You just have to be alert."

Chance's grunt indicated he was unconvinced. "How long have you lived here?"

"I've been in New York for seven years. I came here pretty soon after I finished college. I've been at this apartment for five years."

"Do you live alone?"

"I do now. I had roommates for three years, but after the last one moved out, I was working steadily and decided to live alone." She added ruefully, "Of course, if things don't look up soon, I may have to go back to sharing the apartment."

It seemed the right time to ask her if she had a boyfriend or special man in her life. He doubted she'd consider it too personal a question. He couldn't fathom why he was so reluctant to risk finding out that she did. He remained silent, though the question burned in his mind.

"Here we are," she said. "It's a nice old building." She turned to face him. The streetlamp behind him gleamed off his pale golden hair and obscured the expression on his face as he looked down at her. "Thanks for seeing me home, Chance," she said formally. Why was her voice so absurdly breathless? she wondered irritably. Why did her heart start pounding? Why did he stare so enigmatically at her in the darkness?

"Good night, Ally." His voice was low and husky.

He didn't move. She realized that he must be waiting

for her to get safely inside. Turn around and go, she thought. Now, she thought. But her feet stayed glued to the ground in front of Chance, and her eyes continued to search his darkened face.

"Ally . . ." He muttered something unintelligible, then his hands closed around her shoulders and pulled her towards him. And then she knew why she hadn't gone inside.

Her eyes closed and her head tilted back as smoothly as if the scene had been directed. She felt his lips on hers then; gentle, exploring, warm and moist. She wanted him to kiss her harder, but he teased and played, tasting, testing. His mouth brushed hers again and again with feather-light touches, stroke after stroke, so delicate and quick, they almost couldn't be called kisses. But her fuzzy mind couldn't think of any kiss that had ever excited her so much.

She tried to deepen their kisses, and she felt him pull back to tease her. Suddenly hungry, and uncharacteristically aggressive, she pressed her body against his. She felt him smile with pleasure against her lips.

His arms slid down her shoulders and around her back, pulling her closer. His hands were strong, warm, confident. She gasped. How did he know to touch her like that? Where had he learned to touch a woman so surely, skillfully, suggestively? He massaged her back and stroked her hair and then, finally, he kissed her deeply and slid his velvety tongue into her mouth.

"Mmmmm." She heard the sound before she realized that she was making it. His tongue swept her mouth boldly, as if he had kissed her before, as if he knew exactly how to please her. She pressed her palm against his jaw and felt the muscles working there, felt his absorption in her, his concentration on her. Her mind started to reel giddily.

He broke off their kiss suddenly and pressed her head against his shoulder. He rested his cheek against her hair. She shifted, and the hard bulge she felt against her belly made her gasp. Then she realized how fast they were both breathing. Was she trembling? She was so disoriented, she wasn't sure. He knew more magic spells than she had suspected.

He didn't apologize for his obvious arousal, nor did he try to act on it. He simply held her, and she discovered she was neither embarrassed nor alarmed. Though her reactions weren't as obvious as his, they were just as strong, and she had a feeling he knew.

After a long, cozy moment, he grasped her shoulders and pushed her away unsteadily. He took a deep breath and let it out in uneven laughter. "So much for being a gentleman," he said.

"I might have been safer by myself," she agreed.

"You'd better go inside."

"Uh-huh."

They stood there staring at each other. She wished that she could see his face. She wished he would touch her again. Mostly she wished she didn't feel this way.

"I'll see you tomorrow," he said at last. "I guess . . . we'll need to think about this. Or maybe try it again." He grinned slowly. She could see the white flash of his smile against his dark visage. She could suddenly feel his teeth nibbling on her lips as surely as if he were kissing her again. She swallowed.

"Tomorrow," she choked out, then turned and fled. He really was a sorcerer.

Ally had a long night of tossing and turning and restlessly remembering every detail and sensation of the few minutes she had spent wrapped in Chance's arms. At one point, when sleep had finally opened its arms to her, she had such a vivid dream about him that she awoke with a start, certain he must be in the room with her.

After her initial confusion, she chided herself for believing, even for a moment, that he could cast a love spell on her.

Ally arrived at their rehearsal the next day in a precarious emotional state. She was exhausted from her nearly sleepless night, scared to death of what ghoulish trick

Chance would coax her into trying today, and nervous about seeing him after last night.

So she was outraged to find him cheerfully hard at work, completely absorbed in setting up another illusion with Angus and Zeke, and looking well rested and refreshed. He didn't help his own cause any by greeting her with casual friendliness and then turning his attention back to his work as if nothing different had happened between them.

She started to truly regret, even fear, the attraction that had come to full blossom between them last night. Hadn't she learned her lesson already? She had no judgment when it came to men. She knew better than to trust her instincts—the same ones that virtually seemed to control her whenever she saw Chance Weal.

She hardly even *knew* him. What was she *doing*? What had happened to all her sensible resolutions?

No more actors, she had promised herself. No more men in show business, period—and that surely included magicians. No more infatuation for a guy based on something stupid and insubstantial, like his beautiful smile, his old-fashioned manners, his good looks, his passion for his work, his hot kisses . . . Good Lord, I'm doing it again!

When she saw him approaching her, she braced herself. She must make it clear that last night had been a mistake. She wasn't going to let another man leave his footprints on her back. The mere fact that she was attracted to Chance was enough to make her doubt his character. Experience had finally made her wiser.

"About ready to get to work, Ally?" Chance said as he joined her next to the coffee he had brought into the studio for everyone.

"Yes," she said crisply, professionally.

"Where's the cream?"

She handed it to him, resisting the urge to tell him it was right under his nose.

"You look gorgeous today," he said. He took a long sip of coffee and grinned slowly at her. The intimate light in his eyes made her feel hot. "I guess I still half expect you to look completely different every time I see you."

She raised her brows and tried to look cool.

"You have a very mobile face," he said suddenly. "You could have looked like a . . . a courtesan without all that makeup and costuming."

"That's hardly a compliment, Chance."

"Isn't it? Well, no, maybe not. I just meant that you don't need anything extra to make you sizzle." He leaned forward and whispered confidentially. "Or to make me sizzle, either."

"Chance—"

"I wish Angus and Zeke weren't here right now." His voice was too enticing. She felt herself weakening.

Stiffening her resolve, she put her coffee down rather more forcefully than she had intended. It sloshed over the sides and spilled onto the fold-out table.

"Did you burn yourself?" he asked, quickly putting down his own coffee and taking her hand to examine it.

"No," she said, trying to pull her hand out of his.

"You sure?" He wouldn't let go. Instead, he took a paper napkin and wiped her palm and wrist with tender care. The gesture nearly undid her.

"Quite sure. Stop making a fuss," she snapped.

He went still and peered closely at her. "What's wrong?"

She glanced uneasily over at Angus and Zeke. They were busy. She might as well get it over with right now. "Nothing's wrong. I just think you may have gotten the wrong idea about me, that's all."

"Well, we've admittedly had our ups and downs, but I—"

"No, I mean last night."

He stared at her, waiting for her to continue.

"I didn't expect anything like that to happen, and I don't intend to let it happen again. We're just stuck working together for a week, and that's all," she said. There.

He lowered his eyes and turned away slightly. He picked up his coffee and sipped it with slow deliberation.

Ally's stomach churned; she liked it better when he fought back.

"What brought this on?" he asked at last.

She felt the phrase made it sound like she was overreacting to what had happened between them. "What 'brought this on' was your behavior last night."

His eyes flashed up to her face. Now he looked angry. "*My* behavior?"

"Yes."

"There were two of us there, Ally, and you seemed pretty enthusiastic at the time. In fact, I'd say it was as much your idea as mine." His voice was quiet and even, but she sensed a lot of turmoil.

"I'm not going to make excuses for my behavior," she said, trying to match his even tone. "'It was inappropriate and ill advised, and it's not going to happen again. I suggest we put it behind us and get on with the job at hand." Eager to end the scene, she turned on her heel and walked over to Angus and Zeke.

Chance watched her walk away, resisting the urge to start a fight, drag her off somewhere to change her mind, or just sit down and feel depressed.

Of course, it was perfectly reasonable for a co-worker to suggest they avoid personal complications and just get the job done. But he doubted that had anything to do with Ally's motivations. She just didn't respect him. She had been carried away by the attraction they couldn't deny last night. He had mistaken her trusting, giving response for something more, for a very special kind of magic.

Despite a physical arousal that couldn't be satisfied, he had gone home last night feeling great. And now he knew it was an illusion. He felt the way he had at the age of nine when he had discovered that magic wasn't magic at all, and that magicians weren't sorcerers but merely men who were masters of sleight of hand, diversion, and deception.

But Ally had just made her true feelings brutally clear; she thought he was unworthy of her respect and therefore unworthy of her affection. It would be foolish to even entertain the idea of changing her mind. There had been one woman before whose mind he had tried to change, and that had ended in bitterness and futility. There was no room in Chance's life for a woman who considered him a cheap trickster.

He tried to contain his anger and hurt, and behave professionally that morning. Ally was entitled to her opinion, after all, however erroneous. She was also entitled to tell him not to touch her again, no matter how hard that might be for him. So he was annoyed with himself for being almost incapable of treating her civilly the rest of the day.

Despite the arguments and exasperation of the previous two days, they actually *had* had fun, and enjoyed being together. Today they got far more work done, but they nearly drove each other crazy. Chance was snappish and terse, and his compliments when Ally did something well sounded hollow and cold even to his own ears. The expression in Ally's eyes told him that in addition to being a cheap trickster, he was also an unprofessional macho creep who couldn't deal with a woman who had said no. He hated to think of himself that way, and he wanted to rail at her for changing a good day into a rotten one.

When he finally called it quits for the day, everyone looked inordinately relieved. Chance said he would be staying late to work alone and would lock up by himself.

"We haven't talked about what I should wear," Ally said to Chance as Zeke and Angus tidied up.

"You're not supposed to watch them taking apart the equipment."

"Just answer my damn question and I'll go," Ally said in exasperation.

"Wear whatever you want," he said dismissively, turning away from her and rolling up his sleeves.

"Look, I'm trying to be cooperative. It's *your* act, after all, and I thought you might have an opinion. Don't you think you could put aside your silly personal complaints for just a minute, and—"

Chance whirled around, stung by her tone, her words,

and her unwavering disapproval. "Don't push me, Ally," he warned. "I don't have to take you with me."

"*I'm* the one who's trying to be reasonable."

"You'd better try harder, then." He wanted to give her a taste of her own medicine. "New York is full of unemployed actresses who imagine that their pretty faces and good bodies can land them a job if only they could have a *personal* interview with the director," he said scathingly. "If you want me to help you meet Houston, then you'd better tread lightly around me. Or do you want to go back to using your impressive dramatic training from the inside of a shark suit?"

Ally went pale at the contempt in his voice. Her eyes looked suspiciously misty the instant before she whirled away and fled from the studio, leaving him the uncontested victor on their battlefield.

Victory had a guilty, bitter taste.

FOUR

"What do you mean, we're sharing a room?" Ally demanded.

She kept her voice low, even though they were unlikely to attract much attention in the colorful, noisy lobby of the Wilson Palace Hotel in Atlantic City.

"You were a late addition to the act, Ally," Chance said, holding on to his patience with a death grip. "The room arrangements were made before anyone knew you would be joining me." He hadn't given it a thought until now. "I'm sorry. I never remember to think of details like that."

"This is a big hotel. There must be another room available for me," she insisted.

Chance glanced over his shoulder at the bored face of the bellboy, who was waiting to be told where to take their luggage. "Sorry, Ally. They're booked solid, and they're not going to throw out a paying guest to comp another room for you. Believe me, I tried to talk them into it."

"Why is it so crowded here?"

"They've got celebrities, socialites, and politicians from all over the country here for this benefit this weekend."

"So, as usual, it's the lowly entertainers who get short shrift," Ally grumbled. "But surely there's—I don't know—a maid's room I could stay in, or something like that.''

Her expression made it clear that staying in a broom closet would be preferable to sharing a room with him. It irked him. ''Believe me, if there were a single room in this whole hotel that you could use for free, I'd have found out about it. I tried.''

Ally thought he needn't have made that last phrase sound quite so heartfelt, as if he'd rather share his room with a hungry boa constrictor than with her. ''What about Angus and Zeke?'' she asked. ''When they get here tomorrow, are they staying with us, too?''

''No. They're packing up and leaving tomorrow night, right after the show.''

Ally frowned, realizing that she and Chance would be stuck with each other's company for two nights running. Things between them had been chilly, to say the least, since she had laid down the law with him. Although they had smoothed out the details of her participation in Chance's act, the personal vibrations between them were anything but smooth. She wished she could just stop noticing him.

''All right,'' she grumbled. ''Let's go get changed.''

''Fine.'' Chance signaled to the slightly built bellboy, who followed them to the elevator.

Ally took a last disbelieving glance at the lobby as the elevator doors swished shut. She had never seen anything so vulgar in her life, not even on Eighth Avenue. The hotel's interior was a plush, costly, extravagant nightmare of gilded mirrors, enormous chandeliers, marble columns, thunderous water fountains, and thick Persian rugs redundantly covering red wall-to-wall carpeting. If the decorator had intended to convey anything other than too much money and too little restraint, he had failed miserably.

Their room was on the ninth floor, and they both fidgeted tensely while waiting for the bellboy to finish showing them all the magnificent comforts available to them.

''There's a color television here in the bathroom,'' the lad said, his speech well rehearsed and unenthusiastic. ''It swivels, so you can watch your favorite program whether you're using the tub, the sink, the toilet, or the bidet.''

''Thought of everything, didn't they?'' Chance muttered.

The bellboy, impervious to sarcasm, went on to show them the wet bar, the balcony, the intercom, the complimentary bathrobes, and the entertainment cabinet.

''Complete with radio, television, and stereo, to meet *all* your entertainment needs,'' he proclaimed in a flat voice. ''As a special feature of the television service here at the Wilson Palace, we provide three adult channels free of charge.''

Chance blinked. ''Adult channels?''

''Porn,'' Ally supplied. ''You know: *Cheerleaders in Chains, Vicky Gets Wet, Boldfinger—*''

''Oh, wow, that's my favorite!'' said the bellboy, showing his first sign of enthusiasm. ''I've seen it three times. I love the part where—''

''Yes, well,'' Chance interrupted. Ally could have sworn he was blushing. ''Thank you for your help, um . . .''

''Harvey, sir. If you need anything, just ask.''

Chance pressed a fiver into the boy's palm and urged him toward the door. ''Harvey. Right. Thanks for your help, kid.'' He shut the door behind the boy and leaned against it.

Ally looked around the room. It was a miniature version of the lobby, except that, mercifully, there was no fountain. ''Nice chandelier,'' she said deadpan, looking up.

''Hmmm. Nice marble pillars around the bathtub,'' Chance murmured.

''Nice gold mirrors.''

''Nice red velvet bedspreads.''

Their eyes met, and they burst out laughing. Ally flung herself down on the bed nearest the window and sprawled on her stomach, giggling as she rubbed her cheek against the nubby red fabric. Chance crossed the room and sat down next to her.

"I've seen kennels that were better decorated than this place," Ally wheezed.

"Wilson's got more money than taste, that's for sure." He looked down at Ally and felt the animosity of the past week start to seep away. She looked so lovely when she laughed, her blue-green eyes glowing, her pale cheeks flushing. Her hair was tousled, and her simple black slacks clung to her shapely bottom as she lay on her stomach, face turned up to smile at him.

"Didn't I read somewhere that this is the most expensive hotel ever built?" She chuckled again.

"It's one of them anyhow."

She rolled over on her back and looked up at the chandelier again. "He doesn't need to host charity events to raise money for homeless children. He could just demolish this place and sell off the pieces." She grinned and sat bolt upright. When she spoke again, her voice was a perfect imitation of a professional auctioneer—fast, monotonous, impelled by a stirring, staccato rhythm. "What am I bid for this lovely chandelier, ladies and gentlemen? Who'll say five thousand? Do I hear five, five, five? Gimme a three, gimme a three, gimme a three! I'm bid three! Who'll say four, four, four?"

Chance laughed, noticing the way everything about her changed subtly to fit the role of the auctioneer: her shoulders, her facial expression, the tilt of her chin. She was a true actress.

"It probably would have saved a lot of trouble if he'd just done that," Chance admitted ruefully.

"But then you and I would have missed the opportunity to watch TV from the bidet," Ally reminded him.

"And what a shame that would have been."

They smiled at each other again, and Chance thought that there were a lot of things he might say or do right now, if she hadn't already told him not to. Instead, he heard himself ask, "You got a boyfriend?"

Surprised, Ally answered, "No. Do you?" He laughed, and she added, "I mean, do you have a . . ." She rolled her eyes. " 'Boyfriend, girlfriend.' They're awful words, aren't they? I'm twenty-nine. A little old to date *boys*."

"I'm thirty-two. A little old to date *girls*."

"So do you have a woman?" she asked.

"Not lately." He shrugged. "I've been on the road so much, and . . . Not lately."

"I've been through a dry spell ever since I . . ."

"What?"

She wondered why they were talking about this. Maybe because they were curled up together on her bed like little kids, needing to reach out to each other while they adjusted to this strange place. Maybe he deserved to know the truth. She decided to be frank. "Ever since I decided to stop dating actors. The problem is, I mostly *meet* actors."

"What's wrong with actors?" he asked curiously.

Ally sighed dramatically and flopped back down on her back. "What's *wrong* with actors? Have you got about three hours?"

Looking down at her, he wished to hell that he did. "Actually, no," he said with regret, glancing at his watch. "And neither do you." They had left the city late that afternoon, cutting it close. "We're due at this bash in about a half hour."

Ally slid off the bed. "Can I have the bathroom first?"

"Sure."

She smiled. "Don't worry. I won't take long."

"Okay."

They stared at each other, suddenly both tinglingly aware of the intimacy of sharing a room. Until now, Ally's only thoughts had been about how tense it would be, considering their ill-concealed irritation with each other. But as she looked away from Chance's soft brown eyes, she suddenly recalled the reason for their mutual annoyance— the dark, hot kisses that had triggered this thing between them, the magical feel of those hard, strong hands on her body, shaping her bottom, stroking her back. . . .

"Did you forget something?" Chance asked.

"Huh?" She started as if he'd shouted, then realized

she'd been staring blankly at the contents of her cosmetics case as if she'd never seen them before. Embarrassed, and aware of the weight of his gaze, she picked the whole thing up and carried it into the bathroom with her, slamming the door behind her as if she were afraid he'd try to follow.

Chance stared at the closed bathroom door and fought down the unwelcome impulse to kick it open and follow Ally inside. He heard the water running and tried not to picture her taking off her clothes as she prepared for her shower, tried not to imagine her pulling that black knit shirt over her head, then reaching behind to unfasten her bra and free her soft . . . He shook his head, trying to chase away the visions that entered it uninvited.

After a few more minutes, Ally turned off the water, and there was silence in the bathroom. She'd be drying herself now, he knew, wiping glistening beads of water off her smooth, damp skin, missing a few drops as they rolled down her flat belly. If he were there, would he catch them with his tongue, or would he watch them roll down into the dark triangle of hair that nestled between her thighs?

Chance sprang to his feet as if he'd been stung. Sitting around on a red velvet bed clearly wasn't doing him any good. He flung open his suitcase and began unpacking with vigor. However, since he had only brought enough clothes for the weekend, that task was quickly accomplished, and he again found himself with nothing to do but wait for Ally to come out of the bathroom.

Even if it had been a while since there'd been a steady woman in his life, he knew the ways of women well. She'd be putting on lotion now, pouring it into her palm to warm it up a bit, then spreading it over her creamy white shoulders and the firm, graceful length of her arms. Her hair would be tied up or wrapped in a towel, revealing the delicate strength of her features without the softening frame of those shiny brown waves. The bathroom would smell of her when he got inside. Body lotion, face cream, the citrus shampoo he could sometimes smell on her hair when she brushed by him, the minty scent of her toothpaste, and that warm, unmistakable underlying fragrance of a woman's flesh. The sweetest perfume on earth.

Chance felt the tightening of his body and knew it was definitely time to distract himself. He opened the doors of the entertainment cabinet—which was designed to look like a small pagoda—and turned on the TV.

"Do it! *Do it!* Yes, yes, yes! *Yes!*" cried a buxom, naked actress.

"*Yeah!*" screamed one of her sexual partners.

"Oooh, baby! Ooh, ooh, *ooooh!*" moaned another of her partners.

Chance's eyes bulged. "Adult entertainment?"

"Again! *Again!*" cried the actress.

"Wow," Chance said, as one performer did things with a tongue that was so long and dexterous, it must have undergone special training.

Chance looked up when he heard the bathroom door click. "What are you watching?" Ally asked, coming back into the bedroom. She wore one of the hotel's complimentary bathrobes, its vee neck plunging discreetly to the shadowy hollow between her breasts, which gleamed faintly with residual dampness.

Chance felt his mouth go dry. "I'm not sure. *Boldfinger*, maybe?" Suddenly the phony, exaggerated cries of ecstasy coming from the oversize television didn't seem quite as ridiculous as they had a moment ago.

Ally's eyes widened. "Wow, look at that tongue," she said in amazement. "He must do special exercises or something."

Chance choked on his laughter. They looked at each other. Ally's hair was freshly blow-dried, and she had put on makeup.

"You look . . ." He hesitated, painfully aware of the sighs and moans echoing around them. He glanced at the screen again and then looked away uncomfortably. "You look very pretty."

"Thank you." She lowered her eyes. Her chest rose and fell quickly beneath the terry cloth robe.

"Please, please," someone begged breathlessly.

"You can use the shower now," Ally said, still avoiding Chance's eyes.

"Now! Now! NOW!" the porn actress cried, her head thrown back in abandon, her voice wild with feigned delight.

Chance's skin flushed with mingled desire and embarrassment. "Uh, maybe I should change the channel."

"Uh-huh."

However, Harvey the bellboy had neglected to demonstrate how to operate the high-tech system, and nothing they tried seemed to work. When changing the channel proved to be impossible, they attempted, without success, to turn the TV off.

"How'd you turn it on?" Ally demanded.

"I just pressed the top button."

"Well, it doesn't work."

"Maybe if we tried the remote," Chance suggested, trying to ignore the sighs of satiation coming from the TV.

The remote didn't work either.

"Maybe we should just unplug it," Ally said, getting down on her hands and knees to follow the electric cable to its source. She met Chance nose to nose at the spot where the cable entered the wall.

"There's no socket," he pointed out.

"Can't we just pull it out of the wall?"

"Even if we could . . ." He demonstrated with a hard yank that the cable was sturdier than it looked. He shook his head. "We'd wind up with a bunch of exposed live wires."

"Oh. Can we disconnect it from the other end?"

"Not without some power tools." The cable ran directly through a small hole in the back of the gaudy pagoda.

"Kiss me," Vicky begged. They had learned during the past five minutes that the heroine of the movie was named Vicky.

"Are you *sure* the remote doesn't work?" Ally asked.

"I'll try again."

He helped her to her feet. Her skin was so warm, he felt its heat through the thick material of the robe. He wished he didn't like touching her quite so much.

They pushed every button they could find, on both the TV set and the remote, to no avail.

"Nothing," Chance said, shaking the remote in frustration.

"Here, let me try again," Ally said, reaching for it.

"No, wait a minute," Chance said firmly. "I can make an elephant disappear into thin air. I can saw a woman in half and then put her back together. I can levitate." He gave the remote a savage shake with each sentence. "*Surely* I can turn off one stubborn television."

Ally could see this was turning into one of those male obsessions, like putting together a bicycle on Christmas morning without looking at the instructions, or finding the leak in a car's engine without consulting a mechanic. "Here, give it to me," she insisted.

"Just a minute."

She reached for the remote. They wrestled for it and started laughing again. Their hands locked at last and they stared at each other, breathing fast.

"Stalemate," Ally said.

"*Touch me,*" Vicky begged. "Just touch me."

"Just let me . . ." He noticed that Ally's eyes looked more blue than green in the shadowy light of their darkening room.

"Oh, *yes, touch me there,*" Vicky sighed. Ally glanced at the screen, then back at Chance.

"Let me touch . . . I mean *fix,* uh . . ." Ally's voice trailed off in confusion. She licked her lips nervously.

"Give me your tongue," Vicky whispered seductively. "*Hmmmm.*"

"Here, Ally! You take it." Chance's voice sounded unnaturally loud, even to him. "I'll go speak to maintenance about this while you, uh, get dressed. Okay?"

He was out the door before Ally had time to blink again. He sure could move fast when he wanted to.

"Oh, *baby,* that's so good."

"Shut up, Vicky, or I'll belt you one," Ally muttered.

The room positively vibrated with sexual tension, most of it her own. While Ally believed that not getting involved with Chance was the only sensible choice, she was unhappily aware that she was currently sending him some very mixed signals. The problem was, her brain didn't have complete control over her hormones. All week, while they had worked together in perfect disharmony, she couldn't help noticing him in precisely the way she didn't want to notice him. That lazy softness in his eyes. The way his grin spread across his face, slow and unwilling at first, then speeding up into a flash of uninhibited sunshine. The smooth bulge and flow of his upper arms beneath his shirt, the narrow width of his hips, the easy grace of his movements, and the way the sun played on his butter blond hair all crept into her consciousness no matter how hard she tried to prevent it.

Ally pulled her evening dress out of her garment bag and ground her teeth together. *She* was the one who had decided to take things no further, she reminded herself. She knew better.

She liked to think that her excuse for all the times she had been wrong about men was that she was young and naive. However, at twenty-nine, she didn't think that excuse held much water anymore. As time went by, its corollary was that maybe she was just plain stupid. She had fallen madly in love with her college boyfriend, an acting student, because he had beautiful, lean, long-fingered hands. That was all. She had remained devoted to the jerk for over a year because she liked his *hands*. It was only after the relationship was over that she realized how crazy that was.

After two years of lonely celibacy, she had then gotten involved with another actor. This one claimed her devotion because no one in the world could play tormented postmodern characters the way he could. The problem was, he played them in private, too.

Her problem was, she was a romantic. If a man could make her go all gooey on the inside, she assumed it was fate, destiny, karma; and she never stopped to consider that it took more than beautiful hands or great character roles to make a man worthy of her love and capable of returning it.

"Got a light?" Vicky asked a muscle-bound young man, batting her fake eyelashes at him.

"This is a no-smoking room, Vicky," Ally told her, slipping her evening gown over her head. She and Chance weren't performing until tomorrow, but Ambrose Kettering, Chance's new television producer, had wanted Chance to arrive in time for tonight's gala party. Monty said it was to ensure Chance would be able to attract attention and get his name mentioned in *People, Variety,* and the *Times.* Ally had readily cooperated, since the more time they spent at this place, the more likely she was to find an opportunity to approach Roland Houston.

She was just checking her appearance in the full-length gilded mirror when Chance returned, with Harvey in tow. "Look who I found," Chance said with questionable confidence.

"I thought you were going to get a maintenance man," Ally responded, looking doubtfully at Harvey.

"I decided to follow my grandfather's advice, instead," Chance explained. "Anytime you're having trouble with technology, call a kid for help."

"Hey, I love this movie!" Harvey exclaimed, plumping himself down on the bed Ally had claimed.

"Vicky Gets Wet?"

"No, this is the sequel: *Vicky Gets Wetter.* Has she been kidnapped by the Chinatown warlord yet?"

"Not that I've noticed," Ally admitted. "Can you turn this thing off?"

"Sure." Harvey pressed a button and frowned.

"We tried that," Ally told him.

A brief struggle with the television confirmed Ally's worst fears. Harvey said, "It's broken. We'll have to get a repairman up here."

"Look, we're late already for this bash downstairs," Chance began.

"Oh, wow. Are you here for that? There's, like, a million movie stars and New York socialites and crooked politicians and things here for that," Harvey said. "Are you, like, a politician?"

"No, he's, like, a magician. Can you get a repairman up here right away?" Ally didn't bother to conceal her impatience as Vicky performed an acrobatic and rather improbable feat with the young man who had given her a cigarette.

"A magician? So where's your rabbit?"

Chance sighed. "I'll call Maintenance."

"No, *I'll* call Maintenance," Ally said. "You get changed."

Chance disappeared into the bathroom. To Ally's surprise, he emerged well before she had finished her brief phone call. "So you're a quick-change artist, too?"

He shrugged. "It comes in handy."

She had half feared he would simply wear a newer pair of blue jeans to the formal event, but he looked devilishly handsome in a traditional black tuxedo. More than one woman would be looking their way tonight, she realized.

"Maintenance will have a look at it tonight," Ally told Chance. "Harvey, we're leaving now."

" 'Bye." He was engrossed in Vicky's next conquest.

"Harvey . . ."

"Forget it, Ally." Chance steered her out of the room. "I remember what it was like to be eighteen. You won't get his attention again until the movie's over. Not even," he added with an appreciative look, "in that dress."

As they rode the elevator down to the mezzanine level, Chance surreptitiously admiring the way Ally's pale satin evening dress clung to her body, he reflected that perhaps it wasn't such a bad thing that their television had malfunctioned. At least it had broken the ice between them, eliminating the chill that had existed all week. Ally was smiling openly at him and speculating about whether the repairman would fix the TV or sit down and join Harvey in his admiration of Vicky's adventures.

On the other hand, he couldn't forget the expression on

her face right before he'd had the good sense to clear out of the room and find Harvey. It reminded him of the way she had looked outside her apartment building that night, all soft and willing and interested. He had responded to that look then, and it had earned him a tongue lashing the morning after, as well as a very unpleasant week in general. He wished he knew what she wanted. But then, his grandfather had always said that the next man who figured out a woman's mind would be the very first.

"Here's our floor," Ally said, bringing him back to reality.

The words "cocktail party" hadn't prepared Ally for the spectacle they discovered upon entering the grand ballroom. Helmut Wilson, owner of the Wilson Palace Hotel and Casino, greeted them at the door. Or, rather, they were presented to Wilson by one of the dozen acolytes who surrounded him like bodyguards and waited on him like devoted slaves.

Wilson was the only son of a German countess and an American banker, both now deceased. This new hotel was only one of the Wilson empire's many financial concerns. Recently Wilson had even begun dabbling in the arts. Ally recalled reading that he had lost millions backing a Broadway musical based on a popular novel with a neolithic setting; after the most expensive advertising campaign of any show in Broadway history, the production had folded in just eight days.

Wilson, however, appeared to have emerged unscathed from that experience, Ally noted. He was slim and tan, with slightly silvered hair, perfect teeth, and well-manicured hands. Even without the introduction, though, Ally thought she would have recognized him as the owner of the hotel. He had the same air of overfinanced ostentation. She had never before seen a man who wore so much jewelry on his hands.

"He could sell those diamonds and feed all of Somalia," she whispered to Chance as they waited in line to be introduced.

"Which diamonds? His or his wife's?" he whispered back.

Ally's gaze moved to Celine Gautier Wilson, the French blueblood Wilson had married ten years earlier; her second marriage, his third. "*Hers* could feed the entire African continent," Ally murmured.

A beautiful, well-preserved woman, Mrs. Wilson sported a tan that matched her husband's, as well as a glittering diamond and sapphire necklace that must have weighed five pounds.

"Look at the size of those stones," Chance said softly, gazing at them in awe. "You could cut up each one and still make a killing on the black market."

"What do you know about black-market diamonds?" Ally asked.

"Just what I read." He shrugged. "There are probably a hundred people here tonight thinking the same thing. If those are real and not just a good copy, she's crazy to wear them out in public."

"*Are* they real?" Ally couldn't tell good diamonds from cheap glass.

The Wilsons provided the answer a moment later when the guest directly in front of Chance and Ally, a badly dressed guy with dark, slicked-back hair, had the bad manners to ask, "Are those gems real, Mrs. Wilson?"

"But of course," she said, her accent as rich as cream.

"Surely you've been advised how dangerous it is to wear such valuable jewels in public?"

Ally and Chance leaned forward, shamelessly eavesdropping. Helmut Wilson frowned, and Ally wondered briefly if he was annoyed by the man's questions. When Wilson spoke, however, she realized wryly that no man who had built this monstrosity of a hotel would be offended by vulgar manners.

"We've been advised to have a copy made for Celine to wear in public." Wilson's dismissive expression told them all what he thought of *that.* "What's the point of owning beautiful things if you can't show them off in public?"

The possessive glance he gave his wife made Ally suspect that the woman was included in the list of beautiful things that Wilson owned.

"How much is that thing worth?" the frumpy man in front of Chance asked. Chance rolled his eyes at Ally, amazed at the audacity of some people.

Wilson, however, appeared to enjoy answering the question. "It was appraised in Paris when I purchased it, in the spring. The workmanship places it beyond value, of course," he intoned. "That's white gold, you know. But the stones themselves are worth well over a million dollars."

"Wow!" Ally reddened when all eyes turned toward her and she realized she was the one who had made the uncouth exclamation.

Since they had been noticed, Chance stepped forward, dragging Ally by the elbow, hoping to get the introductions over with. He wanted to find a cold beer and a quiet corner. "Mr. and Mrs. Wilson. Pleasure to meet you. I'm Chance Weal. This is Alicia Cannon. I can see you're very busy, so we'll just—"

"Oh, darling! *C'est lui*—the magician! How marvelous!" Celine Wilson warbled throatily.

"Ah, yes, my dear. You mentioned him." Wilson flashed his perfect teeth at Chance. "When Ambrose Kettering told my wife you would be performing for us, she could hardly contain herself."

She was having a little trouble containing herself *now*, Ally noticed; that gown was awfully low-cut. The woman fawned over Chance, babbling about having seen him perform in Vegas and what an impression it had made on her, and what a thrill it had been to see him again on a recent nighttime talk show. The silly man just soaked it up. But any fool could see that it wasn't *magic* that inspired the woman's enthusiasm as she encouraged Chance to tell her all about himself.

"Ambrose is going to produce a one-hour television special around my work," Chance explained in answer to her questions. "That's how he wound up asking me to perform for you tomorrow."

"We're not performing for *her*," Ally heard herself interrupt in a perfectly even, measured, reasonable tone. "We're performing to raise money for homeless children, Chance."

Everyone turned and looked at her as if she'd just said something wildly inappropriate. Finally Celine broke the silence. "You will be performing with Chance?"

Ally locked gazes with the woman. "Yes."

"I see."

So did Ally. Any woman in the world would have recognized that look. Of course, what Celine didn't realize was that Ally and Chance were not a couple, so there was no question of competition between the two women. No sirree, absolutely not. Celine was free to move in on Chance any time she wanted, if she could ditch her husband. Ally didn't care one bit.

"Where did you learn to speak English so well, Celine?" Chance asked, breaking the awkward silence and turning the full force of his charm on the Frenchwoman. The *married* Frenchwoman, Ally amended silently.

"Oh, you think I speak well, do you?" Celine laughed prettily at this clever bit of repartee.

Ally didn't hear Chance's answer. She was busy thinking that he had some bloody *nerve*, dragging her to Atlantic City and then flirting with another woman right under her nose. Ignoring the rational portion of her brain, which tried to point out that this wasn't an entirely fair assessment of the situation, she turned abruptly to the frumpy man with bad manners, who was still hanging around.

"I'm sorry. I don't believe anyone has bothered to introduce us." She cast a look at Chance and the Wilsons to let them know she blamed all three of them equally for this terrible breach of etiquette.

"Walter Dureau, ma'am," the man said awkwardly, pressing a clammy palm against the hand she offered him in greeting.

"Alicia Cannon. You're an acquaintance of the Wilsons? A fellow philanthropist?"

"Huh? Oh." He tried, rather unsuccessfully, to look worldly and aggressive. "I'm a financier."

"Really?" Ally tried hard to look interested. "And what do you finance?"

"Oh. Things. You know."

She nodded as if she did know, then took his arm and said, "I'm awfully thirsty, Mr. Dureau, and no one has offered me a drink yet."

"Really?"

Dureau didn't offer her a drink either. Instead, he dumped her with some shabby excuse as soon as they were out of sight of the Wilsons, leaving her alone to fend for herself. After procuring a glass of warm, flat, domestic champagne, Ally quickly got lost in the crowd. Chance didn't find her until more than an hour had passed.

"What's the big idea, disappearing and leaving me alone like that?" he demanded.

"Alone?" she repeated, brows raised, voice vibrating with cool surprise. "Didn't the tiger lady keep you company?"

"Tiger . . ." Chance looked at the ceiling, as if the explanation for Ally's behavior could be found there. Then he said the worst possible thing. "I think she's nice. Why don't you like her?"

"What makes *you* like her so *much*?" Ally asked, reaching for a glass of something liquid as a waiter whizzed past.

"I didn't say I like her so *much*, I just . . . What's wrong?"

Her face was screwed up in reaction to the drink she had just sipped. "This is disgusting! Can't a person get an ordinary soda around here?"

Chance grimaced. "The food's pretty lousy, too."

"Food? You've found food?" she pounced.

"Celine showed me where the buffet is. It's pretty easy to get lost in here." He put a restraining hand on Ally's arm, smiling at the way she sniffed the air in search of sustenance. "Trust me. We'd be better off finding a burger joint."

"I don't want to leave just yet. . . ." She glanced around the room again.

"I asked the Wilsons, Ally. He's not coming until tomorrow."

"Roland Houston?"

He nodded, sorry to see the way it made her shoulders droop. A minute later, Ally was rudely jostled by an Arab wearing beautiful white, gold-trimmed robes with matching headgear. When the man didn't even apologize for causing Ally's drink to splatter her gown, Chance grabbed his arm and said, "Hey, watch it!"

The Arab jerked out of Chance's grasp and said to Ally, "Out of my way, woman." His voice couldn't have been more contemptuous if she were a goat.

Chance frowned. "Now, just a minute—"

"Never mind, Chance," Ally said wearily. The man stalked away, followed by two women who were covered head to toe in dark, voluminous robes. Not even their faces were visible.

"How can they see?" Chance asked, staring after them.

"There's sort of a gauzy material over their eyes that they can peer through."

"Are you okay? Why don't we get out of here?"

"Don't you want to see your producer?"

"It can wait. He'll just want to talk about leather."

"What?"

"Remember what I told you? He's got this thing about making me dress in leather and zippers for the television special."

"Oh." It was impossible to keep a straight face. "Well, maybe we should go, then. The evening hasn't been a stunning success. Anyhow, it's awfully stuffy in here, and I heard that there's going to be music soon. Tilly Ramirez."

"Another final, farewell, comeback extravaganza with eight chorus boys and a half-hour medley?" he guessed.

Everyone in American had suffered through at least one Tilly Ramirez spectacle. "Let's go."

After escaping the ballroom, they passed by the entrance to the Wilson Palace Casino. "Why don't we go in here?" Ally suggested.

He glanced uneasily at her. "What for?"

She shrugged. "I've never been in a casino before. Have you?"

"Yes," he admitted. No point in lying.

"Is it fun?"

"Not really, Ally," he said, trying to guide her away from the broad, gilded archway leading to the casino.

"Well, we could play for just a little while, just so I can say I've done it." She resisted the pressure of his hand on her arm.

"It costs money." That ought to stop her.

"Oh, come on, Chance. There must be a five-dollar-limit table, or something like that."

"Ally . . ."

"I've heard that blackjack is the one game where the house doesn't have such an advantage. Do you know how to play that?"

"Yes, but—"

"Then show me!" Her enthusiasm depressed him. He had solemnly sworn never to go near a blackjack table again.

"No, it's really not such a good idea."

"Why not?" She looked genuinely disappointed. "Please, Chance. Let's try to get *some* fun out of this evening."

The pleading look in her eyes, the way she cast interested glances at the lively interior of the casino, and the urging in her voice all tugged at him. Realizing how close he was to doing what she wanted, he gave himself a mental shake and said, "No, Ally. I'm not going in there. And you shouldn't either. Gambling's bad business. A waste of money if you lose, and . . . well, it's not such an honest way to make money, either. Let's go upstairs. Your dress is stained."

"Wait a minute!" she protested, as he virtually hauled her into an elevator. "I don't need your moralistic lectures, Chance, and I sure as hell don't need you manhandling me."

He heard the anger in her voice and knew that he deserved it. He tried a halfhearted explanation. "Look, my grandfather didn't approve of gambling. My father had—"

"Could we leave your family out of this? Don't ever try to tell me what to do, Chance. Got that?"

He slumped against the side of the elevator, tugging at the formal tie and high collar that seemed to be strangling him, undoing them as he spoke. "Sorry, Ally. I got carried away. It's just something that I . . ." He sighed. "Never mind."

Ally's stomach rumbled noisily, and Chance smiled faintly, glad to change the subject. "Hungry?"

"I'm starved. What a sorry excuse for a party."

The elevator stopped on the ninth floor, but the doors only opened slightly. Forcing the doors far enough open for the two of them to exit, Chance muttered, "The party was about as well planned as the electrical system in this dump."

"Things around here don't seem to work very well, do they?" Ally commented absently as she fumbled in her evening bag for her room key. The full import of this remark hit her when she entered their room and found Harvey still sitting on her bed, watching television, while a repairman packed up his tools.

"Isn't it fixed yet?" Ally demanded.

"Nope."

"Doesn't anything work right in this damned hotel?" she demanded.

"Hardly anything," Harvey admitted cheerfully. "They got problems out the wazoo."

The repairman scowled at this inelegant remark and said to Ally, "It can't be fixed tonight, ma'am. You'll just have to make do for the time being."

"Ride me, cowboy!" Vicky cried.

"How long *is* this film?" Chance asked.

"Oh, this is a different one," Harvey said. "The third in the series: *Vicky Gets Even Wetter*. I looked in the program guide and found out that they're broadcasting a Vicky marathon this weekend."

"You say that like it's a *good* thing," Ally muttered. She turned to the repairman. "Why can't it be fixed tonight?"

"Haven't got the right tools to open up the back of that there pagoda."

"Can't we just pull the TV out the front of the cabinet?"

"Sure," the repairman said, not even pausing as he packed up the rest of his useless tools. "If you want an electrical fire on your hands, that is. Hundreds of lives on your conscience. And a possible lawsuit from Mr. Wilson."

Ally morosely studied the television, barricaded in the enormous cabinet and affixed to the wall by a cable. "Isn't there *anything* you can do?"

"Not tonight. Not without the proper tools."

"Can you *get* the proper tools?" Ally demanded.

The man nodded, then added discouragingly, "Maybe. But not tonight, that's for sure."

"But you can't just leave this thing here in this condition," Ally protested, blocking his path to the door.

"You paying for this room?" the repairman asked shrewdly.

"No," she admitted. "But what does that have to do with anything?"

The repairman looked at her with mingled pity and disgust. Chance shook his head.

"That's so naive of you," Harvey said.

After the repairman left, ignoring Ally's pleas to do something immediately about the television set, Chance asked if she wanted to go grab a burger somewhere.

"No. I've got a headache. I think I'll just take a soothing bath and order room service."

"Wouldn't do that if I were you," Harvey said. "The food here sucks."

"Oh."

"And the service is even worse."

"Why is the hotel full, then? Why isn't there another room available?" Ally cried in despair, glaring at the television, the bellboy, and the magician.

"Well, it's full *this* weekend because all of *you* are here. Normally, though, we don't even have enough guests to break even."

"Wilson must be losing his shirt," Chance speculated, removing his own. "God, I hate formal clothes."

Ally looked at his tan, well-muscled torso and felt an entirely unwelcome response stirring in her belly. "Maybe I'll skip room service. Maybe I'll just go right to bed. It's been a trying day."

Chance's eyes locked with hers.

"Bed," he repeated. "Uh, you want the one by the window, right?"

"Oh, *yeah*," Vicky groaned.

"Yeah. The window." Ally swallowed. Maybe she should have opted for a hamburger in a noisy place with fluorescent lights. She suddenly wondered how she would get through a night in this room, with Chance sleeping only four feet away and Vicky's orgasmic sighs echoing around them in the dark.

"Harvey," Chance said. "Take a hike."

"Huh? Oh, come on, can't I at least stay until Vicky does it on the trapeze? It was in the preview, and I really want—"

"Get it on video," Chance advised him, opening the door. "Good night, Harvey."

FIVE

Chance groggily stepped beneath the shower spray, hoping it would help prepare him for a grueling day after what had turned out to be the longest night of his entire life.

Ally was sitting at a wobbly table by the window, wolfing down an unappealing room-service breakfast as if she hadn't eaten in twenty-four hours—which she hadn't. Chance wasn't hungry, but he had thought it prudent to order a half gallon of coffee for himself; he hadn't gotten a wink of sleep.

He supposed that Ally's fresh-scrubbed face and well-brushed hair weren't intended to be seductive, but it had taken all his restraint last night not to sink to his knees and start kissing her thighs right where they disappeared into the ragged hem of her baggy nightshirt.

Remembering the way the shirt had ridden up when she crouched before the television set to fiddle with the controls one last time, he groaned and reached for the shower faucet, turning it to make the water a little colder.

In the end, they had closed the heavy doors of the pagoda-shaped entertainment center. It had blocked out the sight of Vicky and her companions as well as their inane dialogue, but the faint sounds of Vicky's sexual adventures had echoed through the room all night long, heightening Chance's frustration as he counted sheep and mentally rehearsed the illusions he would perform the following evening.

He had tried to avoid looking at Ally's recumbent form, at the way the sheet stretched over her breasts, the way the moonlight streaked across the pillows to highlight her pale skin and caress the dark waves of her hair, the way one smooth arm was flung over her head in abandon.

And then she made it worse. She spoke. "I wonder how many Vicky films there are," she murmured as a muffled cry of ecstasy pierced the night.

"I didn't know you were still awake," he whispered.

"I knew *you* were awake. Do you always toss and turn so much?"

"No. I . . . Never mind."

And so they had lain there in tense silence, trying to ignore the gasps and moans that floated all around them, trying even harder to ignore the desire flowing between them, filling the gulf between their beds and smothering them with its heat.

When dawn had come at last, Chance had leapt out of bed and gone for a five-mile run, somewhat longer than his usual workout, but a blessed relief after a night spent twisted in knots. Ally had finally drifted off during the early hours of the morning, and she only awoke when he returned to the room, flushed and sweat-soaked. One look at her rumpled hair and sleep-softened expression had managed to completely mitigate the effects of his refreshing run, so now he was hoping that fifteen—no, make it twenty—minutes in the shower could help him recapture some peace of mind.

Ally looked up at Chance when he emerged from the bathroom after the longest shower she had ever known any man to take. Not even her last boyfriend, the vainest of leading men, had kept the bathroom occupied for so long. However, one brief glance was enough to confirm that Chance hadn't spent any time preening in front of the mirror. He wore nothing but his usual skintight, faded blue jeans, and a towel draped around his neck. And all the virility that entered the room with him seemed to steal her breath away.

"You ate it all," he said, glancing at the empty plates. That slow, reluctant grin spread across his face. It made her diaphragm ache.

"It was barely enough to feed a rodent," she scoffed. "But it was as bad as Harvey said."

"Maybe we'll go out for lunch."

"We can't. There's that luncheon thing downstairs this afternoon. You told Monty and Kettering you'd be there." She batted her lashes. "*People, Variety,* the *Times.* Remember?"

"Oh, yeah," he said without much enthusiasm. "Well, maybe we could eat before—" He frowned and shook his head. "No, we can't. I said I'd go to the homeless shelter to perform for the kids there this morning." This time he *did* sound enthusiastic.

"Well, good. That's more important than finding me something palatable to eat. I can survive on stale croissants and undercooked eggs for one weekend." She smiled at him.

He glanced at the bedside clock. "In fact, I'd better get going."

She looked at his hair, which was tangled and wet. "Do you want to use my blow-dryer?"

"No, thanks." He smiled sheepishly. "To tell the truth, I'm afraid of those things."

She laughed. "Why would a man who's willing to be set on fire and sawed in half be afraid of a blow-dryer?"

"When I was a teenager, the postmistress in our town got electrocuted with one. She was drying her hair before a date with the high school basketball coach." he shrugged. "Anyhow, she spent four days in the hospital, and I never got over the idea that one of those things could kill you."

Ally shook her head, amazed at the contrasts in Chance Weal, and poured him a cup of coffee. "Did you have a good run? I'm going to see if I can find the health club in this place."

"You must work out pretty often," he guessed. She

was as fit as a dancer. He accepted the coffee from her and thought how domestic this all was. *Coffee, dear? How was your run?*

"Well, it's a lot harder to get roles if you're chubby. And since I'm not willing to eat like a bird, I have to exercise like a fiend. You're sure you don't want me to call down for some breakfast for you?"

"Not hungry. Before I go, I think I'll call maintenance and try to light a fire under them." He didn't think he could live through another night of sharing his room with both Vicky and Ally.

They agreed to meet later in the day, and Ally went into the bathroom to change into her workout clothes, trying not to notice the tingling masculine scents that lingered in there.

Ally made discreet inquiries at registration, but no one could tell her whether or not Roland Houston had arrived yet. It wasn't that the staff were unwilling to share the information; they simply didn't know. In fact, they didn't seem to know much of anything. The more time Ally spent at the Wilson Palace, the more she thought Wilson must be losing millions. She had never seen any place that was so badly run. The health club on the third floor had an impressive array of the most expensive weight machines available, but they were so poorly maintained that half of them were unusable.

Where did money like that come from, Ally wondered, that a man could blow millions on a Broadway flop, neglect an investment the size of this hotel, and still afford to spend more than a million dollars on a necklace—*a necklace!*—for his wife?

"I'll never understand the wealthy," Ally murmured, returning to her room.

Nor could she understand the maid she encountered there, who hopped off the bed and started cleaning, trying to pretend she hadn't been watching *Vicky Gets Soaked* when Ally entered the room. The maid, however, spoke no English, and even Ally's skill as a mime couldn't seem to get the message across that she and Chance wanted extra towels.

She showered and dried her hair. She had become so accustomed to Vicky's sighs that she was even able to take a nap. If she was honest, it was Chance's proximity, and not the muffled sounds coming from the pagoda, that had kept her awake all night. Now exhaustion came over her in a huge wave, and she slept like a log, not awakening until after the time she had promised to meet Chance at the luncheon gathering. She dressed quickly and, finally despairing of ever getting an elevator to stop at the ninth floor, trotted down the service steps for nine floors.

"Sorry I'm late," she apologized to Chance, having spent twenty minutes trying to find him in the huge crowd. "Where's the food?"

"It's a buffet."

"Another one?" she asked despairingly. She had never even managed to *find* last night's buffet food.

"Excuse us," Chance said to three women who all appeared to be hanging on his every word. Ally noticed one of them was weighted down with camera equipment.

"Did you just brush off a photographer?" she asked as he led her away.

"And two journalists. After seeing the way you attacked that breakfast tray this morning, I'm afraid for everyone's safety if I let you go too long without food." He grinned at her and added, "Besides, I didn't brush them off. I was perfectly polite, and I've already spent twenty minutes with them. You'd think they'd want to talk to someone else by now. There are a lot of famous people here."

She grunted noncommittally. He was right about the celebrity quotient of the crowd, but it didn't take much perception to realize why those women were drawn to Chance. His healthy, sunny good looks, his quiet air of self-confidence, and his natural friendliness all made him stand out in any crowd. Moreover, his attire was different enough to be noticeable at this gathering. In the midst of men wearing thousand-dollar business suits or Italian designer casuals, Chance wore his jeans, a plain white shirt, and a faded denim jacket that was worn at the elbows, carelessly mended over one shoulder, and fraying a bit at the bottom.

He noticed her gaze traveling over this attire and said, "I didn't have time to change."

"You look—"

"I always wear this when I do parties, street magic, that kind of thing. It's got lots of pockets."

"It sure does," Ally agreed. Half a dozen that she could see, and probably more on the inside. "Don't worry. You look fine."

He looked around. "You think I should have worn a tie?"

She almost laughed, but his question was serious. "No. I think you look very handsome."

He looked down at her, his brown eyes glowing softly below his dark blond brows. "Very handsome? Is that really what you think, Ally?"

She slipped her arm through his. "Now you're fishing again." But she didn't feel as pert as she tried to sound. Her heart thudded in a heavy rhythm, and the affection that made it ache slightly was as unexpected as it was unwise. Speaking past an inexplicable tightness in her throat, she said, "Where's this food you promised me? Siberia?"

"It's against the wall over there."

But when they reached it, they made a horrifying discovery. "It's all gone!" Ally cried.

"Sorry, miss. There won't be any more. We ordered a little short," said a woman on the catering staff.

"Everything's been eaten? There's not even a crust of bread left?" Ally demanded. "What kind of vultures are these people? I thought the rich had dainty appetites and good manners!"

The woman's derisive snort of laughter made Ally feel naive. Well, this weekend was her first brush with the truly rich, after all. What did she know?

"Maybe we can slip out to the coffee shop," Chance suggested. "I'm kind of hungry, too."

"Ah, Chance! Here you are! I was starting to think we'd never hook up, kid!"

Ally turned to find a tall, fat man bearing down on them. His coal black hair was so improbably thick that Ally wondered if he wore a toupee. A moment later he grasped Chance's hand and shook it vigorously. The man's voice boomed like a loudspeaker as he said, "I understand you did a wonderful job performing for those kids this morning! Just terrific! Wish we'd gotten it on tape. Maybe you can go back tomorrow so we can film it?"

"I don't think—"

"Well, it's something to think about, eh?"

"It seems a little exploitative to—"

"Exploitation? Hey! *Hey.*" The man laughed heartily, though Ally wasn't sure why.

"Ally, meet Ambrose Kettering. Ambrose, this is Alicia Cannon. She'll be performing with me tonight."

"Just for tonight. I'm not on his regular staff," Ally said quickly, hoping this would eliminate any possibility that Kettering would want to talk to her. She found him objectionable.

Chance stiffened beside her, and she realized how her comment must have sounded to him. Before she could say more, Kettering said seriously, "Then maybe you can be objective, Miss Cannon. What do you think of Chance's image?"

"I think . . . I think he's got a great image. But it's really his talent that matters."

"Exactly. That's *exactly* what I think. You're a very clever woman, Miss Cannon."

"Thank you, but I—"

"And I agree completely that his image worked for the *stage.*" Kettering dragged the word out like a guilty secret. "But it's gotta change somewhat for television, don't you agree?"

"Well, no, not really. He's very—"

"You're right, you're right," Kettering said, nodding his head. "And when you're right, you're right. Right?"

"Uh, yes, I suppose—"

"Uh-huh. That's it exactly. I saw it, too. I mean, we don't necessarily want to tamper with a good thing, but then again . . . television's not Ghirardelli Square, is it, Miss Cannon?"

"No, but—"

"You see, Chance? She agrees with me. I agree with her. Now," Kettering said, turning back to Ally, "if you and I could just get Chance to agree with *us*." He sighed and took Ally's elbow, pulling her away so that the two of them faced Chance. Kettering leaned slightly toward Ally, like a comrade, a conspirator, a colleague, sharing the task of dealing with this difficult magician.

"Now, picture it, Ally. I can call you Ally, can't I?"

"Um . . ." She was aware that Chance was turning dark red.

"That blond hair, and the contrast of *black*. Black . . . I don't know . . . leather? Yeah, leather!" Kettering cried, as if just discovering the idea. "Leather looks great on camera. Maybe we'll lighten the hair, just a shade or two. Increase the contrast, enhance the beach-boy look."

"Black leather?" Ally repeated. "I don't think it's him, Mr. Kettering."

"You're right. I couldn't agree more. You're a smart woman, Ally. But, hey, it's prime-time TV. He'll be competing with action-adventure shows. Cops. Guns. Pistols and barrels. Very subliminal stuff. We've got to make a strong statement. We need that female audience."

"But why not just aim for the audience that likes magic?" Ally said.

"Smart. That's smart. I like that. But you think it over and we'll talk again. Just let the thought in, Ally. Huh? Be *open* to it. Black leather. Who knows? Maybe some zippers."

"Think it over? But I'm not even part of his—"

"Hey, here's my good friend, Helmut!" Kettering exclaimed as the Wilsons approached them. Wilson seemed to wince.

"But, Mr. Kettering—" Ally began.

"Forget it, Ally," Chance advised, looking ill.

"But he's . . . That's not . . . I mean, you can make an elephant disappear!" she sputtered.

"Oh, *vraiment*?" cried Celine, approaching them like a heat-seeking missile. "An elephant?"

"Well, yeah," Chance admitted. "But it's not exactly a party piece."

"Ah, but you do have party pieces, *n'est-ce pas*?"

"Yes, I understand you performed at the homeless shelter this morning," Wilson added. "Perhaps since the food is gone and the natives are restless, you would share some of your legerdemain with us now?"

Chance looked uncertainly at Ally.

"Never mind about lunch," she said. "I've lost my appetite." She leaned closer and whispered, "Go ahead and show Kettering that you're too good to go for cheap tricks like dressing up like . . . like one of Vicky's boyfriends."

He looked at her in surprise, since she had only moments ago told Kettering, as clearly and quickly as possible, that she was only temporarily associated with this lowbrow magic act. "Okay." It wasn't a hard decision. He loved performing more than anything else, and never said no.

"I'd be happy to help keep the party going," he told Wilson.

Ally thought it was quite unnecessary for Celine to thank Chance with a kiss on the cheek, but she held her peace.

"What a fine-looking ring, ma'am," Chance said, examining the sparkling rock on Celine's hand. "May I use it for a small demonstration?"

Ally looked at him doubtfully, thinking it was foolish to mess with something that costly, but Celine eagerly pulled the ring off her finger and handed it over.

With wide-eyed innocence, understated grace, and the easygoing friendliness that were all so much a part of him, Chance proceeded to enthrall the crowd that gathered around him. His charm was never more evident than when he worked that crowd, making them laugh at his comments, his deft sleight of hand, and his good-natured teasing. He told the crowd he would make Celine's ring disappear into thin air, a promise that made Ally glance uneasily at Wilson.

As the performance developed, Ally discovered that part of Chance's technique was to heighten anticipation by drawing out the act, building momentum by performing other tricks he hadn't promised.

He started by asking if anyone in the crowd had a scarf or handkerchief he could use, saying he needed one to make the ring disappear. Soon scarves were disappearing and reappearing in unlikely places; Chance even pulled Ambrose Kettering's monogrammed silk scarf out of a buxom socialite's ample cleavage, causing the lady to blush prettily while the crowd laughed again. Other things disappeared, too, including a gold cigarette case and Chance's own watch. He heightened the effect, and the audience's amusement, by looking as surprised as they did every time an object disappeared or reappeared elsewhere, as if this conjuring business were still kind of baffling to him, as if he hadn't managed to bring his magical powers entirely under control yet.

Having found a handkerchief that pleased him, he borrowed Ally's hair ribbon and laid it upon a small drinks tray that a waiter had set down so he could watch Chance's act. With a great deal of flourish, Chance laid the ring atop the ribbon, then covered them both with a large handkerchief.

After two very funny attempts to make the ring disappear, his face becoming utterly crestfallen when missing objects *appeared* under the handkerchief instead, Chance explained that he'd probably been using the wrong magic spell. On his third attempt, the ring was still there, but now—by magic, apparently—the hair ribbon was woven through it, even though everyone knew he hadn't touched either end of the ribbon to draw it through the ring.

"I hate to disappoint a crowd," Chance said sadly. "Do any of *you* know how to make this damn thing disappear?"

Since no one else did, Chance decided that the first thing to do was to get the ring off the ribbon. He asked Ally to hold one end of the ribbon while he held the other. The ring, after some more effort, somehow magically popped off the ribbon without breaking it or passing over either end.

He finally did manage to make the ring disappear, and there was more laughter when Helmut Wilson insisted he make it *re*appear.

"Now, I never promised I could bring it back," Chance warned him.

"Isn't it insured, darling?" Celine asked, making everyone laugh again.

"Bringing things back is a little harder," Chance explained. "I'm not so good at that yet."

Wilson played the straight man very well—and good-naturedly, too, considering what that ring was probably worth. Ally enjoyed his exaggerated reactions as Chance's efforts to conjure the ring produced an egg, a dirty sock, and a garter belt.

"Yours, I believe," Chance said innocently, handing the lacy thing to a pretty debutante. Then he looked over at the waiter. "Could I maybe get something to wet my whistle?"

"Of course, sir."

The waiter gave him a long-stemmed goblet full of white wine. Chance sipped from it and then covered it with the handkerchief. After a few elaborate gestures, he uncovered the glass again and revealed Mrs. Wilson's diamond ring—borne on the stem of the glass. They had to pulverize the glass to get the ring off.

"Sorry about that," Chance said, as if baffled by how that had happened in the first place.

When the growing crowd demanded more, Chance said, "Well, I'm gonna have to start charging you. How about a dollar for my next trick?" He looked slyly at Ally. "Miss Cannon, would you pay a dollar to see me do something else?"

Smiling, and enjoying herself more than she would have

thought possible, Ally fished a dollar out of her purse. Chance folded it up again and again, until it was just a tiny square, taking the whole while. When he unfolded it again, it had changed into a one-hundred-dollar bill.

"Hey!" Ally said, amazed. "Here, let me give you a few more dollars!"

Instead, Ambrose Kettering gave Chance a hundred, instructing him to turn it into a thousand-dollar bill. However, when Chance unfolded the bill, it had turned into an ordinary dollar.

"Oops!" Chance shrugged and smiled beguilingly at Kettering. "Sorry. That happens sometimes."

By the time he finished the impromptu performance, he had returned Ally's bill to its original denomination, despite her protests, and given a one-hundred-dollar bill back to Kettering. To show his appreciation, Wilson invited Chance and Ally to join him for a while in that inner sanctum, that holy of holies, his private penthouse suite.

The Wilsons' private suite was as lush, grandiose, and ugly as the rest of the hotel. To Ally's disgust, there was no food being served up there, only drinks. She had regained her appetite. The Wilsons' various children were there, though Ally supposed "children" might not be the best way to describe them. Helmut and Celine had no children together, but they each had two kids from previous marriages. The four young people, three girls and a guy, were all college age or older. One look at the son made Ally suspect he was a serious drug user. The girls all seemed just plain silly. But then, Ally thought, being raised with this kind of wealth was probably enough to make anybody rather giddy.

"Yes, it's a rough business," Chance admitted in answer to Celine's questions as Ally gave up her search for something edible and joined them in a conversation alcove. "There can't be more than a few hundred guys making their living as full-time professional magicians. I've been one of the lucky ones."

"It's an expensive business, isn't it?" Wilson asked. "Financing an entire magic act?"

"Very expensive," Chance admitted wryly. "The financing alone seems like a full-time job. Our show doesn't go in much for costumes, which saves us some money, but . . ." He shrugged and contemplated his drink. "The props have to be constructed by expert illusion builders. We have to rent trucks and buses, buy airline tickets, negotiate with unions, rent rehearsal halls. Then there are lighting designers and technicians, set designers, illusion engineers, animal handlers, company managers, you name it." He smiled. "It's sure a long way from Ghirardelli Square."

"Who finances you, if you don't mind my asking?" Wilson said.

"Oh, the show makes pretty good money," Chance said vaguely, and changed the subject.

Among the elite guests invited to Wilson's suite, Ally was surprised to notice the Arab who had tried to walk straight through her the night before. When he came over to join them, trailed by the same two veiled women who had been with him last night, Celine spoke with him briefly in French, then turned to Chance and Ally.

"This is Sheik Nesib el Dheilan," she told them. "He wishes to meet you."

"Hi," Chance said uncertainly, returning the man's unblinking, sloe-eyed gaze.

"Hi, there," Ally said, thinking how predatory the man looked as his eyes traveled over her. "We met last night. Sort of."

There was no reaction to this comment. Instead, the sheik said to Chance, "Though the woman is not as comely as my wives, I offer you three camels for her."

"Your wives?" Ally bleated.

The sheik made a dismissive motion, indicating the two dark, silent, berobed figures standing behind him. Ally cleared her throat, prepared to tell Nesib el Dheilan precisely what she thought of such an offer, but Chance stopped her.

"Your offer is an insult," he said. "Twenty camels or no deal. Think it over." He rose to his feet, pulling Ally off the couch, too. "Celine, thank you for your hospitality. We'll see you later."

Ally was sputtering with mingled outrage and laughter by the time they were safely inside the elevator. "Why didn't you let me give that ill-mannered bigamist a piece of my mind?"

"I don't think it's your *mind* that he's after, Ally. Besides, nothing you could say would change the way he's lived and thought his entire life. And I was ready to leave. Weren't you?"

"Yes," she admitted. "Very rich people are . . . well, they're just not that much fun to be around, are they? I prefer actors."

"I thought you'd given up on actors," he teased.

"I've only given up dating them," she corrected. "But in general, I've decided I like them better than multimillionaires."

"I think Wilson likes you."

"I think Celine *adores* you." It came out a little sharper than she had intended.

"She thinks *you're* sweet. She said so."

"Oh, brother."

"Hungry?"

"Now that you mention it . . ."

"I thought so."

The argument started while they wolfed down burgers and fries at a nearby fast-food place. "So how *do* you finance an act like yours?" Ally asked.

"Like I said. The money is reasonably good these days."

"But it wasn't always, right? I mean, you had to start somewhere. Where'd you get the money to acquire expensive illusions, props, trucks, that kind of thing? To make an elephant disappear, you've got to *have* an elephant first, right? Or at least rent one. So how did you get from passing the hat on Ghirardelli Square to making elephants vanish on the main stage?"

"It's complicated," he said, losing his appetite again.

"Explain it to me."

"Why? As you told Kettering, you're just with the act for tonight."

"I only meant—"

"So stop asking questions that are none of your business."

"Jesus, you're touchy!"

"I didn't get any sleep."

"Well, why don't you go back to the hotel and take a nap?" She didn't bother to conceal the irritation in her voice. "I don't need you snapping at me the rest of the day."

"Fine." He threw down his napkin and got up to leave.

"And call maintenance again, if they haven't fixed the TV yet."

His only answer was a curt nod as he walked away. Ally watched him leave the fast-food restaurant with a feeling of consternation. What was the big deal about his original financing? Had he come by it illegally or something? *Men.* She poked her hamburger and wondered where her appetite had gone.

Chance felt bad about snapping at Ally, and he replayed the conversation in his mind as he walked back to the hotel. Hell, it wasn't such a big deal. Maybe he should just tell her. Not everyone would be shocked about the way he had acquired the money, even though his grandfather had been utterly appalled. Some men might even boast about it to a woman like Ally. Looking at Ally made a guy want to boast. More than that. Looking at her made a guy feel hungry and gentle all at once. Sometimes, when she looked at him with those incredible eyes, he didn't know whether he wanted to wrap himself around her and protect her from the world, or throw her down on one of those velvet-covered beds and ravish her. And then *other* times, he wanted to shake her until her teeth rattled.

But their latest argument wasn't her fault. He shouldn't be so touchy. He could have handled it better.

Entering the oppressive atmosphere of the Wilson Pal-

ace Hotel—overpriced, overdecorated, and overcrowded—
only made him feel more depressed. Poor Ally. She'd
come all this way to speak to Roland Houston, and with
the weekend half over, she still hadn't even been able to
learn if he had arrived yet.

Instead of heading for the ninth floor, Chance made a
detour to Wilson's office on the second floor. Wilson had
mentioned he might come down here to do some work
before the evening festivities began. Even if he wasn't in
his office, Chance figured there must be a personal assistant or secretary who could help him. Maybe he'd even
kill two birds with one stone: ask Wilson to help Ally
hook up with Roland Houston, and get him to do something about the television in their room.

When he got to the second floor—he'd taken the stairs,
rather than waiting for one of the few functioning elevators—everything seemed awfully quiet. Chance prowled
around, looking for someone to show him to the right
office. All he found was a security guard who didn't know
which way was up.

"I think everyone's in the grand ballroom, getting ready
for tonight, sir."

"They wouldn't just leave their executive offices empty,
would they?"

"Um, well, there is someone down there. I'm not sure
who." The fellow gestured toward a suite of offices at the
far end of the corridor, near the emergency exit.

"Thank you," Chance sighed, thinking it was a sad
thing when a boy like Harvey turned out to be the hotel's
most efficient employee.

There was no one in the outer office when Chance entered, though the phone lines were ringing and two half-
finished cups of coffee sat on the secretary's desk. How
did Wilson run a multi-million-dollar hotel this way and
manage to stay as rich as Croesus? A noise from the inner
office alerted him to Wilson's presence. He knocked on
the door, which had been left slightly ajar.

"Mr. Wilson?" he said, as the door swung open.
"Sorry to bother you, but I . . ." His voice trailed off as

he came face-to-face with Walter Dureau, the frumpy man from the previous night. The man was sitting at Wilson's desk, poring over some files.

Dureau looked up from his rather compromising position and demanded, "What are you doing here?"

Chance blinked, surprised at the accusing tone. "What are *you* doing here?"

"I . . ." Dureau looked around blankly, as if wondering the same thing. "Helmut suggested I look at an investment proposal. Only, his blasted secretary has disappeared, and I'm having trouble finding the papers he wanted me to study."

"Uh-huh." Chance continued to stare at him unconvinced.

After a tense silence, during which it became obvious that Chance wasn't going to go away and leave him there alone, Dureau said, "But perhaps I'd better wait and ask Helmut to find the papers for me himself."

"Good idea."

"After all, it could take hours."

"That's right. And you'll be missed if you aren't at the show tonight."

"I will be?"

"Count on it," Chance warned. "Shall we go?"

He followed Dureau out of the executive offices and into the elevator, wondering what the little man was hiding.

SIX

"Aren't you going to say something to Wilson?" Ally demanded, following Chance backstage that night.

"Of course I'm going to say something to him," Chance answered irritably. "But not when he's surrounded by fifty other people and a dozen television cameras, okay?"

"I think that Dureau character is as fishy as week-old mackerel. You didn't believe that story he cooked up, did you?"

"About having Wilson's permission to look through his papers?" He shrugged. "Who the hell knows? I'll tell Wilson, and that will be the end of it. Now, can we concentrate on the act?"

They met Zeke and Angus backstage. The two men had driven down from New York earlier in the day and worked with Chance all through dinner, employing their usual precautions to safeguard his secrets.

"Everything that guy says is a lie," Ally told Chance after nodding a greeting to Zeke and Angus. "And he's not even a *good* liar. If he's a financier, I'm Mata Hari."

"Oh, come on, Ally. What do you know about financiers? He's probably exactly who and what he says he is, only he's just cursed with a rotten personality. Now, can we get to work?"

"The question is, who is he really and why is he hanging around this weekend? What's his connection to Wilson? What was he looking for in Wilson's office?"

"No. The question is, are you ready to concentrate on your performance?" Chance said.

"Of course I am. How soon do we go on?"

"We start setting up in about ten minutes."

"Do you think Dureau was looking for money?"

"Will you stop?" Chance begged. "Ally, it's important for me to stay calm and focused before a performance."

"Aye," said Angus.

"Yup," said Zeke.

"Levitating and disappearing are hard work," Chance insisted. "And I need you to stop *nagging* me."

"I'm sorry," she said, realizing how much she would resent anyone disturbing her concentration before she went onstage to play a major role.

Once she stopped pestering him and let him center his mind, Ally recognized that Chance's ability to focus his concentration and ignore distractions was amazing. And there were plenty of distractions backstage that night. True to his reputation, Ambrose Kettering had ensured that his variety show would be BIGGER! BRIGHTER! and LOUDER! than any other. Which did not necessarily make it better, in Ally's opinion.

However, she was impressed that Kettering had managed to convince Lady Mackenzie, the seventy-six-year-old black jazz singer, to come out of retirement for the evening. Ally had a dozen of the singer's albums and was thrilled to see her perform in person. There was also a great political comedian there, though Ally noticed that his wonderful antiestablishment monologue didn't exactly set *this* crowd on fire.

By prior agreement, the entire backstage area was cleared when Chance, Zeke, and Angus began setting up for Chance's act. As usual, Chance was wearing blue jeans, boots, and a plain cotton shirt. He had, however, chosen to wear a new denim jacket that hardly had any worn spots or frayed edges.

"Nice jacket. You're almost overdressed," Ally teased before she followed him out onstage. She saw a grin steal slowly across his face before he turned his back to her and took his place.

The act went brilliantly, and Ally began to understand why it had taken an eternity to rehearse for barely more than ten minutes of actual performance time. All the feats performed with such careful precision were now made to look careless, even accidental. Chance levitated a large metal ball, which then developed a mind of its own and chased Ally around the stage. He taught a handkerchief to dance but then couldn't make it stop, not even after he had put it in a corked bottle. The pinnacle of the act was Chance's own seemingly inexplicable levitation; Ally's role was to simply remove his visible supports precisely as she had been told to and then prove to the audience that he wasn't being suspended by wires. For Chance's final illusion, he magically produced a bouquet of flowers, thanked her for helping him, and presented the flowers to her. When she tried to embrace him, he disappeared into thin air, leaving her alone onstage.

The congratulations from other performers were as resounding as the audience's applause, and Ally glowed with pride for Chance. He was, she admitted, a far cry from the corny, red-caped, rabbit-in-the-hat magician she had initially envisioned.

When Chance was mobbed for autographs outside the green room, Ally found a quiet corner and sat down, realizing for the first time how tiring the past week had been. The emotional ups and downs she'd experienced ever since meeting Chance, the challenge of fulfilling an unfamiliar role in his act, the overstimulation of this weekend's events, and the disappointment of still not having encountered Roland Houston—it all weighed upon her until she wanted nothing more than to relax alone with Chance, away from all these people. Even if he was the source of her ups and downs, she found that she preferred his company to his absence.

Riding high from the pleasure of performing, the success of tonight's act, and the pleasure he had found in appearing with Ally, Chance didn't realize Ally had disappeared until more than an hour had passed. By that time, he'd already signed his name fifty times, given a brief interview, spoken with Kettering, said good-bye to Zeke and Angus as they packed up the major props before heading back home, and even managed to get five minutes alone with Helmut Wilson. He felt like a man who had accomplished everything he'd set out to do, and he wanted a reward. And that *didn't* mean sitting through another two hours of variety acts. He wanted some time alone with Ally, even if they just went to a coffee shop and talked about nothing very important. He just wanted to relax with her, and enjoy what remained of the evening.

He found her at last, sitting alone in a corner, gazing off into space. It was so uncharacteristic that he stopped and stared, wondering if something had uspet her. She looked like a Renaissance painting, like a da Vinci, her face softened by a chiaroscuro effect and her eyes focused on some faraway secret. His gut tightened, and he realized that it wasn't to a coffee shop that he wanted to take her.

She looked a little depressed, and he felt a twinge of sadness when he realized that tonight's triumph, which meant so much to him, hadn't helped her career at all. He was sorry they would never perform together again. She had been wonderful out on that stage. She practically glowed when she stood before the crowd. Her reactions were wonderful, heightening the effect of every illusion, whether she made the audience roar with laughter when she ran away from the pursuing metal ball or reduced them to silent wonder when she gracefully assisted in Chance's levitation, moving like a trained dancer around his floating body.

Feeling tender and protective, he went to sit near her. "Sorry you still didn't get to see Houston tonight," he said softly.

She smiled tiredly and shook her head. "Well, I guess it was always a long shot. He probably decided not to come."

He took her hand, pleased he could give her something she really wanted. "He's here."

She looked at him alertly. "How do you know?"

"Wilson told me. Houston arrived about three hours ago."

"Really? Is he out in the audience?"

"No. He's been closeted in his suite ever since he got here. I gather he's having some kind of long-winded conference call." He rolled his eyes. "I'll never understand big shots. Why come all this way to talk on the phone?"

"Maybe I should leave a message for him," she mused.

"Don't bother. I asked Wilson to take care of it."

"What do you mean?"

He smiled and squeezed her hand. "Since Wilson said he was grateful for my telling him about Dureau—"

"So Dureau *didn't* have Wilson's permission to look through his papers?" she pounced.

He shook his head. "Wilson says he hardly knows the man and never spoke to him about an investment proposal."

"Aha! I wonder what that greasy little man is up to."

"Forget about it, Ally. It's none of our business."

"But—"

"*Anyhow,* Wilson asked if he could do anything for me in return, and I said I'd like him to set up a meeting between you and Houston tomorrow morning."

Her grip tightened so hard, he winced. "You *did*?" She frowned. "But can he do that?"

"Wilson? Why not? Houston's a guest in his hotel, right? Anyhow, I figure a man worth hundreds of millions of dollars can do just about whatever he decides to do, don't you?"

"I don't know, but I figure *you* can do just about anything you decide to do." She smiled and touched his cheek. "Thank you, Chance."

He swallowed. "Do you really want to hang out here any longer?"

She shook her head. "No." She looked down at the funky outfit she had worn onstage and repeated, "No. I want to put on jeans and a sweat shirt and get away from all these people.''

"Let's go back to the room to shower and change.'' He chuckled and added, "And then, if I know you, you're going to want to go get something to eat.''

"Oh, yes! I'm starving!''

Chance grinned, pleased to see her usual exuberance returning. They both lost the flavor of enthusiasm, however, when it became apparent they'd never get an elevator. It seemed that only two elevators were still working. One of those hovered permanently between the fifteenth and twentieth floors, and the other had such a huge crowd in front of it that Chance and Ally gave up waiting for it after fifteen minutes.

"Thank God I run in the mornings,'' Chance panted as he hauled himself up yet another flight of stairs. "Otherwise, I'd have had a heart attack somewhere around the seventh floor. You and your bright ideas,'' he added unfairly, forgetting that he, too, had been in favor of taking the stairs.

"Almost there,'' Ally grunted between deep, controlled gulps of air. "If you stop talking so much, you'll conserve oxygen.''

"We should have stayed in some motel at the edge of town. It would have been so much more comfortable,'' Chance huffed. "Or gone home with Zeke and Angus.''

"Too late for such a long drive,'' she panted.

"But *this* is okay?''

"Here we are,'' Ally breathed. "Ninth floor.''

They pushed open the heavy metal fire door and stumbled into the hallway. "I think maybe we should just call it quits and stay in for the rest of the night,'' Chance suggested windily.

"Agreed.'' Ally opened the door to their room. "Harvey!''

"Hi, guys,'' Harvey said from his reclining position on Ally's bed.

"How'd you get in here?'' Ally demanded.

"Pass key.''

100 / LAURA RESNICK

Chance shook his head in disgust. Some hotel.

"But what are you doing here?" Ally asked.

"Avoiding the front desk," Harvey said frankly. "With all those elevators broken, there's no way in hell I'm going to carry somebody's bags up ten or twenty flights of stairs."

"I can understand your point of view, Harvey," Chance said, collapsing into a chair, "but couldn't you avoid the front desk from some *other* place in this hotel?"

"Oh, baby, I *love* you!" Vicky cried.

"Well, it's the end of the Vicky marathon," Harvey explained. "I didn't think you guys would begrudge me this chance to see it, considering that I managed to solve your television problem."

Ally's eyes widened. "You've fixed the TV?"

"Not exactly. Wilson's chauffeur used to hot-wire cars, and he said disconnecting a TV would be no problem. So we took apart the cabinet, using his old tools, and disconnected the thing. Then we got some of the other bellboys to help us switch it with the TV in Mr. and Mrs. Pollingsworth-Biddle's room."

"I'd have settled for just having ours disconnected," Ally said. "But since no one else was able to solve the problem, maybe the chauffeur should switch jobs with the television repairman."

"Why'd you put our TV in someone else's room?" Chance asked.

Harvey grinned maliciously. "Mrs. Pollingsworth-Biddle is a nasty old bitch who runs us all around like slaves and doesn't tip. So now she's stuck with a porn channel she can't turn off for the rest of the night."

"Oh, really, Harvey," Ally said critically. "How could you?"

He blinked innocently. "Well, if you really think I've done such a terrible thing, I suppose I can always arrange to have the televisions switched again before she finds out about it."

"Uh, Ally . . ." Chance said. "Let's not be too hasty about this, okay?"

"But, Chance—"

"Look, for all we know," he reasoned, "*Mr.*
Pollingsworth-Biddle might be very grateful for this opportunity to . . . stimulate his wife. Maybe they've never
taken the time to view adult films together. Have you
thought of that?"

"No, but—"

"And maybe it will have a softening effect on Mrs.
Pollingsworth-Biddle. For all we know, Harvey may have
just put the zing back into their marriage." Chance's dark
brown gaze was as blandly innocent as Harvey's.

Ally tried hard to conceal her smile. "Let me just make
sure of one thing. I can turn this TV off whenever I want
to?"

"Absolutely," Harvey said. "Just let me watch the end
of the movie, and I'll prove it to you."

Chance glanced at the screen. "Good God! Vicky's getting *married*?"

"Yeah. Isn't it cool?" Harvey said. "She found true
love."

"Does he know about her past?" Ally asked delicately.

"Some of it. He's the guy that saved her from the Aztec
harem in the last movie."

"Aztec harem?" Ally repeated. "But, Harvey, Aztec
civilization was—"

"Forget it, Ally," Chance advised. "Sometimes you
just have to let art *be*."

"Yeah," said Harvey.

"She's got some nerve wearing white," Ally muttered.

"I think I'll take a shower." Chance disappeared into
the bathroom.

When Vicky's honeymoon night took a predictable
course, Ally asked Harvey, "Are things always like this
around here, Harvey? Everything broken, a staff that
doesn't know what's going on, lousy food, and so on?"

"Always," Harvey said without looking away from the
TV screen.

"But isn't Wilson losing a lot of money?"

"You don't read business journals much, do you?" Harvey guessed.

"Do you?" she asked curiously.

Harvey nodded. "I'm working on my bachelor's degree in business." He sat up and looked away from the screen when the credits started to roll. "Wilson is into debt more steeply than some Third World nations. He's spread himself too thin. I figure he hasn't got the money it would take to put this place into shipshape."

"But he just bought Celine that incredibly expensive necklace. Where'd he get money like that?" Ally asked.

"Who knows? The ultrarich operate differently, Miss Cannon. He probably bought it on credit." Harvey shrugged. "When Wilson's empire goes down the toilet and he's reduced to living in a twenty-room Long Island mansion, with an income of a mere two hundred thousand dollars per annum, people will call it a tragedy. And most of those same people walk straight past homeless children and handicapped beggars every day in New York City without giving it a second thought." Harvey sneered and added, "Some tragedy."

Chance emerged from the bathroom, and Ally decided to follow his example and take advantage of the hot water at the Wilson Palace while it was still working.

Wearing a complimentary bathrobe and drying his hair with a towel, Chance turned off the TV and suggested Harvey leave.

"You don't want to see what's on next?" Harvey asked.

"No, Harvey. We're tired."

Harvey glanced at the closed bathroom door. *"Ohhh,"* he said knowingly. "I thought at first that it was strictly business between you and the lady, but I guess I was—"

"*Lady* is right, Harvey, and a gentleman doesn't speculate on a lady's . . . um . . . Never mind."

"Don't worry. I won't say a word to the other guys. Honest."

"Good night, Harvey." Chance closed the door firmly in the boy's face.

"Did Harvey leave?" Ally asked, coming out of the bathroom.

"I wonder if I was ever that young," Chance murmured, going to the pagoda cabinet and closing its doors.

Ally looked at him from under her lashes. "I'll bet you were," she said. "I'll bet you were doe-eyed and eager and always falling in love." She could picture it perfectly.

He thought back. "Well . . ." That slow grin spread across his face. "But my grandfather would have tanned my hide if he'd ever caught me lounging on a lady's bed and watching *Vicky* movies."

"You always mention your grandfather, but never your parents."

"Never knew my mom," Chance admitted, sliding into one of the chairs by the window and letting his long legs sprawl lazily. "They say she ran off when I was just a year old. Left me with my father in some dump in L.A."

Ally's jaw dropped. She sat down on the edge of her bed, directly in front of him, and stared at him. "I had no idea." Belatedly she murmured, "I'm sorry."

"I don't remember it." He shrugged. "Anyhow, my father took me to a small town in northern California, where he'd grown up, and dumped me on his father. After that, I only saw my dad once in a while. He died about fifteen years ago. Too much liquor, too little of everything else."

"Did your . . . Was your father an only child?"

"No. I had two aunts and an uncle. All nice, hardworking people with kids." He sighed and looked at the ceiling. "The popular interpretation was that my father just had bad blood, and there was nothing you could do about that."

She was silent for a moment, picturing him as a boy. "Did they worry about you inheriting his bad blood?" she asked at last.

"Sometimes," he admitted, his expression wry as he looked back with an adult's perspective. "When I was fifteen, I got caught with the sheriff's daughter in the backseat of her car. She was eighteen. An older woman, you see . . ." He grinned more broadly, remembering. "It was my first time, and kind of embarrassing, to be honest, even *before* her father aimed his Colt .45 right at my private parts."

Ally couldn't help laughing, though she supposed it hadn't seemed funny to any of them at the time. Chance continued, "And when I was sixteen, Billy Whittaker and I got drunk on moonshine we'd made in his basement and then busted up Ellie Cameron's annual slumber party."

He looked at her with sleepy eyes. "And when I did things like that, everyone in town would shake their heads and say, 'It's his father's bad blood showing up. Damn shame.' "

"What did your grandfather say?"

His face brightened. "He said, 'Boys will be boys,' and things like that. He grounded me, he assigned me the worst chores imaginable, and he scolded me in a voice that could pierce through solid steel. But he never thought I was guilty of anything other than high spirits and overactive hormones."

Except the one time, Chance thought, still regretful. It was the only time he'd ever thought Grandpa was really ashamed of him, and the memory stung even now.

"You were very close, weren't you?" Ally guessed.

"Yeah. He's the one who took me to my first magic show. I was six. That's the day it became my lifelong passion. He always encouraged my interest. We'd often drive as far away as San Francisco, about three hours from home, just to see a good show. And my Christmas and birthday presents were always new magic tricks, books, and magazines."

"Then he encouraged you to turn professional?"

Chance rested a hand on his flat belly and thought over her question. "No. Not really. He just always encouraged me to pursue my goals. When I was eighteen, I left for college on a math scholarship, thinking I would eventually be an engineer or something. It was only after nearly three years of college that I finally realized there was just one thing I wanted to do with my life."

"So he supported that decision, too," Ally surmised.

"Yes. And he was the only one who did. Everyone else tried to talk me out of it. They all thought I was crazy: relatives, friends, teachers, girlfriend." The woman's defection had hurt most of all; at twenty-one, he had believed himself to be in love. He had even contemplated asking her to marry him.

"But you went ahead and became a magician anyhow."

He shrugged. "It was . . . a calling." He looked sharply at her. "You must know what that's like. No girl's family can be happy about her becoming an actress."

"Mine wasn't," she admitted. "They only agreed to let me enroll in college as a drama major because I threatened not to go to college at all, otherwise. I told my poor mother I'd simply leave for New York right away and try to be an actress without any contacts or training if they interfered with my plans. Since I was eighteen at the time, and more naive than most eighteen-year-olds, I'm sure it struck terror into the poor woman's heart." She tilted her head and remembered those emotional scenes with a twinge of guilt. "So I got my way."

"I've noticed you're pretty good at getting your way," he teased. "God help Roland Houston if he tries to thwart you tomorrow."

"I appreciate what you did for me, Chance." Her voice and expression were serious, her hair softly highlighted by the lamp-glow behind her. "I . . . Why did you go out on a limb for me like that?"

She smelled clean and sweet after her shower, and it was becoming harder and harder to keep his eyes from straying to where the flaps of the bathrobe revealed a flash of thigh. "It wasn't so far out on a limb, Ally. The guy offered a favor, and I asked." His voice sounded husky in his ears.

She looked down at her knees, clearly dissatisfied with his answer. He wasn't so satisfied with it, either. Suddenly everything became crystal-clear to him. They were two consenting adults, alone together behind a locked door, and they both wanted the same thing.

"I only wondered . . ." she began.

"I wanted to do something nice for you," he whispered.

"Why?" Her voice was even softer than his.

Their eyes locked, and all the unsatisfied aches of a lifetime drew them together. He slid out of his chair, knelt before her, and took her hand. Her slim fingers folded cautiously around his.

"Hasn't a guy ever just wanted to be nice to you?"

She lowered her gaze and watched his thumb brush lightly across her knuckles, stirring her senses with a touch that might have seemed impersonal, but which, instead, seemed heart-stoppingly intimate.

"Not often," she admitted. "Not really."

"Well . . . maybe that's because you don't always make it easy," he teased gently, taking her other hand, working his magic on both of them now with featherlight strokes.

"Maybe I just always get involved with the wrong men," she countered, trying to maintain her emotional balance. She hadn't realized he could be so gentle, hadn't suspected that his gentleness could make her quiver like an animal.

"What's wrong?" he whispered, his eyes hot and tender.

"Hmmm?" Her breath was suddenly out of control, and every heavy inhalation carried his clean, musky scent to the center of her body.

"You're trembling."

"I am?"

He moved in closer, pressing his chest against her knees, and leaned his forehead against hers. "You're not afraid of me, are you?"

"No, but what are you doing?"

"I'm making my move," he murmured.

"I, uh . . . Chance, I don't think . . ."

"I know you said you didn't want to." His lips brushed her cheek, so warm, so enticing. "But are you still sure . . ." he kissed her forehead ". . . you'd really rather . . ." he planted a kiss in the palm of her right hand ". . . go to bed alone . . ." he slid his arm around her waist, pulling her closer, letting her feel the heat of his desire, the strength of his wanting ". . . and lie four feet away from me all night long . . ." he kissed her lips, letting his tongue flicker lightly against her hungry mouth ". . . all twisted in knots?"

"Um . . ." She moved involuntarily, leaning into his next kiss, parting her lips in silent invitation.

"Oh, Ally, is that *really* what you want?"

"No," she whimpered.

He swept her up against his chest and kissed her hard, the force of his momentum carrying her with him until they lay sprawled across the bed, mouths melding, hands seeking, legs entangled. Her robe parted easily beneath his questing hands, and he sought the softness of her skin with eager, hungry caresses, stroking her smooth thighs, her satiny belly, her womanly hips, and his mouth demanded her surrender again and again. He had never felt so driven to touch, to hold, to possess. The need to explore every inch of her consumed him, his instinctive urgency warring with the tenderness he felt when she sighed and murmured his name.

Ally felt his urgency, felt the swelling demand of his body as he writhed to get closer to her, felt his self-control crumbling away. The hot insistence of his tongue, exploring her mouth and mating wildly with her own tongue, made her dizzy with pleasure. The urgent heat of his palms on her skin made her whimper with desire. Her hands wrestled clumsily with the knotted sash of his bathrobe, then plunged inside to revel in the delicious textures of his naked body. His back was as smooth as marble, his chest hard and rough with wiry golden hair, his buttocks taut and responsive beneath her grasping fingers.

His hands tugged impatiently at her robe, yanking it off her shoulders and away from her body, trapping her arms by her sides. She arched against him, struggling to pull her hands out of the heavy sleeves.

"Ally, Ally . . ." he murmured heavily, his open

mouth moving over her neck and shoulders, his arms locked tightly around her. "I want you . . . this . . . every inch of you. . . ."

Her nipples were so sensitized that even the touch of his harsh breath upon them made them tingle, made her cry out and stretch to come closer to him, her arms locked helplessly at her sides. His tongue was wet and velvety, fanning the fire in her loins, making her feel cherished and ravished at once. She freed one hand at last and tangled it in his hair, pulling his head closer, urging him to do whatever he wished with her, whatever he would. She had never in her life felt such total abandon, such consuming need, and she would let nothing stand in the way of this man's devouring her.

When she freed her other arm and slid it between his legs, his whole body shook. His arms tightened around her, and his mouth grew rough on her breast. She didn't care. She welcomed his roughness, encouraged it, bathed in it. She wanted to be rough, too, wanted to drive him to the edge, exhaust him, make him as much a slave to this thing between them as she was.

"Yes," he hissed through clenched teeth when she spread hungry kisses across his chest. "Oh, God, yes," he sighed weakly when she teased his male nipples with her tongue and suckled him as he had done to her. "Please . . . I mean . . . Ally . . ." he choked when she massaged his abdomen and nuzzled the steely-hard flesh that rose from his loins.

He rolled her beneath him then, his words incoherent and his face intent, and she spread her legs willingly beneath his questing hand.

"Oh!" She threw her head back and rose up spasmodically against the pressure of his palm, closing her eyes against the torment of his clever fingers.

"Chance, please," she begged, clutching his shoulders, pressing fervent kisses against his neck. "Please," she whimpered, trusting him, knowing he wouldn't disappoint her.

He pulled her thigh over his hip, sank against her, whispered her name . . . and then froze.

"Chance . . ."

"Wait." His chest was going in and out like a bellows.

"What?" she sighed, stroking his heaving rib cage, loving every part of him.

"Condoms," he whispered into her mouth.

"Hmmm?" She pulled him closer and . . . she froze. "Condoms?"

"I think I brought some." He raised his head and frowned. "Oh, hell, where did I put them?"

Ally sagged against the pillows, her body screaming in protest, her brain returning to reality.

"Wait here," he whispered, giving her another kiss before he slid off the bed. His robe flapped around his body as he went into the bathroom, presumably to investigate his shaving kit. He came back to bed a few moments later, tossed several foil packets on the bedside table, and sat down next to her. "Sorry."

"It's okay."

"I, uh, actually know how to pull one out of thin air," he said with a wry smile, "but it takes a little advance planning."

"Really, it's okay. I don't expect . . ." She sighed.

"I wanted to be one of those smooth guys who unwraps a condom and slips it on so discreetly, the woman hardly even notices."

She blinked. "*Are* there guys like that?"

He grinned sheepishly and shrugged. "I don't know. But it's, you know, how a guy *envisions* doing it." He put a hand on her shoulder. "But I got carried away."

"So did I," she admitted softly.

He touched her rumpled hair and watched her pull her robe over her body. "Still in the mood?" *He* still was; some things, a man just couldn't hide.

"Yes, but I, uh . . . um . . ."

His soft, gold-lashed gaze remained on her as she struggled to a sitting position. "But now you're having second thoughts."

She nodded and swallowed. "It's not because of this." She gestured to the condoms lying on the bedside table, their sterile wrappers gleaming beneath the lamp-glow. "From a woman's point of view, you did everything right, Chance," she sid quietly, because he deserved honesty from her. "I don't fantasize about men who are so smooth and in control that they've already choreographed the 'condom sequence.'"

"Oh." He smiled as he toyed with the hem of her robe. "Well, maybe I won't work on smoothing that out, then."

"And the fact that you thought of it proves that . . ."

"Yes?"

She drew a steady breath. "That I can trust you. That you're . . . I don't know, an adult. Responsible. Considerate. You know." She was babbling.

"But?"

"But I don't think I trust you enough to go to bed with you right now." It came out in a rush.

"Oh."

The silence was thick with lingering desire as he struggled with her decision. To break the tension, she finally said, "Is there any particular reason why you brought these with you this weekend? Or do they just go wherever you go?"

He glanced from the foil packets to her. "I didn't have designs on your person, if that's what you mean." He lowered his eyes after a moment and added more honestly, "Well, maybe I *did,* but that has nothing to do with . . ." He gave up and said simply, "No one has any business being careless."

"You're right." She rested her forehead against his shoulder.

"Why don't you trust me?" he whispered.

"It's not that I *don't* trust you, exactly. It's just that . . ." She sighed and turned her head so that her cheek rested against his shoulder as she spoke. "I guess I'm paying for past mistakes. And though it's not fair, that means you wind up paying, too."

He rested his cheek against her hair. "What mistakes?"

"Well, to put it succinctly, my father calls me a 'bum magnet.' "

"Sounds painful." His voice was dry.

"Every man that I've ever cared about was self-centered, unemployable, or untrustworthy. My last boyfriend was all three."

"I see."

"That's why I've been living like a nun, so to speak, for nearly two years."

"Two years is a long time between drinks," he murmured.

"Yes, but I didn't want to go back to that same well."

"There are others," he said quietly.

"So I've been told." She shrugged and rubbed her face sleepily against the nubby fabric of his robe. "But I didn't care. I was too burned-out." She chuckled. "Until you touched a match to my kindling."

"So are you just gonna smoulder, or can we get a blaze going here?"

"I don't know," she admitted. "I just don't trust my own judgment, Chance. And I've never known anyone quite like you."

He pushed her away slightly to look into her face. "Maybe that's your answer, Ally. I'm not like the guys you're talking about."

She clasped and unclasped her hands, her nerves taking over in the absence of sexual gratification. "I hardly know you. We shouldn't even be staying in the same room."

"I—"

"Everything's happening so fast, and I have so much to think about all at once. And anyhow, what's going to happen tomorrow, when we're finished here?" She was babbling again.

"I'm not asking for a one-night stand."

"And . . . and I *hate* this room! I *hate* that pagoda! I don't want to wake up with you tomorrow when that awful maid ignores the 'do not disturb' sign and bustles in, or maybe it'll be Harvey and Wilson's chauffeur. . . ." She could hear herself getting hysterical.

So could he, apparently. "All right, shhhh, shhhh." He folded his arms around her and rocked her gently, waiting for her frantic breaths to subside into soft sighs. "It has been kind of a tense weekend. Maybe we should just . . . try to get some sleep." Above her bowed head, Chance rolled his eyes. He was as likely to fall asleep right now as he was to levitate to the moon. However, Ally had clearly reached the end of her rope, and he wanted to comfort her more than he wanted to convince her to comfort him.

"You're so tough, you make me forget that actresses are pretty sensitive," he murmured against her hair.

"I'm sorry," she said miserably. "I didn't mean to, you know, lead you on. . . . I know it must be hard—"

He choked on his laughter. "Well, yes, it still is," he admitted ruefully.

She made a sound somewhere between a giggle and a sob. "I meant . . ." She shrugged and rubbed a hand across her face. "I just meant that I'm really sorry about . . . this. Tonight."

"I'll let you make it up to me another time," he promised. "When you've realized you can trust me."

"Do you think there'll be another time?"

"I'm counting on it." He brushed her hair away from her face and added, "Tomorrow you'll see Houston, and then we'll get out of this hotel. Everything will start to look better once we're free and clear. Okay?"

"Okay."

He stood up, carefully closing his robe, and added, "I've been pretty wound up, too, I guess. It'll be good to make our escape. We'll even try to leave early."

"Good."

"Go to sleep now."

"All right." She was settling in when she noticed him pull a blanket and a pillow off his bed. "What are you doing?"

Heading for the bathroom, he said, "I'm going to sleep in the tub tonight."

"The tub?" she repeated blankly.

His eyes met hers, and the expression in them rekindled her banked fires. "I'm being a good sport about this, Ally, but the truth is, I'd rather be dragged across a field of broken glass on my stomach than spend the next eight hours lying four feet away from you and listening to you breathe."

And even though she felt bad, she couldn't help smiling when he closed the door behind him.

—— SEVEN ——

Chance wandered aimlessly around the lavish farewell brunch buffet, wondering how Ally's meeting with Roland Houston was going. Unable to sleep, Chance had left the room well before dawn. Since it was too dark to go jogging in a strange city, he had restlessly prowled the corridors of the hotel for over an hour. When the sky had finally grown light enough, he'd gone out for another five-mile run. If nothing else, his acquaintance with Alicia Cannon was certainly keeping him fit.

Upon his return to the room, she had asked him where he had been for so long. He told her and apologized for having unknowingly awakened her when he'd slipped out of the room, but he didn't think she even heard his answer. She was nervous about her meeting, and in the mysterious manner of all women, she was studying her reflection in the mirror as if it were a mortal enemy.

She had then proceeded to go in and out of the bathroom trying on all her clothes. Three times each. And then in different combinations and with different accessories. He was thankful she'd only brought a garment bag and an overnight case with her. He couldn't imagine going through this ritual with her entire wardrobe, particularly after she became annoyed with him for not voicing a clear preference.

"They all look good to me. *You* look good. Stop worrying," he said.

She looked at him as if he had just suggested she should mutilate a small, helpless animal. *Women*, he thought. Giving up, he had gone to take a shower.

The memory made him smile, though, because in her high-strung and demanding way, Ally Cannon was a hell of a lot of fun. A hell of a lot of woman, too. He wished . . .

"Ah, well, what's a few more nights on the tiles, after all, in the grand scheme of things?"

"Excuse me?"

Chance blinked, then felt his face grow hot when he realized he had voiced his last thought aloud. Mr and Mrs. Pollingsworth-Biddle had just joined Chance near the bar to tell him how much they had enjoyed last night's performance.

"Sorry, ma'am. I was drifting." He smiled. "Didn't sleep much last night."

"Neither did we," admitted Mr. Pollingsworth-Biddle with a look of utter bone-weariness. Mrs. Pollingsworth-Biddle giggled. It was a most astonishing sound.

Chance worked hard to keep his face straight. So Harvey *had* put some zing back into this society marriage. "Aren't you finding your room comfortable?" he asked solicitously.

"Oh, the room is *wonderful*!" Mrs. Pollingsworth-Biddle enthused. "Simply *marvelous*. In fact, we've decided to stay on an extra day or two, haven't we, dear?"

"Ungh," said her husband.

"How nice," Chance murmured.

"And after that, we've accepted an invitation to the Wilsons' yacht party. Will you be there, young man?"

"Uh, no, ma'am." He hadn't been invited, but he figured he'd rather walk through the Bowery alone at two o'clock in the morning than be imprisoned aboard a fancy yacht with this crowd for an afternoon.

"Oh, what a shame," Mrs. Pollingsworth-Biddle said, oozing insincerity. "They always invite such a pleasant crowd."

"Ah. No riffraff?" Chance guessed.

"Ungh," said the woman's husband.

"Maybe next time," Chance said absently, looking around. Not many familiar faces today. The Wilsons were conspicuously absent, as was Walter Dureau. Chance wondered if Wilson had had Dureau thrown out of the hotel after learning the man had been rifling through his office. Ambrose Kettering was nowhere to be seen, either. However, early morning rumors were circulating that Kettering had lost a bundle in the casino last night after leaving the benefit performance; Chance supposed the guy was holed up in his room this morning, nursing a hangover and a bad case of the blues. Gambling was a dirty business.

"Aren't you having anything to eat, Mr. Weal?" Mrs. Pollingsworth-Biddle asked, picking daintily from the plate she balanced in one hand. Her husband was gobbling his food like a young athlete in training for the big event.

"No, ma'am. I thought I'd wait for my associate, Miss Cannon."

"Ah, yes, of course."

Chance tried not to glance at the buffet. He was starving. Ally's stomach had started growling right before her meeting, too. However, he figured that this food—even if it lasted until Ally arrived—probably wouldn't be much better than anything else they'd eaten in this accursed hotel. He already had all their luggage stowed in the car, and he hoped they'd leave as soon as Ally's meeting was over, and eat on the road.

"Well, since you're not eating, perhaps you could perform a little sleight of hand for us," Mrs. Pollingsworth-Biddle suggested.

"Huh?" Eyes trained on the door, awaiting Ally's longed-for appearance, Chance had missed what the woman said. When she repeated her request in the haughty tone of royalty addressing the court jester, he shrugged and said, "Sure."

"Ungh," said the husband, which appeared to be a sign of approval.

What should he do? Chance reached into one of his many pockets and pulled out a condom packet. "Oops."

"What is that?"

"Nothing, ma'am." He slipped the packet back into his pocket with the others he had scooped off the bedside table in his last-minute search of the room before checking out. "Ah, here we are," he said, pulling a coin out of another pocket.

Though coin tricks are among the oldest forms of legerdemain, they are still extremely effective. The Pollingsworth-Biddles were vocal enough in their amazement to attract a small crowd as Chance made things appear and disappear as if by magic.

When he finished the brief performance, Mrs. Pollingsworth-Biddle asked Chance some typical questions about magic, and he answered, as usual, with polite evasions, feeling lonesome for Ally. It would indeed be a relief to get away from here. There was something rotten about the whole situation at the Wilson Palace, but he couldn't quite place his finger on it.

"Ah, here's Celine Wilson now," Mrs. Pollingsworth-Biddle said, catching sight of the woman's strangely haggard face as she shoved her way into the room. "We've been wondering where she was, haven't we, dear? It's so *outré* for the hostess to be absent from her own brunch; don't you agree, Mr. Weal?"

"Well, I—"

"But then, you and Celine have grown rather close in the two days you've been here, haven't you?"

"No, I wouldn't say—"

"She's either right by your side, or else she's talking about you to everyone else. She's really quite . . . *fond* of you, isn't she?"

Harvey was right about this woman, Chance decided. Pure poison. That pleasant smile didn't fool him, nor did it take the acid out of her insinuations. "I think that's a slight—"

"Thieves! Thieves! *Voleurs!*" Celine Wilson screamed, plunging into the crowd, still wearing last night's evening gown. Everyone turned and gaped. It was just about the most dramatic entrance Chance had ever seen. *"Mes diamants! Mes bijoux! They are gone! Stolen!"*

Shrieks and gasps from all over the room punctuated this announcement.

Chance said, "My French isn't so—"

"She's been robbed!" Mrs. Pollingsworth-Biddle cried. "Her necklace!"

"What?" Chance exclaimed. "That five-pound piece of ice she was wearing the other night?"

"Yes!"

"My beautiful necklace!" Celine wailed. *"Volé!"*

"Stolen?"

"Robbed!"

"Good God!"

"Pinched," Chance murmured, his brain working furiously. "This place will be crawling with cops in a half hour." The thief knew it, too. Perhaps he had already disappeared. Of course, any enterprising thief may have stolen such a well-publicized chunk of change as Celine Wilson's necklace, but Chance already had a suspect firmly in mind. He wondered if there was any chance that Walter Dureau hadn't already made his escape. Since participating in the general hysteria that now overwhelmed the crowd wasn't going to solve anything, Chance decided to go look for Dureau.

"Will you excuse me, ma'am? Sir?" Without waiting for an answer. Chance took his leave of the Pollingsworth-Biddles and exited the ballroom.

He knew better than to ask the staff at registration whether or not a guest had checked out; they'd be lucky if they could even find the computer's "power on" switch. Instead, he proceeded to the bell captain's station, where Harvey lounged indolently.

"Harvey, do you know a guest named Walter Dureau?"

"Dureau?"

Chance described him.

"Oh, yeah, the nervous, greasy little guy who wants a receipt for every tip?"

"Really? You're kidding me." Chance blinked. "No, never mind about that now. Is he still here?"

Harvey shrugged. "Maybe. Why not check his room?" Harvey also knew better than to bother asking at the registration desk.

"Where is it?"

"Twenty-two fifteen."

Chance frowned. "Isn't that directly below Wilson's suite?"

"That's right. What do you want Dureau for?"

"Just a hunch," Chance muttered, hoping he could find a functional elevator.

The hysterical crowd from the ballroom started spilling out into the main hallway. "Holy Mother of God, what's going on?" Harvey demanded.

"Just keep an eye out for Miss Cannon, okay? I don't want her to get caught up in all of this."

"Sure, but—"

But Chance was already halfway to the elevators.

Ally rode the elevator up to the twenty-second floor, grateful that one—if *only* one—elevator was working. She had emerged from her promising but inconclusive meeting with Roland Houston to find chaos reigning in the lobby of the Wilson Palace Hotel, and then bumped into Harvey, who assured her that there was nothing to worry about.

"I'm not sure what all the fuss is about," he said, looking around. " 'Theft' is all I've been told. I'm just the lowly help after all, so no one—"

"Where's Chance?" Ally interrupted the boy.

"Twenty-two fifteen."

"What's he doing there? We're supposed to eat now. I'm starving. Oh, never mind. I'll go up and get him myself. Thanks, Harvey."

The elevator made a grinding noise between the nineteenth and twentieth floors. Ally shifted nervously, thinking she'd try to talk Chance into taking the stairs on the way down. When the elevator came to a halt on the twenty-first floor, she decided it was an omen and got off.

Finding the emergency stairs, she climbed the rest of the way to the twenty-second floor and entered the hallway, looking for Room 2215.

After a hair-raising ride up in the only functional elevator, Chance found Room 2215. Surely it was no coincidence that Dureau had taken a suite directly below Wilson's quarters. As he stared at the door of Dureau's room, it occurred to Chance that he was a magician, not a cop. If Dureau was in there, what was he going to do about it? Maybe he should call hotel security.

But then again, he reasoned, maybe he should determine if Dureau was still in the room before creating a stir. He'd heard somewhere that jewel thieves weren't dangerous, crazed killers, but skilled professionals. There was even a popular belief that they didn't carry weapons, though Chance was skeptical about that. Even so, he decided to take a small risk before summoning hotel security, who probably already had their hands full with that mob scene downstairs.

Using odds and ends from his pockets, he quietly picked the lock and cracked open the door. No wonder Celine's necklace was stolen, he thought disgustedly. He'd seen sturdier locks on dollhouses.

That was when he heard the voices. Moving as carefully as he did when performing his most dangerous illusions, he inclined his head toward the crack in the door and listened.

There were two speakers, both male. Their voices were faint, as if they were far from the door. Still, Chance didn't think it wise to risk opening the door any farther.

"Am I right about the necklace?" said one voice. It was Dureau. No doubt about it. The nasality was unmistakable.

"Don't you think we have more important things to discuss?"

Chance blinked. The second voice sounded awfully familiar, but surely he was mistaken. It didn't make sense.

"Oh, come on, Wilson," said Dureau.

What the hell was going on? Chance leaned closer to

the door and closed his eyes in concentration, straining to catch every word.

"I didn't expect this," Wilson said.

Expect what? Chance wondered. Expect Dureau to steal the necklace?

"This complicates everything," Wilson continued.

"You surprise me," Dureau said. "I didn't think you'd be squeamish about murder."

Murder?

"Squeamish? On the contrary. It'll be a pleasure."

"I rather thought so," Dureau said dryly.

"Chance? What are you doing?" Ally asked.

He nearly jumped through the ceiling. Instead, he plunged headlong through the doorway, involuntarily dragging Ally down into a messy heap on the floor when she made a grab for his jacket.

"Chance!" she cried.

"Who's there?" Wilson's voice sounded about as cordial as the bark of an attack dog.

"Chance?" Dureau repeated from the next room. "The magician?"

Chance was on his feet in a split second, spinning Ally around and shoving her out the door. "We've got to get out of here!"

He looked over his shoulder to see Wilson emerge from the bedroom portion of Dureau's suite. He held a very large gun in his right hand. One good look at it made Chance feel ill. Instinctively using his skills at misdirection, he threw the first handy object he could grab—in this case, Ally's purse—directly at Wilson's face, lunging sideways in case the man pulled the trigger. Twenty years of practice probably saved his life, since the surprise move worked. Wilson's reflexive grab to catch the purse made him drop the gun, giving Chance the time he needed to slam the door and shove Ally toward the emergency stairs.

"Chance, what's going on?" she demanded, staggering as he forced her down a flight of stairs.

"No time to explain! Just *run*, Ally."

"But why?"

"Don't ask questions! Just *do* it!"

They made a mad dash down a dozen more flights of stairs, by which time he assumed Ally had run out of breath for asking questions; he had certainly run out of breath for answering them.

"Wait," she finally panted, digging in her heels and coming to a complete stop somewhere around the tenth floor. "What are we running from?"

"You didn't see it?" he demanded, breathing hard.

"See what?"

"The gun."

"What gun?"

"The one pointing directly at us."

"Someone was pointing a *gun* at us?" He nodded. Without another word, Ally started running down the stairs again.

By the time they reached the lower levels, their descent was essentially a controlled fall. When they arrived at the ground floor, Ally stopped for breath again. "Why . . . isn't . . . he . . . chasing . . . us?" she asked between gulps of air.

Chance grunted. "Maybe . . . he's still . . . waiting for . . . the elevator."

For some reason, this set her off into peals of laughter.

"Ally . . . not now."

"Sorry . . . sorry. We've got to . . . report this."

When they opened the fire door and stepped into the lobby, they found things even more chaotic than before. Socialites and celebrities were milling all over the place, the check-out desk was mobbed by a vast herd of guests who were suddenly eager to leave, and the bell captain's station was buried beneath a pile of designer luggage.

"Hotel security," Ally suggested, still struggling for breath.

"No!" Chance grabbed her hand and dragged her toward the main doors.

"What? Chance!"

"No!" he repeated, wiping sweat off his face with his jacket sleeve. How could he tell the Wilson Palace security people that Wilson himself was running around with a gun? No, he had to go directly to the Atlantic City Police and tell them about Wilson and Dureau. He only wished he knew what he was going to say. It made no sense. It would probably sound crazy.

"Chance!" Ally cried, struggling against his grip on her arm. "We can't just *leave*."

"*Nothing* is getting me back inside the hotel, Ally."

Outside the main doors, a doorman approached him and asked solicitously, "Taxi, sir?"

Ally said, "No, thank you. We have a car."

"Yes, we'll take a taxi."

"What? But, Chance—"

"There's no time, Ally. We've got to get out of here!"

"We can't—"

Her protest was interrupted by the wail of sirens, followed closely by the screech of tires. Within seconds, three blue-and-whites and an unmarked police car all pulled up in front of the Wilson Palace Hotel and Casino.

"The police," Ally said with relief. "Now can we stop running?"

"There he is!" cried a voice from behind them. Chance whirled to find himself facing Mrs. Pollingsworth-Biddle.

"He who?" Ally asked, even though the lady was clearly pointing at Chance.

Four husky security guards rushed forward and seized Chance, shoving Ally roughly aside.

"What's going on?" asked a dark-haired man in a trench coat, emerging from the unmarked car.

"That's the culprit, officer! That's your man. Helmut Wilson just identified him!" Mrs. Pollingsworth-Biddle cried.

"What do you mean, 'identified him'?" Ally demanded in confusion.

"Mr. Wilson's stuck on the top floor, sir," said one of the hotel security guards, addressing the dark-haired cop. "This fellow," he added, jerking Chance by the shoulder, "just threatened him with a gun."

"That's crazy!" Ally snapped.

"He stole the diamonds, officer," Mrs. Pollingsworth-Biddle cried.

"What diamonds?" Ally said.

"Celine's diamonds," Chance said wearily.

"I don't get it," Ally said, looking at him plaintively. He sighed. "Let's just say I'm having one of those days."

The trench-coat cop, despite his Italian looks, turned out to be named O'Neal. Ally felt almost sorry for him, since he was clearly having a difficult time trying to bring order to chaos and to make sense out of insanity. She and Chance were shown into a small sitting room near the casino. The room seemed to grow even smaller as it filled up with people: another plainclothes detective, four uniformed cops, the four hotel security men who had brought Chance there, Mr. and Mrs. Pollingsworth-Biddle, Harvey, one of the hotel receptionists, and Celine Wilson. Ally was relieved when Sheik Nesib el Dheilan was asked to leave the room, since he had no information regarding the matter at hand; the arrival of that man and his two heavily veiled wives had turned the thick crowd into a sardinelike assembly. However, before leaving, the desert prince made his displeasure known.

"That woman is not worth twenty camels!" he told Chance.

"Nineteen, then," Chance countered.

"What's going on?" Detective O'Neal demanded.

"It's a long story," Chance answered.

"Five camels and two goats," the sheik offered, looking Ally over with a coldly assessing gaze. She wondered if he'd go as high as three goats.

"All right," O'Neal said to a patrolman. "Get this guy out of here. And his bodyguards, too."

"Those are his wives, Detective," Ally corrected.

O'Neal stared doubtfully at the retreating figures. "That's anybody's guess, Miss Cannon. He could have two of the ten most-wanted hidden in those things, and who would know?"

He had a point, Ally thought, wincing when another patrolman trod on her foot in passing.

"Why doesn't someone tell me what happened here?" O'Neal suggested, taking a seat.

It was a big mistake. Half a dozen different people answered at once, all raising their voices to be heard above one another, and all refuting what everyone else said.

"All right, that's enough!" O'Neal shouted, trying to be heard above the din. "Now, let's get this straight. Mr. Weal threatened Mr. Wilson with a fistful of diamonds?"

The roar of protest produced by this misstatement caused another five minutes to be wasted. O'Neal paused in his efforts to control the crowd, and washed a couple of little white pills down with a swig of soda. Ally thought he looked rather red-faced, and wondered if he had high blood pressure.

"Then what exactly *did* happen?"

"My jewels, they are *volé*!"

"The necklace," Chance said, trying to shake off the heavy hands of two beefy security guards. "Someone stole her diamond necklace."

Ally gasped. "Your necklace was stolen?"

"This innocent act is appalling!" hurled Mrs. Pollingsworth-Biddle. "No wonder you're reduced to working as a magician's assistant."

"Now, just a *minute*," Ally said.

"I thought you said you *liked* the act," Chance said, clearly stung to the quick.

O'Neal cleared his throat. "Could we please—"

"No. Wait a minute," Chance said. "I want to know just what Mrs. What's-her-face means by that."

"You have the manners of a hyena," Ally snarled at the woman.

"This man has shamelessly wooed and dazzled Mrs. Wilson with his attentions this weekend," Mrs. Pollingsworth-Biddle began. "Putting her under his spell, drawing her into his web—"

"Oh, *mon Dieu!*" Celine cried. "Do you mean to say

. . . Have I been deceived in this man? But he made me feel so . . . ''

"You're a married woman, Celine," Ally reminded her sharply. "Anyhow, Detective O'Neal, that's rubbish. Mr. Weal has spent most of this weekend with *me*." Realizing how that sounded, particularly when she saw a wink pass between two uniformed cops, Ally amended, "I mean, you know, we're working together this weekend, so he's hardly been out of my sight."

"Don't you see? *She's* his alibi." Mrs. Pollingsworth-Biddle rolled her eyes at the audacity of it all.

"What's the matter with you?" Harvey said to the woman. "I thought you got laid last night."

It took O'Neal several minutes to bring the room back to order after this outburst. Mrs. Pollingsworth-Biddle, dismissing O'Neal's announcement that he would interview them all one at a time, continued her tirade.

"Having set his sights on the necklace and made poor, dear Celine trust him," she began, "he then—"

"Give me a break," Harvey said.

"Mrs. Polly-Biddle," O'Neal said.

"This man has been making jewels disappear all weekend," the woman said.

"Excuse me?" said the detective. "Have someone else's diamonds been stolen?"

"No, no." Chance said. "I make things disappear. It's my job." When this drew a cold, speculative stare from O'Neal, Chance licked his lips and said, "Maybe I should rephrase that."

"You'll have your chance, Mr. Weal."

"Where's Wilson?" Chance demanded. "He's the one who phoned security and said I'd attacked him. He knows more about the diamonds than anyone else. He's up to his ears in this. Why isn't he here?"

"Mr. Wilson has a weak heart. Can't come down until one of the elevators starts working," said a security guard.

"A likely story," Chance muttered. "And what about Walter Dureau? We're all sitting here wasting time while

Wilson and Dureau are . . . are . . . Well, to be honest, I don't know *what* they're doing."

"Wilson and Dureau?" Ally repeated incredulously. "Together?"

"Didn't you hear them?" Chance demanded. "Didn't you see . . ." Seeing her blank look, he broke off in frustration and turned back to O'Neal. "You've got to find them."

O'Neal assured Chance that he would. However, it was clear from his response that he considered Chance's wild comments about Wilson to be the least of his concerns. Ally supposed that was to be expected. Wilson was, after all, a fabulously rich, socially prominent member of the community, and his wife's priceless necklace had just been stolen. She wished she understood what was going on.

"And when Celine announced that she had discovered the theft of the diamonds," Mrs. Pollingsworth-Biddle said, "what were the first words out of this man's mouth?"

After an expectant pause, O'Neal sighed again and said, "What, ma'am?"

"He said that the hotel would soon be 'crawling with cops.' And then he made a hasty exit from the ballroom."

"Is this true?" O'Neal asked Chance.

"Yes, but I can explain that. I figured that Dureau—"

"I'll tell you one thing—Mr. Weal was planning a hasty exit from the hotel," piped up someone at the back of the room. They all turned to look at the receptionist. "He checked out before breakfast and had all his luggage put in his car, ready for a quick getaway. Ask the bellboy."

"Well, son?" O'Neal said, turning to Harvey.

"Well, yeah, I helped him stow the luggage in his car. But if *you* had spent two days in this hotel, you'd be just as—"

"Search the car!" cried Mrs. Pollingsworth-Biddle.

"You want to search the car? Get a warrant!" Ally snapped, growing exceedingly impatient. "I'm telling you, he didn't do it; read my lips. And while we're standing around here wasting time, the real thief is getting farther away every minute.''

"Not necessarily," Chance said gloomily.

"He has all the skills needed to pull off a job like this. I've seen *To Catch a Thief*. I know what I'm talking about," said the hotel receptionist.

"What did we ever do to you?" Ally demanded. It was as if the girl had a *vendetta* or something. "Look, when did the jewels disappear, Celine?"

"Yes, when *did* they disappear, Mrs. Wilson?" O'Neal looked a little embarrassed, as well he might. It shouldn't be Ally's job to get things back on track there. Thank God she had once played a cop.

"I was wearing them last night," Celine began. "I became very weary suddenly. So tired, dizzy even, that it was an effort to reach my suite of rooms. I only got as far as the couch, then all is blackness in my memory.''

"Drugged or drunk?" Harvey wondered.

"Drugged," Ally guessed. "The thief counted on those diamonds not making it back into the safe."

"Could we continue?" O'Neal said testily.

"When I awoke," Celine said, starting to weep again, "the necklace was gone!"

"Where was your husband during all this?" O'Neal asked.

"He is, how you say, a party animal."

"Is that how we say it?" Ally muttered.

"I do not think he came to bed last night." Celine gave a beautiful, sad, sweet smile. Ally wanted to punch her. "Last night, everything was so exciting, such a triumph for him, you see."

"There. That proves my point," Ally said, slicing ruthlessly across this poignant moment. "Chance Weal was in our room all night long. He never left it until . . ." Her voice trailed off suddenly and she blinked several times. Blinked hard. "Oh, God."

"You've remembered something, Miss Cannon?" O'Neal surmised. "Mr. Weal *did* leave the room?"

Ally looked at Chance. He winced and said a bad word. Ally cleared her throat. "Well, actually . . . um . . ."

"Yes?"

"Ah-a!" cried Mrs. Pollingsworth-Biddle.

"He went jogging. Before dawn. He, uh . . . jogs," Ally said. trying to sound convincing.

"Jogging?" said the youngest security guard. "Not hardly. I saw him prowling all around the corridors. I had just come on duty, early shift." He grinned sheepishly. "I'm working extra hours, you know, trying to save up enough to buy an engagement ring for—"

"Never mind the autobiography," O'Neal interrupted. "You saw Mr. Weal prowling around, you say?"

"I wasn't prowling." Chance sounded outraged. "I was . . . Oh, hell, it was still too dark to go jogging, so I was just—"

"Do you always get up in the middle of the night to go jogging?" O'Neal inquired.

"No, of course not. And it wasn't the middle of the night, it was just before—"

"Why were you up and about so early on this particular occasion?"

"Because I couldn't sleep."

"A likely story," sneered Mrs. Pollingsworth-Biddle.

"Put a cork in it, you skinny witch," Ally said.

"Ladies, please," O'Neal pleaded, looking red-faced again. "Why couldn't you sleep, Mr. Weal?"

"Because . . . uh . . ." He met Ally's gaze for a moment, reddened slightly, and looked away. Finally he shrugged.

There was a lengthy silence. At last O'Neal said, "All right, Mr. Weal. You've apparently shown interest in the necklace this weekend. You may have unusual skills which would assist you in stealing—"

"Come on," Ally interrupted. "Sleight of hand is not the same as—"

Looking at his notes, O'Neal said, "I gather Mr. Wilson told his security staff that, prior to Mr. Weal's attacking him—"

"Chance didn't attack anyone!"

O'Neal continued, "That Mr. Weal opened the door by picking the lock."

"Forget it. He can't pick a lock. Can you, Chance?"

"Mr. Weal?"

Chance cleared his throat and looked at Ally. He hadn't felt like this since the sheriff had caught him with his pants down more than fifteen years ago. "Well, actually . . ."

"Oh, Chance." Her face fell.

"It's just something I, you know, learned for escapes and . . ." He tried a halfhearted smile. "Well."

"Good grief." She sighed wearily. "I wish you would have just lied."

"Why?" said Mrs. Pollingsworth-Biddle. "Lying hasn't worked for you today, young lady."

Raising his voice to be heard above the ensuing argument, O'Neal continued, "In addition, Mr. Weal, you appear to have been prepared to make a hasty exit from the hotel, and you behaved suspiciously when you realized the police were on their way."

"I didn't behave suspiciously, I—"

"We apprehended you in the act of fleeing," O'Neal reminded him. "You've also been accused of assault with a deadly weapon by Mr. Helmut Wilson, a prominent and respected citizen. Furthermore, there's a chunk of time this morning that you can't account for." O'Neal snapped his notebook shut. The gesture made Ally's heart sink. "I'm afraid I'm going to have to take you and Miss Cannon in for questioning."

"You should be questioning Wilson," Chance insisted, rising to his feet.

"I don't believe this!" Ally exclaimed. "You can't seriously believe—"

"What about my necklace?" Celine wailed.

"I'm going to divide my men into teams, Mrs. Wilson. One team will question the staff and the guests, and the other will organize a search. If your diamonds are still in this hotel, we'll find them. And if they're in Mr. Weal's car . . ."

"Are we under arrest?" Chance asked disbelievingly. "Are you *arresting* us?"

"You better not *touch* that car without a warrant, pal," Ally said, practically hopping up and down with outrage. "I know my rights, O'Neal. I've *played* a cop, and if you take one wrong step, I'll see you prosecuted to the full extent—"

"Miss Cannon," O'Neal interrupted loudly. "I feel a headache coming on. Could you please not talk quite so much?"

In answer to Chance's question, O'Neal explained that they weren't under arrest and that they hadn't been charged with anything—yet. He eyed Ally, however, as if he'd like to charge her with aggravated verbal assault. "We're just going to question you. For now."

"Oh, yeah!" Ally said, disliking the implications in his tone. "Well, just think about these two words. O'Neal: habeas corpus. Got that?"

"Ally, please don't antagonize him." Chance forgot his civilized intentions a moment later, however, when a patrolman took Ally's arm. "Keep your hands off her," Chance snapped, "or I'll make you wish you'd never even *seen* her."

"Buddy, I *already* wish I'd never seen her," said the patrolman, but he let go of Ally and gestured politely for her to precede him out the door. Ally held her head high as she walked past a gloating Mrs. Pollingsworth-Biddle.

"Gosh, Mr. Weal," Harvey said as Chance was escorted past him. "Is there anything I can—"

"Not at the moment, Harvey. Thanks, anyhow." On his way out of the room, he nearly walked straight into a tall, thin, long-haired, bearded aesthete wearing even shabbier clothes than his own faded duds.

"Ally?" The guy lowered his dark glasses long enough to take a good look at Chance's companion, who was being hovered over by two big cops. "What's going on?"

Ally drew in a sharp breath, and Chance saw her face redden. "It's just a slight misunderstanding, Roland. The police want to question me."

"Oh, no! The fuzz?" Houston replaced his dark glasses and fell back a step. "My God, Ally! Can I help?"

"Maybe you could call Monty Jackson and tell him I'm in trouble?"

"Of course. Anything! We're children of the sun, Ally. They can't lock you away. Don't let these swine break and bend your beautiful spirit! Don't fall prey to their fascist imperatives! Don't—"

"Uh, Roland, they just want to question us for now," Ally said placatingly, giving him a little shove toward the bank of nearby pay phones.

"Never quite got over the sixties, did he?" Chance guessed, watching the guy skitter away.

"He's an anarchist. But a very good director."

"Uh-huh."

"Can we continue?" O'Neal asked testily.

"Let's get on with it," Chance muttered.

They drew a lot of stares as they walked through the lobby. Guests of the Wilson Palace didn't often get escorted out by a small crowd of armed, uniformed men.

"Hey, Chance! What's going on, kid?"

Chance winced when he recognized Ambrose Kettering approaching them. "Might as well just kiss my television special good-bye now," he mumbled to himself.

"We're questioning this man, sir, and would appreciate being allowed to get on with our business," O'Neal said, looking very annoyed by now.

"Whoa there, boys!" Kettering said jovially. This time Ally winced. "What's the trouble?"

"It's routine, sir," said O'Neal, trying to hustle his suspects past Kettering.

"Routine?" Ally snapped. "This sort of farce may be routine for you, O'Neal—"

"Are these kids under arrest?" Kettering asked.

"I am not a kid!" Ally told Kettering testily.

"Ambrose," Chance began. "I'm sure this will all—"

"Because this boy is due in Los Angeles in a few weeks," Kettering told O'Neal.

"Maybe so, sir, but he also—"

"I think we can work something out," Kettering said, oozing confidence and bonhomie. Ally thought the man looked particularly hung over today, but expensive tailoring and a good tan can make up for a lot of nature's flaws. She thought his hair looked slightly askew, however.

"Uh, Ambrose," Chance said uneasily, "I don't think—"

"What do you make per annum, Detective? Round figures," Kettering said, drawing O'Neal slightly apart from the others.

"Excuse me?" O'Neal said.

"Do something," Ally instructed Chance, sensing disaster ahead.

"How'd you like tickets to the show?" Kettering asked O'Neal. "It's this kid's first television special. Live audience and everything."

"Sir, let me warn you that you're making a big—"

"Round-trip airfare for you and the wife, complimentary suite at a first-class hotel . . . I can probably even get you onto the set of your favorite television show." He put a familiar hand on O'Neal's shoulder. "And all I'm asking in exchange is that you don't interfere with this kid's schedule. What do you say?"

"I'm going to spend the rest of my life behind bars," Ally said woodenly.

"It won't be so bad," O'Neal said to her nastily, shaking off Kettering's hand. "You'll eat three squares a day and learn a trade. As for *you* . . ." O'Neal pointed at Kettering, stared hard, and finally shook his head. "Oh, what's the point? Come on, Mr. Weal."

"Ambrose, I think it would be better if you just let me handle this," Chance said as he was hauled away.

"And if I lock you up and throw away the key," O'Neal added to Chance and Ally, "just remember that you have your friend to thank for that."

"He's no friend of *mine*," Ally insisted. "Anyhow, O'Neal, I know my rights!"

"Ally, please . . ." Chance pleaded.

"I have a headache," O'Neal grumbled.

Later on, Chance would never be quite sure exactly what made him do it. He was innocent and believed he could prove it, even though it was starting to look like doing that might take a bit of time and a good lawyer. Maybe it was the thought of Ally, languishing in a jail cell without his protection. If worst came to worst, he was pretty sure he could escape from a jail, but he couldn't leave her locked in a cell with tough women criminals who might not shrug off her flashes of temper. Besides, who knew how long O'Neal would keep them there, whether he would decide to charge them both, or what kind of bail might be set for them? Aside from the problem of the missing diamonds, Wilson was accusing Chance of assault; and it was pretty obvious that a multimillionaire hotel owner's word carried a lot more weight than that of a visiting magician. Wilson could easily frame Chance for whatever he chose to accuse him of. And who were Wilson and Dureau planning to murder?

Maybe it was just the confusion and panic of the moment that drove him to it. Everything had happened too fast; he hadn't had time to think clearly, let alone figure out what to do about it all. Maybe it was just pure instinct. Whatever the cause or motive, when he saw his opportunity, he seized it. After a lifetime of refocusing his audience's attention, this came so easily that O'Neal would probably suspect he had rehearsed it.

"The diamonds!" Chance shouted.

A simple cry, an economical gesture, and everyone was looking the other way. In that split second, he grabbed Ally's hand and ran.

EIGHT

Ally wasn't sure why she cooperated when Chance took her hand and dragged her into the casino. Maybe it was just instinct. He was the only person who seemed to still be on her side. Or maybe it was because she felt pretty sure that Ambrose Kettering had just destroyed the possibility of her being released before the century was out. O'Neal had been practically purple with outrage by the time Kettering was done with him, and Ally had little doubt about who would ultimately suffer for that.

So she and Chance plunged into the casino, hoping to be obscured by the crowd. They had only gone a few yards when she heard the shouts behind them.

"Police! Freeze! Halt!" the cops shouted, as well as all the other things that cops usually said in such situations.

Her insides twisted with dread as she realized what could happen next, but it seemed too late to stop running. The cards were dealt. There was nothing to do now but play out the hand.

"Through here!" Chance jerked her arm painfully and dragged her past a bank of slot machines, recklessly shoving through a crowd of middle-aged women, all trying their luck. The ladies' concentration on the one-armed bandit was so focused that they never even seemed to notice the magician and actress pushing through their ranks, closely followed by a herd of armed policemen.

"Freeze!"

Ally ran faster, truly terrified now.

Theft. Armed assault. And, of course, resisting arrest.

"Oh, God," she moaned.

She heard screaming behind her and realized that someone had finally noticed the police, whose guns were exposed as they ran through the crowd.

"Stop, or I'll shoot!" O'Neal warned.

"Chance . . ." she panted.

"He won't shoot. Too many people. Come on!"

"Everyone hold still!" O'Neal cried.

Hardly anybody could hear him, since casinos are not notoriously quiet places. Anyhow, the people who *could* hear his order did exactly the opposite and starting running around frantically.

"Where's the exit?" Ally asked.

"Jackpot!" some lady cried.

"We need a diversion," Chance said, leading the way past a row of blackjack tables.

Ally glanced over her shoulder, then she tripped. "Ow!"

"Are you all right?" Chance was already hauling her to her feet.

"Hey, buddy! What's going on?" The man who asked this quesiton was blocking their path. An incredibly large person, he was wearing a tuxedo and appeared to be a hotel employee.

"God Almighty," Chance said respectfully.

Ally looked way up at the man's face, gauging his size advantage. He outweighed the two of them put together. They'd never get past him.

A diversion, Chance had said.

She stuck her hand in the pocket of her peach-colored blazer and spoke in her most convincing Brooklyn accent. "I've already killed the bellboy, buddy, so don't think I won't blow you away, too," she snarled, using the same tone she'd used upon murdering her character's pimp in *Northern Comfort*.

Chance's eyes went so wide, she thought he'd forgotten to keep breathing.

"Okay, lady, let's stay calm," the big guy said, gaze fixed upon the threatening shape in her pocket.

"Hands up and start backing toward the exit," she growled. "Unless you want all these nice people to get a good look at what a thirty-eight can do to a new tuxedo."

The man raised his hands and started backing up.

"Ally . . ." Chance looked uneasily over his shoulder.

"Tell the cops they better stop right there," Ally ordered the man. It came out: *Tell da cops dey bedda stop roit deah.*

"Don't come any closer!" the big guy shouted. "I got three kids!"

O'Neal came closer anyway, so Ally warned him, "Two more steps and I'm gonna blow him away. I mean it, O'Neal! Don't push me! Don't you *push* me! I'll do it, O'Neal!"

"She'll do it!" the big guy cried. "What's one more stiff to a woman like her?"

"What?" O'Neal said, stopping in his tracks. "She's not armed." He blinked and his jaw dropped. "Is she *armed*?"

Ally laughed nastily. "The big detective didn't think to search me."

"Don't overdo it, okay?" Chance said out of the corner of his mouth.

"We're getting outta here now," Ally warned. "Anyone tries to stop us, this guy is dead meat." Under her breath, she added to Chance. "Get *behind* me, you idiot. Don't you ever go to the movies?"

"What? Oh!" As they backed toward the exit, he whispered, "What do we do once we're outside?"

"Didn't you have a plan when you decided to break and run?" she muttered.

"I thought we'd just run," he shot back. "I didn't know we were about to become Bonnie and Clyde."

Realizing that misleading the cops might be a good idea, Ally raised her voice enough for her hostage to hear every word clearly. "As soon as we're clear, we're gonna make a break for the car. Thank God you put the luggage in there this morning."

"The car? But, Ally— Oof!" An elbow in his ribs prevented him from finishing. He winced and murmured, "You're so impetuous."

"Okay, Prince Charming," Ally said to her hostage, "we're going out the door. You cause any trouble, and . . ."

"No trouble, lady. I'm not paid enough to cause trouble. My take-home isn't even four hundred a week, I—"

"Never mind the autobiography," Chance advised.

When they reached the doors of the casino, they released their hostage and looked for a way to disappear quickly. As luck would have it, O'Neal hadn't had time to call for backup, and no one outside the casino seemed to know they were fugitives. They jumped into the first taxi that rolled up and ordered him to take off.

"Where are we going?" Ally asked Chance.

"I don't know. There hasn't been time to think."

"The police?"

"You can't be serious." He cast a warning glance at the driver. The less anyone knew about them, the better.

"Then let's go back to New York and sort things out from there."

"You folks know where you want to go?" asked the cabby.

"West Ninety-third Street in Manhattan," Ally said.

"Lady, how about I just take you to the bus station, okay?"

"The bus station? Can't you take us all the way to New York?" she asked plaintively.

"Sorry, lady. My shift's over in an hour."

"How about dropping us two blocks from the station, in that case?" Chance suggested.

"Why not right *at* the station?" Ally asked.

Chance shook his head. Ten minutes later, she realized why. They watched the bus station carefully, hiding behind magazine racks at a newsstand about half a block away. Two patrol cars were parked outside the station, and several uniformed policemen were obviously on the lookout for them.

"Dammit," Ally said. "No bus for us, I guess."

Chance sighed heavily, his mind spinning. "I could hotwire a car, but I think we're in enough trouble already."

"No doubt they've got the nearest airport covered, and all the car rental agencies, too. Forget about trains . . . How are we going to get out of town?"

"I've got an idea," Chance said.

"No. Absolutely not," Ally said.

"Look, we've already tried it this way, and they just won't stop for a guy. And if we stand around here much longer, O'Neal and his men are going to find us."

"This was *your* idea," she reminded him. "I will not initiate such a degrading transaction."

"You're gonna find a jail cell a whole hell of a lot more degrading."

"*I* wasn't the one accused of burglary and assault with a deadly weapon," Ally pointed out through gritted teeth. "*I* might have been released without being arrested."

He felt guilty, because he realized that was true. He should have left her behind when he'd made his break for freedom. However, there was no turning back now. "Maybe so, but *I* am not the one who threatened a hostage with a thirty-eight right under O'Neal's nose."

"There was no thirty-eight!"

"But you and I are the only two people in the whole world who know that, Ally. So maybe we should get a move on." He gestured to his roadside position. "Ready to give it a try?"

She sighed. "Oh, all right." She scowled as she joined him on the shoulder of a secondary road leading out of town. "Who would have thought I'd be reduced to hitchhiking? My mother would have a breakdown if she could see me now."

"Think of it as research," he suggested. "You might play a part like this one day."

A stony stare told him what she thought of that advice. She stuck out her thumb and tried, without success, to get a ride. After ten minutes of steady failure, she took off her pretty peach blazer, mussed her hair, hiked up her skirt, and borrowed Chance's handkerchief.

"What are you going to do?" he asked.

"Lie down," she ordered.

"What?"

"Lie down."

"But it's all muddy."

"Chance, just do it."

Wondering what she had in mind, he lay down on the shoulder of the road.

"Try to look, you know, ill or injured or something."

"Uh-huh." He did his best.

They heard another truck coming. Ally stepped out into the middle of the road, ignoring Chance's protest, and waved her handkerchief in the air. The truck stopped, since the alternative was killing Ally. The driver stuck his head out the window.

"Are you nuts, lady? Are you out of your mind? Are you—"

"Oh, please, sir, please," Ally cried in a southern accent that made her sound all helpless and fluttery. "Please, sir, as you are a Christian and an American and a gentleman, I *beg* you to help us." It came out: *Ah baig yuh ta halp us.*

"Uh . . ." The truck driver scratched his head and paused to stare at the lovely young woman, who wore only a short skirt and a sheer, silky blouse, and who begged for his gallant assistance in a voice like warm honey. "What's the problem, miss?"

"We have been set upon by gangsters!" Ally cried. "They found us at the roadside fixing a flat tire. They took our car, our money, everything! And they harmed my poor brother."

Ally wept real tears into the handkerchief. The driver

huffed and puffed about this terrible incident and came down from his cab to pat Ally awkwardly on the back and help Chance into the truck. Never having been much good at accents—or tall tales—Chance left all the talking to Ally and confined himself to pained grunts.

"We'll go to the police," the driver said decisively.

"Oh, sir, no, oh, no, oh, please!" Ally's voice mounted in volume, causing the driver to wince. "If you could just take us north. North to where our dear mama awaits us."

The driver frowned. "North? But I thought you were southerners."

"We are, but Mama opened a pastry shop in the city, and we've been just ever so happy there," Ally said quickly.

"The city? Philadelphia?"

"Uh—"

"Then you're in luck, miss, because that's where I'm headed. I can take you all the way."

"But—" Ally gasped when Chance elbowed her sharply.

"Thank you," Chance murmured. As long as they had safe passage out of Atlantic City, who cared where they would wind up?

The ride passed uneventfully. Chance pretended to be asleep most of the way. At Ally's suggestion, the driver dropped them off at a gas station on the outskirts of Philadelphia.

"I'll call my mama from here, and she'll come get us," Ally assured the driver, thanking him profusely for his help.

"Good luck with everything, miss."

After the truck had pulled away, Ally turned on Chance. "What's the big idea? We should have gotten off *miles* ago! I don't want to be in Philadelphia!"

"What's wrong with Philadelphia?"

"It's not home, that's what's wrong with it."

"Oh." He frowned, feeling guilty again. He had forgotten that New York City was home to her. "All I thought about was getting away from Atlantic City."

"Maybe we'd better talk about this."

"I think we'd better keep moving, Ally. There'll be plenty of time to talk once we're sure we've lost them."

And so they hitched another ride, this time in the back of a chicken truck. The smell made Ally pass out; or perhaps it was just exhaustion. In any event, it was hours later when she finally awoke. A sharp jolt had thrown a heavy object on top of her, and she struggled against it, panicking as she felt herself smothering. The heavy object mumbled and snuggled closer, and she recognized it.

"Chance, you're crushing me," she croaked.

"Hmmm?" He raised his head and sniffed. "What's that smell? Is that *you*?"

"No, that's not me. That's the charming mode of transportation you chose for us. Remember?" She shoved at his chest, and he rolled away.

"Oh, yeah. It's all coming back to me." He closed his eyes in an apparent effort to make it all go away again.

"Chance." Ally forced firmness into her voice. "I'm tired, I'm filthy, I'm scared, and I'm so hungry, I could eat one of my own shoes. We've got to stop somewhere and figure out what we're going to do."

He nodded. "Okay. You're right. We've got to talk, to come up with a reasonable plan. Let's get off at the next town."

"Where are we, anyhow? We should have gotten into New York a long time ago."

When the truck finally stopped, they got out, moving swiftly and trying not to inhale too deeply. They were in some desolate little town that looked like it hadn't changed a bit since the Depression.

"There's a coffee shop." Ally pointed. "Let's get something to eat."

They sat on wooden chairs and leaned their elbows on a chipped laminated tabletop. Ally ordered a roast beef sandwich, french fries, a salad, a chocolate shake, a bowl of vegetable soup, and a glass of ice tea, saying she would decide later what to get for dessert.

"I think the first thing we should do is call Monty," Ally said between mouthfuls of food.

"All right," Chance agreed, eating his burger and onion rings with similar concentration. When they were done eating, they changed some of Chance's money for quarters, found a pay phone near the door, and called Monty's weekend number.

"Ally?" Monty cried. "What's going on? What have you done? Where are you?"

"We're . . ." Ally realized she didn't know. "Where are we?" she asked Chance.

"I think I saw a sign that said we're in Chicken Neck, Pennsylvania."

"That's Turkey Foot," corrected a waitress, who was shamelessly eavesdropping. Chance tried to look menacing, but he apparently didn't do it as well as Ally, since the waitress ignored him and continued to listen in.

"Somewhere near New York, anyhow," Ally said. "We're on our way home."

"New York City?" the waitress asked. Chance nodded. "Nowhere near the city," the waitress corrected.

"Oh?" Chance said.

"This is western Pennsylvania, honey. I'd say you're a good five hours from New York City. Maybe more."

"What?" Ally said.

"What? What?" Monty asked frantically.

"We seem to have taken a wrong turning," Ally said wearily. "We're hitchhiking, and you just sort of have to take what comes along."

"*Hitchhiking?* Good God, Ally!" Monty cried.

"Do you have a map?" Chance asked the waitress. "Maybe you could show me where we are." He gave her his most charming smile. She smiled back and led him into the staff room, where a grease-stained map was pinned to the wall. Ally found him there about ten minutes later.

"What did Monty say?" he asked.

"It's pretty grim." Looking glum, she added, "I'll give you the details later."

He took that to mean she would wait until they were alone. Outside the coffee shop, he asked, "What now?"

"Monty suggests we press on to another town. The more we keep switching directions, the harder it will be for anyone to find us." She sighed wearily and started walking down the road that led out of Turkey Foot, her head bowed and her shoulders slumped.

I got her into this, Chance thought, walking dejectedly behind her.

Their next ride, a Vietnamese immigrant, took them as far as a little town called Stinking Creek.

Chance took one whiff and said, "Guess how the town got its name."

"At least there's a motel."

"Ally, I was just wondering . . ."

"Hmmm?" She looked exhausted.

"Well, since I threw away your purse when we were trying to escape Wilson . . . do you have any money on you?" Chance figured he barely had enough cash to pay for a motel room, and maybe some breakfast. If Ally didn't have any money, they couldn't hold out for long. Yet he had decided that returning to New York probably wouldn't be safe either.

"I don't know." She fished around in the pockets of her blazer and finally came up with a single dollar bill. She held it up, and the expression in her eyes told him she had already guessed the state of their finances.

"Let's see how much a room costs," he suggested quietly.

"Chance . . ." Her hand on his arm was warm, despite the growing chill of the night air. The bite of the wind reminded him that it was nearly October.

"What?"

"Could you . . . Maybe you could . . ."

"What, Ally?" he asked, wondering at her diffidence.

"Maybe you could turn it into a hundred dollars?" she

asked, suddenly looking like a child who believed in all his magic, instead of the sophisticated actress who had scorned his hocus-pocus.

He smiled, wondering at the sweetness that welled up in him when she looked at him like that, wide-eyed and trusting. He took her dollar and said, "Well, I don't know about turning it into a *hundred* dollars, but I think I can do something with this."

A few moments later, he turned over a fifty-dollar bill to her—the last cash he had. Her eyes sparkled for a moment, and she admitted ruefully, "It . . . it actually makes people feel a little better sometimes, doesn't it?"

"That's what I like best about it," he said.

Fifty dollars turned out to be enough to get them a motel room, a couple of toothbrushes, and a simple dinner. They retired early to their dingy room, with its sagging bed and broken TV set. The shower water was only lukewarm, rather than hot, but it felt heavenly to Ally, who wished she didn't have to get back into dirty clothes the following morning.

After his own shower, Chance pulled his jeans back on, then started towel-drying his hair as he returned to the bedroom. He found Ally curled up on the bed, wearing only a white hotel towel, her dark chestnut hair falling in damp waves around her shoulders. She was fiddling with the TV remote, to no avail.

"We don't seem to have much luck with televisions," she remarked.

"You're afraid we're on the news," he guessed.

She lowered her eyes. "Monty says things look pretty bad." Her voice was a thin whisper.

He sighed and joined her on the bed, reclining on the pillows she had propped against the headboard. She sat with her bare legs folded under her, her smooth white shoulders gleaming in the faint yellow glow of the bedside lamp. "Don't be afraid," he murmured. "It'll be all right." He hoped he was telling the truth.

"Why do they think you stole the necklace? Why do they think you threatened Wilson with a gun?"

He thought her hand was shaking when she tucked her towel more securely over her breasts. Reaction to the day's events was setting in fast, now that they were alone and temporarily safe.

"Wilson threatened *us* with a gun—"

"But I didn't see—"

"And somehow he's involved with the theft of the diamonds." He rubbed a hand across his face. "But I just don't get it."

"Monty says . . ." She cleared her throat and tried again. "Monty says that he thinks we might be arrested if we turn up in New York. He'd gotten four phone calls about us before I phoned. We're in a lot of trouble, Chance."

"I know. I'm sorry. I shouldn't have let you get involved. If I had left you behind, they would have probably questioned you and then let you go."

"Maybe. Anyhow, it's done now." She swallowed. "I want . . . I want to go home, despite what Monty says. We're innocent, and we can—"

"We can't, Ally." He took her hand in his, wishing he didn't have to tell her this. "It's too dangerous."

"The longer we keep running away—"

"No, you don't understand."

"I don't understand *any* of this!"

"I overheard Wilson and Dureau talking about murder."

She stared at him. "*Our* murder?"

"No. I mean, I doubt it. They didn't have any reason to want to murder us." He paused significantly. "At the time."

Her eyes widened. "Are you saying that they do now?"

"*They* may think they do. They don't know how much I overheard. They're probably only sure that I haven't told the cops anything important yet."

"Then . . . you've got to tell the police exactly what you heard."

"I intend to, Ally. But we've got to be careful. Don't you understand how powerful these men are?"

"Chance, Wilson doesn't have control of every cop on the entire eastern seaboard."

"No, of course not. He doesn't even have control of Atlantic City. O'Neal is an honest cop. But all the reputation and influence is on Wilson's side. With one brief phone call from his suite, he had everyone convinced that I was a dangerous criminal."

She blinked, and her shoulder slumped again. "Oh."

"And I'm pretty sure Wilson saw you with me outside of Dureau's suite. He's bound to know you ran away with me." He sat up and pulled her closer. "Ally, I'm afraid of what might happen to you if we go back to New York now."

Ally let him draw her closer to the alluring heat of his body. The intensity in his brown eyes was more compelling than any promise, any avowal, any oath or declaration. He looked like a protector at the moment in her life when she most wanted protection. His golden hair as wildly tousled as a lion's mane. His muscular chest looked broad and hard and capable. The width of his shoulders and the strength of his arms offered shelter and safety in the most windblown night of her life.

"I'm afraid," she admitted, her voice a soft intrusion into the solemn silence of their communion.

His warm, hard palm slid up her arm to her shoulder. "I won't let anything happen to you."

She raised a hand to his face and traced her fingers across the stubble that was starting to roughen his normally smooth jaw. "I . . ." Her breath started to come faster. She recognized the look in his eyes—possessive, intent, sensual—and knew what he wanted, what he intended. She withdrew her hand. "This isn't what I . . ."

He inhaled deeply and moved closer. "Touch me," he murmured, reaching for her hand again and drawing it to his chest. "I dream of you . . . touching me."

His eyes were dark, like the cave of all her fears, like the bottomless well of all her unsatisfied desires. Thick-lashed, heavy-lidded, full of deceptive innocence, rich with the secrets of a man, his eyes called to her. And so she tumbled forward, recklessly answering the dark promise of their call, willingly surrendering to their power.

His arms closed around her. As her towel fell away, she felt the heat of his bare chest against hers, hard where she was soft, rough where she was smooth. Every sensation was heightened, as if she had never done this before, as if he were the first man to ever touch her.

She had no doubts, no second thoughts, no rational disclaimers. She had ached for him too long to deny him any longer. She was too in need of comfort to turn away. She craved the raw sensations he offered, hungered for the forgetfulness that enveloped her the moment his arms drew her against his body, yearned to use his magic to shut out the horrible mess her life had become during the past few hours.

Danger lurked all around her. And though he had exposed her to it, she clung to him for protection. His arms, which rippled beneath her hands with magnificent animal strength, would keep trouble away. His back, which arched with graceful beauty as he pulled her beneath him, was strong enough for any burden.

"Yes, yes," she murmured, surrendering everything to him, offering herself up like a pagan sacrifice. *Devour me, consume me, leave nothing for them to find tomorrow.*

His mouth was warm and damp, then hot and wet; his kisses were sweet and seeking, then hard and demanding. She arched her back luxuriantly, throwing her arms overhead and wrapping her fingers around the bars of the headboard, as he sought her breasts with rough, hungry kisses. Their legs tangled restlessly as his velvety tongue laved her nipples, making them ache with sensation. His teeth were gentle in their nibbling, his mouth ferocious in its suckling, his hands restless in their kneading and caressing.

Frantic now, too impassioned to wait, to let him linger, she fumbled with the fastenings of his jeans. He winced as she slid his zipper down, then they both sighed with pleasure when her hands slipped inside and found the bold male shaft which quivered impertinently as she freed it from the confinement of his pants.

She had always been slightly shy before, hesitating during the most intimate moments, waiting for her lover to take the lead. But something about this man had changed all that. Whether it was the fire he caused to blaze deep inside of her, the obvious pleasure he took in every detail of her body, or simply his complete acceptance of her, faults and all, she felt no shyness or hesitation now as she drew him between her legs and showed him exactly what she wanted.

"Wait," he whispered, breathing heavily, trembling at her touch.

"No." She arched toward him.

He almost laughed, but groaned instead, returning her kiss, stroking her tongue with his own. "There's a condom . . . Oh, God, that's so . . ." He closed his eyes and ground against her, responding to her urging. "In my jacket."

She squealed with surprise when he rose from the bed, carrying her with him. She wrapped her arms and legs around him and clung to him as he crossed the room. When they reached the rickety chair upon which his jacket lay, he removed one supporting hand from her bottom and fumbled in one of the pockets until he found what he was looking for.

Ally hadn't thought of protection. She hadn't thought of anything beyond having him inside her. Later she would feel foolish, later she would chastise herself for such idiocy. Right now she could only feel this need burning in her belly. They sank into the sagging mattress together, completely uninhibited, and she lavished her affection on him while he struggled with responsibility.

"Okay," he breathed after a moment.

"Oh, now I'm not in the mood," she sighed.

He laughed and rolled across the bed with her, and everything seemed perfect. She knew this was absolutely right. Even this dingy motel room suddenly seemed like a honeymoon suite at the most exotic resort hotel. This was what she had waited for, looked for, longed for, through all those lonely nights, disappointing dates, and fruitless relationships. This was the garden for which she had ventured through the wilderness, all those long years.

She sighed his name and spread her legs for him, welcoming him home, guiding him into the place he would always belong. After her first long thrust, she became weak with delight, mindlessly crying out, pleading, praising, and reveling in the sound of his own rich, breathless voice doing exactly the same thing as he kissed and touched and held her. He made love the way he did everything else, with such skill and grace and concentration.

The slight friction of his hairy chest against her breasts, the sweet taste of his mouth, and the welcoming weight of him between her thighs all heightened the pleasure he incited with his deep, rhythmic thrusts until the tension building in her body exploded, sending her senses reeling as erotic sensations spilled through her in hot, dazzling waves.

"Ohhh . . ." She wept for the beauty of it, weakly absorbing his shudders as the storm swept through him, leaving them both gasping in its wake.

She didn't think about the morrow, or the morning, or even the next five minutes. She thought only about how extraordinary it was to have found such a gift where she once never would have looked for it. Utterly exhausted, she fell asleep snuggled against him, smiling when she noticed he liked to sleep facedown.

NINE

"I don't want to hitchhike," Ally said firmly.

"Then what *do* you want to do?" Chance worked hard to keep his voice even. Ally had alternated between silence and churlishness ever since waking him up this morning. Standing fully dressed beside the bed, she had looked rather like a drill sergeant. When he'd tried to kiss her, she'd acted like he had bubonic plague. It was not the reaction he'd expected after last night.

Last night. He tried not to think about it. When he looked at her now, it hurt too much to remember the way she had come to him then, so willing, so eager, so ready to belong together.

"I want you to explain again what happened yesterday." She sounded challenging.

"Okay. But can I explain it *after* we get a ride? I don't want to hang out here much longer."

Their eyes locked. She looked away first. She bit her lip. He'd bitten her lip, too, only much more gently. He'd done a lot of things last night, and she had seemed to love them all. What the hell was wrong?

"Okay," she said at last. "But then, no more prevaricating."

"No *more* prevaricating? When, I ask you, have I prevaricated?"

She didn't answer, just gave him one of those looks that made him want to strangle her. She'd given him about half a dozen such looks during their tense breakfast at the motel. He'd already asked her several times if she was upset about last night. He'd finally given up asking, since her expression suggested that if he had to ask, then there was clearly no point in explaining it to him.

"We should take that road," Ally said, pointing east. "The main road out of town has some construction a few miles ahead, and not many locals are using it."

"How do you know that?"

"I asked around this morning."

He frowned. "When?"

"While you were still sleeping."

"You left the room while I was sleeping? Why?" He wasn't sure that was so smart. What if her picture was being circulated in the papers today, or something like that?

"I had some thinking to do."

"I don't think I want you wandering around alone like that."

She stared speculatively at him. "Oh? Why not?"

"I thought that would be pretty obvious, Ally." She wasn't making it easy to be patient.

"Obvious?" She turned her back on him and started walking down the road they would take out of Stinking Creek.

"Yes, obvious."

"Well, I know the explanation you gave *me*, Chance. . . ."

He grabbed her shoulder and spun her around to face him. "Now, what the hell does that mean?"

"Don't you manhandle me!"

"I'm not—" He released her shoulder, closed his eyes, and clenched his jaw. "Sorry. Now, why don't you tell me what you mean?"

"I got up and went for a walk this morning to think things over, because there are a lot of loose threads and unanswered questions here."

"Then go ahead and ask them."

A truck rolled by them. Ally stuck out her thumb. Chance grabbed her hand and pulled it down.

"What are you doing?" she demanded.

"Forget about getting a ride. We're staying right here until you tell me what's going on in that Machiavellian mind of yours."

"I do *not* have a . . ." She took a deep breath and said, "What were you doing on the twenty-second floor? What were you doing leaning against that door like an eavesdropper?"

"I was eavesdropping!"

"Why?"

"Why?" He blinked as he realized that, in all the confusion, there actually were a lot of things he hadn't told her. "All right," he said in a more conciliatory tone, "let me explain." He frowned. "No, there's too much. Let me summarize."

He condensed the events as best he could, explaining the reasoning that had led him to Walter Dureau's suite, including Ally's own suspicions of the man. He told her why he had picked the lock on the door, and what he had heard when eavesdropping.

"Why didn't *I* see Wilson and this gun?" she asked.

"Well . . ." He tried to remember the sequence of events. It had all happened so quickly. "I had already pushed you out of the door. You must have had your back to us when I threw the purse at him."

"Uh-huh." Her tone was not exactly friendly. "And what about Celine's necklace?"

"What *about* Celine's necklace?"

"You have no alibi for the time it was stolen."

"Do I need one?" he asked incredulously. "For *you?*"

She swallowed and turned away, walking along the roadside again. He walked right by her side, but she kept her gaze firmly fixed ahead. "There just seem to be a few too many coincidences, Chance. You happened to sleep in the tub—"

"Have you forgotten *why* I decided I'd be more comfortable in another room?"

Her cheeks reddened. "No, but . . . with you sleeping in the bathroom, I wouldn't notice you were gone, would I, if I happened to wake up in the night?"

"You'd notice if you needed to *use* the bathroom," he pointed out irritably.

"And you were awfully quiet when you sneaked out of the room around four o'clock in the morning."

"I was quiet because I thought you were asleep! I didn't want to wake you."

"The thief wouldn't have wanted to wake me, either."

"Fine. Should we suspect every person in Atlantic City who tried not to wake you that night?"

"This isn't funny, Chance."

"No, it sure as hell isn't."

"You knew the black-market value of those diamonds."

"What?"

"The first time we saw them, you said—"

"Ally, I don't know their black-market value! I don't know anything about diamonds *or* the black market. But any fool could see—"

"It was a strange comment; don't you see?"

"If you're going to start suspecting everyone at the Wilson Palace who made strange comments, you'll need three months just to write down all their names."

"And Mrs. Polly-what's-her-face was right. You did behave suspiciously."

"You can't be serious."

"You kept saying things like, we would 'make our escape,' and get 'free and clear.' "

"Everybody says those things." He couldn't *believe* they were having this conversation.

"You disappeared when you realized the cops were on their way. After we ran away from Wilson, whom I *didn't* see—"

"Oh, for—"

"—You tried to escape the hotel without speaking to security, without getting caught by the cops."

"Are you serious?" He saw that she was. "Jesus, Ally, I can't believe you really suspect me!" He put a hand on her arm to stop her forward progress and made her turn to look him in the eye. "Do you really believe this?"

She shifted uncomfortably. "All I know is there are some inconsistencies, Chance." She licked her lips. "You expressed interest in the diamonds. You *did* spend a lot of time with Celine."

"Oh, come on, you—"

"You can't account for your whereabouts when the diamonds were stolen, except to say that a security guard caught you prowling in the halls. You were eager to leave the hotel that morning, and you ran away from the police when they wanted to question you."

"But I—"

"And let's face it, Chance, that receptionist was right; if anyone in the world has the skills to steal that necklace, it's you. Sleight of hand, lock picking, quick changes, secret escapes, sudden appearances and disappearances, misdirection . . ." She spread her hands. "You're a master of deception and diversion. Who could do it better than you?"

He shook his head, staring at her in disbelief. "Why do you think I'd do a thing like that?"

"I wondered about that all morning, waiting for you to wake up. It's crazy, I thought. Why would he do something like that? He's a great performer, a successful entertainer. Why would he want to steal something? And then I remembered."

"Remembered what?" he demanded.

"That conversation in the Wilson suite about how expensive it is to finance a magic show. You never did say where you got all the money it must have required, Chance. Maybe even now you don't earn quite enough to cover all your expenses?" She raised her brows inquisitively and waited for his answer.

He returned her gaze, having absolutely no idea what to say. It had never once occurred to him that she would suspect him. After last night—*don't think about last night*—he would do anything for her, face any danger for her, risk anything on her behalf. And here she was, theorizing that he had stolen and lied and betrayed her trust, and God only knew what else.

"Don't do this, Ally," he pleaded.

"If O'Neal goes ahead and searches your car, what will he find, Chance?" Her voice was hoarse, her face tense.

"Dirty clothes and a couple of props I didn't send home with Zeke and Angus the other night." His voice was tight, his hands clenched into fists.

She looked away. There was a long, taut silence between them. Finally Chance turned away from her and started walking back toward the center of town. She followed him.

"Where are you going?" she asked.

"There must be a sheriff in this one-horse town."

"What are you going to do?"

"It's what *you're* going to do."

"What? What are you saying?"

"If you really believe this story you've just concocted, then you have no choice, Ally. You've got to turn me in."

"Turn you in?" she shrieked.

He winced, having grown accustomed to her more modulated tones. He shrugged off her hands when she made a grab for him and kept stalking back toward the center of Stinking Creek.

"Wait, let's talk this over!" Ally insisted.

He turned then and faced her, letting his own anger have full rein. "Why? You've made up your mind. What else is there to think about, Ally?" He purposely intimidated her, towering over her, forcing her back several steps.

She looked panicked. "But it's just . . . just a theory, dammit! What about the gun they accused you of having?"

"Maybe I made that disappear, too," he snapped. "I certainly know how to." He turned away again.

"But wait!" she cried, catching up to him. "What

about the danger? You said we'd be in danger if we were found."

"Yeah, but if you turn me in and tell them I'm the thief, then *you* won't be in danger anymore. The police and Wilson and Dureau will have exactly what they wanted: someone to pin the theft on. Everyone will know you're not involved, and Wilson will figure you don't know anything about what happened on the twenty-second floor. And no one will believe anything I say about them after that." In fact, the idea had its merits for everyone concerned, except possibly Chance, who didn't want to spend the next ten years in prison.

Ally stopped in her tracks. Chance walked ahead for another fifteen yards before he finally turned to face her. She made an uncharacteristically awkward gesture. "I can't do it, Chance. I can't turn you in."

He strode back to her, bearing down on her. "Why not, Ally? If you believe the incredible story you've just concocted, then you have no choice. I'm a thief, and possibly violent. You're not safe with me, and neither is anyone else. You've got to turn me in."

"Oh, stop it," she snapped. "I know you're not violent. And I know I'm safe with you."

"How do you know that?" he snapped back.

She hugged herself with her arms, warding off the chill wind that whipped across the road, and looked away from him. "You wouldn't hurt me after last night," she said hoarsely.

"Funny you should say that," he replied quietly. "Because I thought the same thing, and you just hurt me like hell."

There was a heavy silence between them. Finally Ally said. "It's not what I want to believe. Chance."

"Really? You sounded pretty enamored of your theory a few minutes ago."

"Can't you look at it from my point of view?"

"Your point of view is too confusing for me to follow, Ally. You defended me to the cops, you helped me escape, and you made love to me last night like there was no one else in the whole world. But now you think I'm guilty." He stomped away from her again. *"Women."*

"I'm not turning you in, and that's final," she called after him.

"Then what do you want to do now?" he asked over his shoulder.

A pickup truck approached from the west and screeched to a halt near Ally. "Hey, lady, you goin' my way?"

Four hours later, just outside a charming metropolis called Dead Mare Hollow, Ally insisted they sit down on a fallen tree trunk and rest awhile. She had never realized how exhausting hitchhiking was. Chance sat several feet away from her; it seemed like miles, considering how perfectly their bodies had fit together the night before. She felt more lonely than she'd ever felt in her life, and she wished there were some sure way to bridge the gulf between them.

The morning had been like a nightmare, waking to realize how much she hadn't asked him, how little she really knew. As she had lain wrapped in the sturdy warmth of his arms, feeling the soft caress of his breath against her neck, she had started to realize with dread that he could be the guilty party. Indeed, as she had pointed out, he was the ideal suspect.

There were definitely pieces of the puzzle that didn't fit. For one thing, she couldn't believe that a man who touched her with such tenderness, who cradled her so protectively in his sleep, had threatened Wilson with violence. Anyhow, she had been on the twenty-second floor with Chance, and knew he hadn't been carrying a gun. But had Wilson? Or had the millionaire merely recognized Chance as the jewel thief, and had Chance invented the gun to force Ally to run headlong down twenty-two flights of stairs with him?

Ally sighed in confusion and watched a couple of hatchbacks drive past. No point in jumping to her feet. Chance had taught her that one of the first rules of hitchhiking was that you never got into the back of a two-door car. She wondered when in his past he had learned so much about hitchhiking.

Maybe, Ally acknowledged, she was allowing personal experience to prejudice her viewpoint. Just because every man she'd ever been involved with before was a lying, no-good, low-down rat, it didn't necessarily follow that Chance was, too.

He sure *seemed* different. Last night she wouldn't have mistaken him for anyone else in the whole world. No one had ever made her feel the way he did.

She looked over to where he sat, absently playing with a coin, making it appear and disappear. He made it look so easy, so natural, that a person could forget the thousands of hours of practice he had put in on even his simplest tricks. He was a man of dedication, of character. Surely he wouldn't stoop to theft?

She sighed, wishing she knew what to do, painfully aware that she had offended and hurt him with her accusation. Would things ever be right between them again?

"Blackjack," he said suddenly, without looking up. He snapped his fingers and the coin disappeared again.

"What?" she said blankly.

"That's where I got the money." He reached for something in the air, and the coin reappeared. "Playing blackjack."

She blinked. "Are you saying you financed your act by gambling?" she asked incredulously.

He nodded and turned the quarter into a penny.

"That's . . . a lot of winnings," she said carefully, not sure what to think.

"I have a system. I'm a—whaddya call it?"

"A counter?" she guessed.

"Yeah." He shrugged, never meeting her fascinated gaze. "It works pretty well most of the time. Unless, of course, you get caught." He looked up briefly, then looked quickly away and turned the penny back into a quarter. "Casinos don't like counters. I got caught a few times and thrown out."

"That hardly seems fair, just because you have the ability to keep track of the cards."

He shrugged. "That's the way gambling works, Ally, whether it's a fancy place like the Wilson Palace or a friendly game in the back room of your neighborhood bar. The house always ensures it has the advantage. That's why gambling's such a profitable business for casinos." He added quietly, "And such a bad business for gamblers."

"I can understand that maybe this isn't the image you want in your professional life, Chance," Ally said carefully. "But why are you so closemouthed about it privately? When I wanted to go into the Wilson Palace Casino, you acted like you didn't approve."

"I *don't* approve. But it's not my business to tell you what to do. I'm sorry."

Considering their current problems, his apology for that incident struck her as almost funny. "How can you not approve, if that's the way you earned—"

"It's a long story, Ally."

"So summarize. You're good at that."

He almost smiled. Instead, he waved a hand and made the quarter defy gravity. "Well . . . my father was a gambler. It was like a disease with him, Ally. They say it's why my mother left him. My grandfather gave him a lot of chances. Maybe too many. The old man finally threw my father out of the house once and for all when he caught him stealing from me."

"From you?"

"Grandpa had opened a savings account for me and put money into it every week, for my college education. When I was twelve, my father came to stay with us again, for a while. Over three or four weeks, he cleaned out the savings account and gambled away the money. So Grandpa sent him away and told him not to come back until he was through with gambling." Chance shrugged, gaze focused on his coin tricks. "But he was never through with it, and I only saw him once more before he died."

"Oh, Chance." Her sympathy made her heart ache.

He cleared his throat. "So, of course, my grandfather made me promise I would never, ever gamble. But you know boys. I tried it, just because it was forbidden. And after all, my father had named me Chance for good luck, so how could I lose?" He smiled sadly, and Ally had a painful, vivid recollection of the day she had ridiculed his name. "I figured out pretty quickly that games of chance are just designed to clean out a man's pockets. But I discovered that I was very good at any game where the odds were reasonable. During college, I taught myself to win at blackjack."

"Because you were so good at math." She recalled that he had said something about a math scholarship.

"And I needed the money. My father had gambled away twelve years of savings, after all, so even with my scholarship, things were pretty tight."

"So rather than ask your grandfather for more money when you needed it, you started playing blackjack like a professional," she guessed.

He put his coin away and pulled a deck of cards out of another pocket. His cheeks were dark red. "Yeah. And when I realized I wanted to take my magic show out of Ghirardelli Square and into the big time, I . . . I made sure I won a lot of money."

"Did your grandfather ever find out?"

He nodded, and she saw his hands clench around the deck of cards. "It was the year before he died." He was quiet for a long moment, remembering. He took a deep breath then and said. "It was the only time in my life he was ever ashamed of me. I hadn't seen him that angry since the day he threw my father out of the house. I thought he'd never forgive me." Chance looked down at the dirt between his booted feet. "He made me ashamed of myself. Not just for breaking my word and gambling, but for lying to him all those years, too. Lying by omission."

"Did you stop then?" she wondered.

"Yes. I promised him. Never again. It was over." He

shrugged. "Luckily I had a manager by then and was able to get backers. I didn't have to finance everything myself anymore. But . . ." He looked up, finally meeting her gaze steadily. "I'm not proud of what I just told you, Ally. But it's the truth. It's how I got the money, and it's why I never talk about it. And I'm trusting you not to tell anyone else."

"I promise," she said quietly, wishing she could hug him, wishing things between them now were as right and open as they had been last night. "I'll never tell anyone. It'll be our secret."

He looked at her for a long moment, and then a slow smile spread across his face. Subdued, but undoubtedly, a smile. Ally answered it tentatively. "If I know you," he said, "you're hungry again."

"I am, actually. But we don't have any money left."

He looked at the deck of cards in his hands. "I think we can fix that. Come on."

She followed him as he rose to his feet and started walking away. "Where are we going?"

"Back to Dead Mare Hollow." He shook his head. "I don't even want to think about how the town got its name."

"Chance! Look at all the money we made!" Ally cried, counting their newfound wealth as they sat together in Dead Mare Hollow's only coffee shop.

He looked at the collection of wrinkled dollars and grimaced. "I used to do a lot better in Ghirardelli Square."

"Well, we're a long way from there," Ally reminded him. She felt better than she had since awakening. Not only did they have money enough for food, but she realized that, whatever happened, they could keep themselves fed and dry until they decided what to do. "You were a big hit," she told Chance.

"So were you."

It had been his idea to stage a street show in Dead Mare Hollow's main square. Chance had performed card tricks and coin tricks, and had enthralled the crowd with his ability to cut up the local newspaper into twenty pieces and then completely restore it. Ally had contributed her fair share to the act, too, mostly relying on stunts she had learned for a musical flop she had appeared in two years earlier: juggling, fire-eating, and a few minor acrobatics.

She shifted in her seat and winced.

"Something wrong?" Chance asked.

"I'm in no shape to do cartwheels and flip-flops." She put a hand gingerly to her mouth. "And I think I burned myself."

"Maybe you should stick to a safer routine next time," he advised.

"It's funny how quickly you can lose a skill," she mused.

"That's why I practice every day," he said absently, looking across the room at their waitress.

Ally thought how strange it was that, under the circumstances, they could sit here simply talking shop. She supposed it was because, performers to the core, they both felt good about having just given a successful performance. It was in their blood, and it bound them together. But then Chance's relaxed expression changed to a frown.

"Something's wrong," he said.

Ally looked up to see their waitress approaching them. "She's got no food in her hands. Where's our food?"

"I think you two better come with me," the middle-aged waitress said, her double-knit uniform clinging to her ample figure like a second skin. Her face was alight with excitement.

"What's going on?" Ally demanded.

"That was some show you folks put on out there a little while ago," the woman said. "A little too good, you know? It attracted a lot of attention, such talented performers suddenly turning up in the main square of Dead Mare Hollow."

"Oh, no," Ally groaned. "Why didn't I think of that?"

"You were weak with hunger," Chance said. "Dammit."

"Sheriff heard some interesting news this morning. After seeing you two, he made a few phone calls."

"How do you know that?" Ally asked.

"I grew up in a town like this," Chance said. "Everyone always knows everything."

"Oh."

"But I've always had a soft spot in my heart for the underdog," the waitress said. "If you give me your word that you didn't hurt no one . . ."

"On my honor, ma'am," Chance said, giving her his best wide-eyed country-boy look, "we haven't done anything wrong, except maybe run away from the police when they pulled out their guns."

"That's what I figured,." The waitress nodded with satisfaction. " 'Merl,' I said . . . That's Merl over there, by the way." She pointed to a chubby, apple-cheeked man who grinned at them through the grill cook's window. " 'Merl,' I said, 'a talented boy like that, with such nice manners, he wouldn't do nobody no harm. And that pretty girl with him, I just don't believe the terrible things the sheriff said about her,' I said to Merl."

"What did the sheriff say about me?" Ally asked indignantly.

"Ally, not now," Chance said.

"Come on, you two. Me and Merl have decided to help you make your getaway. Don't you worry about a thing."

"Worry? Who's worried?" Ally said, ignoring Chance's dirty look and following the waitress out the back door.

She stuffed them into the backseat of her old Chevy and drove to a crossroads about thirty miles outside of town. "You ought to be able to get a ride to just about anywhere in the world from here," she told them.

Ally looked at the empty rural crossroads and doubted it.

"We can't thank you enough, ma'am," Chance said. He kissed the woman on the cheek. She swatted him playfully and giggled like a schoolgirl, then wished them luck and drove off. "I wish we could have done something nice for her."

"Are you kidding? This is probably the most excitement she's had since the Johnstown flood."

"That was well before her time, Ally. What put you in such a good mood?"

"I'm hungry."

"Oh." He looked around at the darkening landscape. Three fields and a barn. No house, motel, or restaurant in sight. "Well, we'll get a ride to the next town, find a room, and lay low for the rest of the day. Okay?"

"Okay." She hunched her shoulders against the cold as the sun dipped behind the clouds. And then what? They couldn't go on like this indefinitely, hitchhiking aimlessly around the Northeast in an effort to keep one step ahead of the law.

A trucker picked them up around dinnertime and offered to take them as far as Whooping Crane Branch, wherever the hell that was. Two hours later, he let them off at another crossroads. Whooping Crane Branch boasted a post office, a gas station, and a coffee shop with an OUT OF BUSINESS sign on the door. The gas station and post office were closed for the evening and wouldn't reopen until tomorrow morning. Chance and Ally washed themselves in the little creek that ran alongside the town. Ally clenched her teeth as the icy water made her shiver. Why had she never before noticed how cold September nights were? Slightly cleaner than before, and hungrier than ever, she dejectedly followed Chance as he set off to find some place they could bed down for the night.

TEN

The barn was old and musty and drafty, but it was better than sleeping out in the open. By the time they found it, Ally wanted nothing more in life than to lie down and curl up into a ball, so she wasn't inclined to be critical to its lack of facilities.

"I didn't know there were so many empty places in America," she said wearily, sitting on a wooden bench as Chance explored the dark interior of the barn. "We must have walked for miles."

"No, just a few hundred yards," he called from the hayloft.

"How could there be no house, no car, no nothing for miles around?"

"You talk just like a New Yorker." He sounded amused. "This is nothing. Out west is where it's really empty. There are places out there where you could go for days without seeing another living soul."

"If you're trying to cheer me up, you're failing miserably," she grumbled.

He came back down to the ground floor a few minutes later. It was so dark, she could barely make out his features. "Come up to the loft," he invited softly. "It's a little warmer up there, and I made you a bed out of straw and part of a horse blanket."

She groaned. "I feel like I'm stuck in an old Claudette Colbert movie and can't escape."

"You'll feel better once you've had some sleep."

"The only thing that will ever make me feel better again," she said, "is a hot shower, a change of clothes, and a really big pizza with everything on it." She softened a bit when he led her to the makeshift bed he had made. It was scratchy and lumpy and unsanitary, not to mention rather damp, but she could tell he had tried hard to provide her with some comfort. "Thanks, Chance. This seems very, uh, very nice."

"Why don't you lie down and get some rest?"

When he let go of her hand, she heard something skittering and shuffling above them. "What's that?"

"Just birds," he soothed.

"Or mice?"

"Birds," he repeated, probably lying.

"Where will you be?"

"Just over there." He pointed to another pile of straw.

She peered into the darkness. "It doesn't look very comfortable."

"I've slept like this before."

"When?"

"When I was growing up."

"Tumbled a few girls in haylofts?" she guessed.

"A few." In the darkness, she couldn't tell whether or not he was smiling. "Try to get comfortable, Ally."

"All right."

She nestled into the rough, damp blanket and listened to him moving around, getting ready for bed. The moon had risen, and now its alabaster rays peeked coyly through the slats and windows above them, highlighting golden strands of Chance's hair as he bent his head to remove his boots. She heard them hit the floor one after the other. Thud, thud. Then he took off his jacket.

"Aren't you cold?" she murmured. "I'm so cold." Her raw silk blazer, sheer blouse, and torn stockings weren't much protection against the night air.

"You're cold? Here, take my jacket."

"No, that's okay."

"Take it, Ally. The straw will keep me warm." He knelt beside her and spread his jacket gently across her, tucking it in around her chin and shoulders. "Better?"

"Yes." She wished she could see his eyes. "Chance, we can't keep on going like this forever."

"I know. We've got to come up with a plan."

"Yes."

He lowered his head. "Have you given any more thought to turning me in?"

"No! I won't do it."

"Have you decided to believe me? One hundred percent?" He sounded doubtful.

"I want to believe you."

"That's not good enough."

"Your story rests entirely on . . . on your word."

"That's right. It does." His voice was uncompromising. "I need that to be enough for you, Ally, even though I don't expect it to be enough for the cops."

Her throat got tight, and she felt tears welling up in her eyes. It was such a big step, especially after so many failures. "If you knew the kind of men I've known . . . My last boyfriend, two years ago, stole money from me to pay his Equity dues. The guy before that didn't love me nearly so much as he loved my rent-controlled apartment. And—"

"Stop it." His voice was harsh, devoid of the sympathy she wanted from him. "Stop it, Ally. I don't want to hear about those bums, not right now. I'm not going to take the rap for them, do you understand?"

"But, Chance, I just don't—"

"No, Ally. Did you learn from your mistakes, or not? Did you want me last night for the same reasons you once wanted some jerk who stole your money?"

"No," she admitted. "Last night was different."

"You waited for two years, and then you chose me. I wish things hadn't happened this way, but they did. So now you've got to decide what you believe about me, Ally, and you don't have much time."

She sighed and remained silent, wishing she could make a clear choice, wishing she could end this internal battle between her past and her present. She felt Chance shift on the blanket and start to rise. She reached out to stop him. "Chance, don't go." He hesitated, and she urged, "I'm still cold. Hold me."

She felt him tense. "You know that if I touch you, it won't end there."

"Okay."

He threw off her restraining hand. "Stop it," he growled. "We can't. Not with this thing between us."

"I can never understand you," she said irritably. "It's usually the man who doesn't want disagreements to interfere with sex."

"Your suspecting me of being a criminal is more than just a *disagreement*," he pointed out. He lowered his head and sighed. "This morning was bad enough, Ally. I can't go through the same thing twice."

"Don't you want—"

"Of course I want to." The moonlight highlighted his profile and silvered the golden stubble covering his jaw. "But I won't."

"You need a shave," she murmured.

He made a sound that might have been a laugh. "Listen to me," he said at last, his voice strained. "If we sleep together now, it won't be like last night. Not if you can't trust me. You didn't hold anything back then, and neither did I. That's why it was . . . the way it was." His voice was husky when he added, "That's why, no matter what happens, I'll always remember it."

"So you're not going to kiss these silly ideas right out of my pretty little head?" She almost wished he would.

He took her hand again, careful not to touch any other part of her. "Would that work with you?"

"Well, if anyone could do it," she whispered, "it's you."

"After all the things you said this morning, I'm not sure if that's a compliment."

She smiled and drew his resisting hand up to her cheek. "After last night, it's definitely a compliment."

"Don't," he whispered, pulling their joined hands back to a less tempting position. "Last night was more than good sex."

"Yes," she admitted. "And now you want a leap of faith."

"That's as good a name for it as anything else. I thought I was in love once, Ally, a long time ago. But she couldn't make a leap of faith either, and everything between us fell apart after that."

She sat bolt upright. "Have you been in this situation before?"

There was an awful silence, and she feared she had said the wrong thing. Then, to her relief, he laughed. "No. No, this situation is definitely unique in my experience."

"Then what are you talking about?"

"When I was in college," he said. She settled back into the blanket as he continued, "I was twenty-one and thought I was a man. I also thought I was—"

"In love," she said tersely, not liking the idea of him loving some nameless, faceless woman more than a decade ago.

"Yes. I even . . . Well, I guess I thought I'd ask her to marry me, and we'd live happily ever after. She seemed to have the same idea."

"So what happened?"

"I decided to drop out of college and pursue a career as a magician. She was shocked and bewildered at first, then furious when I made it clear I wasn't going to come to my senses and go back to school. She had thought she'd be marrying an engineer, a guy with a normal life—"

"A guy with a steady paycheck and full benefits," Ally said cynically.

"A guy who'd be home most of the time, who could have a regular life and . . . You know."

"I know." There were things that didn't matter very much to people like her and Chance, things like daily routine, weekly paychecks, and lifetime conventionality. But those things mattered an awful lot to some people, and Ally could understand why, even if she didn't feel the same way.

"She'd always been polite about my interest in magic as a hobby."

"But her attitude changed when you decided to make it a career," Ally guessed. It didn't surprise her. Everyone in her family had reacted that way when she'd decided to become an actress.

"*Changed* is an understatement. She became scathing about it. I hadn't known that she was merely tolerating my interest in magic because she thought I'd 'outgrow' it. She was so contemptuous, so superior. . . ." He sighed and admitted, "She sounded a lot like you did when I met you, Ally."

"Oh, Chance." She wanted to weep. It would have stung less if he'd slapped her. How could she have been so careless, so insensitive? "I'm sorry," she said huskily. "I was so feverish and hysterical the day we met. And later on, I was so wrapped up in my own problems. I can never excuse . . ." She looked away and repeated, "I'm sorry."

"I know you are." His voice was quiet, weary, depleted. "And maybe I'm not being entirely fair, either. Maybe, I'm making you take the rap for her, too. But the truth is, Ally, you're the first woman I've gotten involved with since then who had that same negative attitude."

"But things are different now."

He almost laughed again. "Yeah, things are a lot different now. We're fugitives now."

"Yes, but—"

"Look, I know what I want. I want to clear my name and get on with my life. And I want you to be with me, really *with* me, for both things. But you've got to decide what you want. There's no room left for half measures. Not between us, Ally."

"All right," she agreed. "That's fair. I'll sleep on it. Alone."

He squeezed her hand. "Okay. And I think I'll go . . . pace for a while."

This time she was the one who almost laughed. She watched him put on his boots and disappear into the darkness, then closed her eyes and tried not to think about how cold and hungry she was.

"Where's the last place they're likely to look for us?" Ally said, climbing down from the hayloft and following Chance out of the barn and into the sunlight the following morning.

"I'm way ahead of you. The Wilson Palace. That's where I'm going. I decided last night, while I was—"

"Pacing. I know. I heard you clumping back and forth for hours."

"Sorry."

"It's all right. Great minds think alike. If we can just get a ride to—"

"Not *we*. Me. You're going back to New York City."

"What?"

"When you get there, get ahold of Monty, and don't let him out of your sight. He seems to be the only reliable man you know."

"Well, *really*."

"Make a statement to the police, saying that I forced you to run away with me—"

"That won't work. Remember? I threatened that big guy in the casino."

"Oh, right. Well, then say that you ran away with me because you were confused, and I didn't let you—"

"Will you stop being so damn noble? I'm going with you to Atlantic City."

"No way."

They argued about it all the way back to the main crossroads.

"Hey," Ally cried, "the gas station's open! Maybe they sell candy bars."

They didn't, and neither did the post office. But a kind trucker offered them a lift to Wilmington, Delaware.

"That'll put me near the Atlantic City Expressway," Chance said, studying a map in the gas station.

"*Us*, Chance. It'll put *us* near the Atlantic—"

"Why are you so all fired up to go with me?"

"Because I believe you."

He stared at her. "You do?"

"Uh-huh."

"Are you sure?"

"Uh-huh."

"You don't sound sure."

"I'm *sure*," she snapped. "What do you want, a Shakespearean declaration?"

He rolled his eyes. "Forget I said anything."

"I believe you're a man of your word. Especially after what you told me about your family and the gambling you did."

"That's what convinced you?" he said incredulously. "The most shameful story in my past convinced you I'm innocent?"

"Yes." And as for the rest, Ally had decided to simply tackle their problems one at a time.

He shook his head. *"Women."*

They heard a horn honking. "Sounds like our ride is ready to go," Ally said. "Shall we?"

"Ally, wait. This might be dangerous."

"That's why I'm not letting you go alone. You do have a knack for getting into trouble, Chance."

He was still smoldering over the unfairness of this comment when they climbed into the cab of the truck and pulled away from the gas station. The drive to Wilmington was mercifully uneventful, though Chance figured he'd never again want to hear country and western music after this trip; however, at least the twangy blare of the music prevented Ally from having to concoct another of her melodramatic stories for the driver. They arrived in Wilmington within a couple of hours, found a phone, and called Monty.

"Just wanted to let you know we're alive and well, if not clean or well dressed," Ally said into the receiver.

"Where have you been?" Monty cried.

"We spent the night in a place called Whooping Cough Creek."

"That's Whooping Crane Branch," Chance corrected.

"Lovely little spot. I may retire there."

"Enough, Ally! Have you seen the papers? Do you know what they're saying about you?" Monty demanded.

"Whatever they're saying, it can't be worse than what the critics said after I played a nun in that neo-anarchist off-Broadway thing last year."

"Ally, this is not the time to mope over bad reviews," Chance chided.

"We need your help, Monty," Ally said.

"Yes, I'm already trying to find the best criminal defense lawyer in New York," Monty assured her.

"Hopefully we won't need his services. We're working on a plan."

"Oh, no." Monty's voice was thick with dread. "I think we've all suffered enough, Ally. Please, don't do anything rash."

"I just need you to call the police and tell them we've decided to turn ourselves in. Tell them we'll be at your house by tonight."

"What are you really going to do, Ally?"

"We're going to catch the bad guys ourselves."

"Oh, Ally, no! If you won't think of yourselves, then think of me! Think of my heart, my blood pressure, my liver, my intestines!"

"Please don't get scatological on me, Monty. It's so unbecoming."

"Ally!"

"Just do as I've asked. If things go as planned, we'll be back in New York by next weekend."

"And if not?"

She bit her lip. "Then maybe you'd better keep looking for that lawyer." She said good-bye and hung up the phone. "He'll do it," she told Chance. "Not willingly, cheerfully, or happily, but he'll do it."

"Good. With Wilson's connections, he's bound to learn within an hour or two that we're headed for New York."

"So he'll have his watchdogs keeping an eye out for us there," Ally concluded. "Leaving us free to case the Wilson Palace."

"Theoretically."

"You needn't sound so gloomy. I think it'll work. Especially if we're disguised."

"Disguised?" he asked suspiciously.

"Trust me."

It was late afternoon by the time they arrived in Atlantic City. They found a pay phone at the back of some video arcade and used the last of their quarters to phone the Wilson Palace. Posing as a society lady, Ally asked to speak to Harvey on the pretext that she wanted to thank him personally for all his assistance during her recent visit to the hotel.

"Harvey, act cool," Ally instructed when the boy came on the line. "It's me, Alicia Cannon."

"Holy moly!" Harvey cried, loud enough for Chance to hear.

"I told you that calling him would be a big mistake," Chance muttered.

She ignored him. "Harvey, we need your help."

"Holy moly!"

Chance rolled his eyes. "Forget it, Ally."

"It'll work," she insisted.

"What can I do, Miss Cannon?"

Ally winced. "For God's sake, don't use my name!"

"Oops! Sorry, Miss Ca . . . Er, sorry."

"I have a plan. Now, listen carefully."

Ally purchased some makeup with the cash she and Chance had earned in Dead Mare Hollow the previous day, then they awaited Harvey in the lobby of another hotel. The smell of food coming from the hotel's coffee shop nearly drove Ally insane, but she and Chance had more important things than their stomachs to worry about right now.

Harvey was nearly an hour late. When he finally arrived, he explained that his tardiness was due to the trouble he'd had stealing the necessary items and sneaking them out of the hotel without getting caught.

"Security at the Wilson Palace is usually as leaky as a tune net," the boy said, "but everyone has been so jumpy since you guys made your escape."

"Thanks, Harvey. These things look perfect. Chance, go find a men's room and get changed," Ally ordered. He scowled and obeyed, leaving her alone with Harvey.

"What else can I do, Miss Cannon?"

"We'll need a detailed map of the hotel. Broom closets, cleaning supply storage, that kind of thing." When he was done showing her as much as he could from memory, Ally said, "Thank you. Now you'd better get back to work before you're missed."

"You're going after Wilson, aren't you? Mr. Weal said he was up to his ears in this business."

"And Dureau."

"Dureau? Are you sure about that?"

She frowned. "Yes. Why?"

"He's been missing since you and Mr. Weal got into trouble with the police. Never checked out, never paid his bill. Well, not as far as anyone knows, anyhow. Things get lost pretty often at the reception desk," Harvey admitted. "But his car is still in the garage, and none of the guys carried his luggage out for him. They'd remember."

"Hmmm. I wonder what he's up to." She frowned as she thought it over. Finally she said, "You'd better go now."

"I guess I'll see you at work, huh?"

"But don't let on that you know us. If anything goes wrong, no one must know you've helped us. Understand?" He nodded, but there was a heroic gleam in his eyes that made her uneasy.

After Ally changed into the cleaning uniform Harvey had stolen for her, she went into the men's room to find Chance. "What's taking you so long?" she demanded.

"What are you doing in here? You can't come in here," he insisted.

"Oh, don't be such a slave to convention." She took a good look at him and burst out laughing "Harvey got the size wrong, I see."

"It's not funny." He glowered at her, but he didn't look very threatening, wearing a white cleaning uniform that was about five sizes too large for him.

Ally soothed his wounded ego as she started industriously rolling up his cuffs. "Not much we can do about the waistband without a needle or safety pins," she remarked. "You'll just have to tighten your belt and hope it'll hold up the trousers." Unfortunately, she started giggling again.

Wearing a martyred expression, Chance removed a series of truly astonishing items from his denim jacket and stuffed them into the various pockets of his baggy white coat and pants. Ally bundled up their clothes in the bag Harvey had brought and stuffed them in one of the bathroom cabinets. Although she personally didn't care if she never again saw her ruined silk outfit, she knew Chance was very attached to his old denim jacket.

"We'll come back for this stuff later," she assured him. "Let's go."

"Not yet. Even in these clothes, we could still be recognized." She pulled out the bag of makeup she'd bought.

Chance frowned at her. "What's that for?"

"Come here in the light, where I can see better." She tugged him forward.

He dodged her hand when she tried to brush some brown eye shadow on his face. "What do you think you're doing?"

"Hold still, will you? I'm changing the shape of your face. With a little skillfully applied makeup, a hat, and a change in posture, we could walk right by Wilson and not be recognized."

"Aw, Ally, don't put that stuff on my face."

"This will be over sooner if you stop complaining and hold still."

She wasn't entirely satisfied with her efforts, since he rejected the dark lipstick she wanted to use on his mouth. However, once they were both fully made-up and wearing the caps that matched their uniforms, even Monty wouldn't have known them without looking closely.

"Now, just remember to keep your shoulders stooped and your face down," she instructed, demonstrating. "Get into your character."

"I feel silly," he muttered, trying to emulate her posture.

The bathroom door swung open and two hotel guests staggered in. "Oops!" said one of them. "We'll come back when you're done in here."

His companion, whose expression suggested he was in more dire need of the facilities, asked, "Is there another men's room on this floor?"

Ally pointed vaguely in the other direction.

"Thanks." The two men left.

"You see? We're convincing."

Chance grunted. "Let's find some cleaning equipment, in case we bump into someone a little less drunk or a little more observant."

They left the hotel, crossed the alley, and entered a side door of the Wilson Palace. Then, using Harvey's map, which they discovered had been drawn on the reverse side of a half-completed fan letter to the star of the *Vicky* movies, they found a storage room for cleaning supplies. Armed with suitably convincing gear, they climbed the stairs to the second floor, where the executive offices were.

"Wilson's office is down there," Chance murmured. "There was hardly any security the day I found Dureau up here."

"Well, Wilson wouldn't need security against his own confederate, would he?"

"I wish we'd thought of that at the time."

As before, there was one security guard on duty on this floor. Ally recognized him as one of the men who had apprehended Chance the morning the diamonds had disappeared.

"Stay in character," she whispered. It worked. The guy didn't pay any attention to them as they walked right under his nose.

As they approached Wilson's suite of offices, the door opened. Ally's stomach tightened. It was already past seven o'clock, late enough in the day that she had supposed the offices would be deserted. When Wilson himself emerged a moment later, Chance muttered. "Oh, hell. I don't believe this."

"Stay calm," Ally whispered. "Focus on your intent."

"My intent?"

"To clean things."

"Oh." He slumped his shoulders and lowered his head.

Wilson saw the two of them and frowned. "What are you doing on this floor?" His tone was cold.

"Excuse me, sir," Ally said to Wilson in a heavy Hispanic accent. "We gotta get in there. We gotta clean in that there room."

"Hmmm? Oh. Well, be sure to lock up when you're done."

They entered the room, and the door closed behind them. In heavily accented English, Ally ordered Chance to start vacuuming the floor, complaining bitterly about the mess that had been left behind for them to clean up. She kept up the chatter for nearly two minutes while Chance industriously vacuum-cleaned the room. Only then did they risk peeking out into the hallway to make sure that Wilson hadn't suspected anything. She locked the door behind her, then alerted Chance.

"Coast is clear," she said above the noise of the vacuum cleaner. "Let's get started."

They left the vacuum cleaner roaring in the outer offices and tried the door to Wilson's inner sanctum. "Locked," Chance said. "He figured we wouldn't be able to get in here."

"Can you open it?"

"Of course." True to his word, he swung the door open less than twenty seconds later.

"That's a very handy skill," Ally observed.

"It has been lately," he said ruefully.

Having no idea where to start, or what they were looking for, they moved quickly and just hoped they wouldn't overlook an important clue if they saw one. Chance picked the locks on the desk and the filing cabinets, then assisted Ally in looking through the files and papers she found.

It seemed a long time later when Ally turned to Chance, feeling discouraged. "I don't see anything interesting. Maybe Wilson removed whatever Dureau was looking at that day."

"Wait a minute, look at this." Chance showed her some insurance forms. "Wilson recently took out a huge policy on that necklace."

"But that only makes sense, Chance. Something that valuable . . ."

"But he said he bought the necklace in the spring. Why would he wait until last month to insure it?"

"Maybe it's a second policy." Ally frowned. "Wait. Harvey said Wilson was broke and had huge debts. The kid was pretty sure Wilson must have bought the necklace on credit. Maybe he couldn't afford to buy a policy when he got the necklace."

"But maybe he scrounged up the money for a policy when he realized the necklace would be stolen soon."

Her eyes widened. "You're saying he and Dureau planned it together? That far in advance?"

"I'm not sure." Chance tried to remember exactly what he had overheard the two men say that day. So much had happened since then.

"Keep looking," Ally said. "The insurance policy isn't proof of anything."

"Fortunately, that's true," said an unpleasant voice.

They both whirled to see Wilson standing behind them. He had crept up on them under the covering noise of the vacuum cleaner—which they'd been using to cover *their* noise. It seemed so unfair. Ally wished they had thought of a better plan. Then her horrified gaze dropped to the weapon in his hand. "So *that's* the gun you were talking about," she said to Chance.

"I don't believe this is happening to me," Chance groaned.

Sudden recognition contorted Wilson's face horribly. "My God, it's you! But you're supposed to be turning yourselves in to the police in New York right now."

"It worked," Ally said. "Monty came through."

"You mean you didn't recognize us in the hallway?" Chance asked. "Then what made you come back here?"

"It finally dawned on me that there was something strange about this. We had a cleaning staff up here yesterday. No one ever cleans two days in a row in this hotel."

"I believe that," Ally said. "The service here is terrible. Are you aware—"

"Not now, Ally," Chance said, his gaze fixed on Wilson's gun. There was once a great magician who had dodged bullets as part of his act. Chance wished he had bothered to study the technique. Desperate to keep Ally safe, he said, "Let the girl go, Wilson. She doesn't know anything."

Ally and Wilson both turned disgusted gazes upon him. Chance didn't know which of them looked more appalled at the stupidity of this remark. He felt his cheeks grow hot and mumbled, "Sorry. It just, you know, seemed like the right thing to say."

"Entertainers," Wilson sneered in disgust. Then he bellowed "Luther!"

A few moments later, the burly security guard appeared in the doorway. "Mr. Wilson!" he cried. "I'm sorry, sir! I thought they were cleaners!"

"It's all right, Luther. We're going to put them in the Blue Wing."

"What do we do now?" Ally whispered to Chance.

"With that other guy?" the security guard asked.

"I'm thinking," Chance whispered back.

"No," Wilson said. "Next door."

"Well?" Ally said.

"Nothing's coming," Chance admitted. He only knew

that he had to get Ally out of here, and he had just a few seconds to do it.

"All right, let's go, you two," Wilson said.

"Wait a minute," Ally said. "Aren't you going to tell us what this is all about?"

Wilson looked surprised. "No, of course not. If you haven't figured it out, why should I enlighten you?"

"Don't you want to brag about your cleverness?" she prodded.

"Excuse me?" Wilson looked puzzled.

"Don't you ever go to the movies?" Ally demanded. "The bad guy always tells the good guys all his plans before he kills them." She paused and then added hastily, "Or, rather, before he locks them up. Killing is really unnecessary. Especially in this case."

"I'm busy," Wilson said. "And while it's been interesting, Miss Cannon, I can't say I'm very eager to deepen the acquaintance. Shall we go?"

"Did you have to use the word 'kill'?" Chance muttered.

"It just slipped out," she apologized.

"Quiet," Wilson snapped.

"Let's go," said Luther, the beefy guard, pointing his own gun at them. He looked pretty nervous as he prodded Ally.

"Don't push, buddy," she warned. "My friend here can make you vanish like *that*." She snapped her fingers. "I've seen him do it to guys bigger than you. He can even make elephants disappear."

Luther hesitated, looking from Ally to Chance and back again. She nodded knowingly and said, "Yep. Like *that*. Just a little hocus-pocus, a little prestidigitation—"

"That's enough, Miss Cannon," Wilson warned.

Ally circled Luther, talking the whole while. Chance made a show of looking him over, as if gauging how much energy it would take to make him disappear. He hoped Ally understood; one of them had to get away, to go for help, and it had to be her. When the moment was right, Chance threw a tangle of knotted, colored scarfs over Luther's head, causing him to flinch. It was all they needed.

"Run, Ally!" Chance kicked Luther's feet out from under him and turned to knock Wilson's gun away. The man was stronger than he looked. They were still struggling when Chance heard Ally scream. Forgetting his concentration, forgetting everything but the instinct to go to her, he let himself get distracted.

There was a brief searing pain at the back of his skull, then everything went black and silent.

ELEVEN

The pounding in his head gave way to a softer sound. Darkness was all around him. He fought his way through it, drawn toward this new, soothing sound. It was water in the desert, shelter in the rain, comfort in the void.

"I'm here, Chance. No, don't try to get up. Hold still. You don't want to move just yet." The voice broke on a sob. "Can you hear me?"

A beautiful voice. Throaty, melodic, husky.

"You're going to be all right. I'm sure you're all right. Please tell me you're all right."

It sounded familiar. Sweetness filled the black emptiness, and he struggled to open his eyes.

"Are you awake? Can you hear me?"

"Ohhh." Another voice, very close by. Gravelly and vague. "Ungh."

A hand touched his cheek. He felt embarrassed when he felt fingers rasp across the stubble there. Why hadn't he shaved? His grandfather had never let him leave the house in such a state.

"Oh, Chance . . ." A weight against his chest. Soft hair under his chin. That voice, so familiar. The scent of her hair brought her name to his lips.

"Al-lee . . ." Good God, that awful sound was *his* voice.

"Yes, yes! How do you feel?"

He opened one eye. Lights blinked wildly at him, as if he were caught in an electrical storm. The ceiling above him tilted. He closed his eye again. "Lousy."

"I don't know anything about first aid. I'm so sorry." She sounded desperate. "Do you think you have a concussion?"

He shifted slightly, trying to see if anything hurt besides his head. "Don't use . . . that word."

"We have to consider it."

"No, we don't," he said stubbornly. He was a little stiff, but everything felt normal except for his head. He tried opening both eyes this time. After a few interesting hallucinations—which bore some resemblance to the dancers at Caesar's Palace in Las Vegas—his vision cleared and he was able to focus on their surroundings. "Where the hell are we?"

Ally sat up and looked down at him. That's when he realized he was stretched out on a double bed. Considering how uncomfortable it was, he guessed they were still in the Wilson Palace. "We're in something called the Blue Wing," Ally informed him. It looked kind of like their former room at the Wilson Palace, only everything was ugly and blue instead of ugly and red. "They took us through a series of dark service stairs and deserted hallways, so I wasn't able to get my bearings. Anyhow, I was a little distracted at the time. Luther had just clobbered you with the butt of his gun, and you were gushing blood while he hauled you along."

"Spare me the details," he requested, noticing the wet, stained, messy towels on the floor beside the bed. She must have cleaned him up while he was unconscious. Just as well. He hated the sight of his own blood. "How long have I been out?"

"On and off, for about three hours. You started mumbling and rolling your head after about fifteen minutes, but you haven't been lucid until now."

"What time is it?"

She checked her watch. "Nearly eleven o'clock."

He sat up and winced. It felt like he'd just been hit over the head with a sledgehammer.

"Maybe you should lie back down," Ally suggested uneasily.

"No, I'll feel better if I get up for a bit." He hoped it was true. In any event, he doubted he'd feel any *worse*. He looked down and noticed that he was only wearing his T-shirt and the ridiculously loose trousers stolen from the cleaning supplies room. "They took away my coat." He had put most of his things in its pockets.

"Wilson said he didn't want you pulling any more tricks."

"Are we locked in?"

"Yes."

Chance emptied the pockets of his ridiculous trousers. He found chewing gum, a handkerchief, three quarters, a few condoms, a penny, and a compact toothbrush. "Damn. Do you have a credit card on you, Ally? A few hairpins? A ballpoint pen?"

"No. I have nothing but what I'm wearing." She had washed off her character makeup in the bathroom, and now wore only the simple white cleaning dress. "Anyhow, Luther's right outside the door, Chance. With a gun." She didn't need to add that even if Chance could figure out a way to open the door, he was in no condition to overcome the big man on the other side of it. "Do you think we can get out of here some other way?"

He searched the room quickly. The windows had been boarded up. The walls and ceiling were solid, both in the bedroom and the bathroom. The vents were far too small to be escape routes for anything larger than a rat. "We're stuck here until someone opens that door," he admitted.

"Oh." She sat back down on the bed and regarded her folded hands with a resolutely calm expression.

Realizing how frightening their capture and imprisonment must have been for her, especially with him injured and unconscious, he put an arm around her and drew her close. She started to tremble in reaction, dropping her brave front. "Did they hurt you?" he whispered fiercely.

She shook her head. "No. But Wilson said they *would*, if either of us caused any more trouble."

"I wonder how long he plans to keep us here?" He stroked her silken hair.

She took a deep breath. "Tell me the truth. You said you think Wilson and Dureau are already involved in murder. Do you think they're going to kill us, too?"

She deserved honesty. She wouldn't even be here if he hadn't gotten her into this mess. "I don't know," he admitted. "But it seems to me that if Wilson wanted to kill us, he should have done it before: two dangerous fugitives caught red-handed in his private office. He could claim he had killed us in self-defense. . . ." He shrugged. "I'm not sure, Ally. I'm sorry."

She turned her face in to his neck and nuzzled him. "I'm just glad you're all right," she whispered. "When you crumpled into a heap in that hallway, I thought . . ." She swallowed and tightened her arm around his neck. "I thought he'd killed you, or shattered your skull, or ruptured your—"

He kissed her hard, as eager to stop her unpleasant words as he was to taste the nectar of her mouth. She responded eagerly, willingly, wholeheartedly.

"And when you were lying here unconscious," she breathed, between quick, soft kisses, "I kept thinking that I just wanted to be good to you, wanted to make you feel—"

"Yes," he whispered, rubbing his forehead affectionately against hers, glad to be alive, glad to be with her, despite everything. "Be good to me, Ally. Let me be good to you."

She held his face between her palms and kissed his cheeks, his eyelids, his forehead, his chin, making him feel cherished and cradled. She rubbed her soft cheek against his roughening jaw and smiled away his apology. "You look sexy with a five-o'clock shadow."

"I haven't shaved since we checked out of this rotten hotel."

Her hands found the hem of his T-shirt, and she worked

it up, running her hands over his flat belly, his chest, and his shoulders, then pulling the shirt gently over his head, mindful of his injuries. "Does your head hurt?"

"It hurts a little less every time you touch me."

They exchanged a long, wet kiss, and he started unbuttoning her baggy dress, pleased to find only her sheer bra and panties underneath. He traced the lacy cups, enjoying the way her nipples peaked beneath the satiny material. "It's peach. Like that blouse you were wearing."

"I like everything to match. It's a compulsion."

She inhaled deeply and arched lazily toward him when he cupped one breast in his palm. Their eyes met, and it was just the way it should be. She looked tender, excited, and uninhibited as he dipped his hand between her thighs to feel the heat there. She was ready to share herself openly and freely with him. Their lips met again, and their kiss blocked out the ugliness of this bedroom, the terror that lurked outside the door, and the horror of their situation. Whatever Wilson and Dureau intended, whatever their hired goons might eventually do, Chance knew that these moments were sacred and inviolable. Nothing was as powerful as the way he and Ally could make each other feel.

Her hands moved to his belt buckle, and he stroked the soft skin of her arms as she unbuckled, unbuttoned, and unzipped, taking her time about it, brushing her knuckles lightly, teasingly, across his groin again and again, smiling intimately at him when she felt the growing hardness there.

"And I believed you when you said there was nothing up your sleeve," she teased.

"That's not my sleeve," he pointed out.

"Lie back," she suggested, placing both hands on his chest and easing him into the pillows. Once he was reclining, it took her very little effort to pull off his baggy trousers and his briefs.

"You have such a beautiful body," she murmured, kneeling beside him.

"Clean living. And what's your secret?"

"Good genes."

She ran her hand across his chest and brushed her fingertips over his flat male nipples, teasing them into rigid peaks the way he had teased hers. She smiled at his deep sigh, enjoying his pleasure, wanting to ease the ache in his head and the worry in his eyes. She knew he felt responsible for her, felt he had failed to protect her. She wanted to make him understand just how much of a man she knew he really was.

"Take off your bra," he murmured.

She lowered the straps over her shoulders, basking in the heat of his gaze. She had never before enjoyed taking off an undergarment as much as she did now, and she stalled, lingering over the moment, flushing with pleasure at the impatient caress of his hand on her thigh.

"Are you a breast or a leg man?" she asked, pulling the lacy cups half an inch lower. His gaze followed their descent.

"That depends. Are we talking about chicken, turkey, or women?"

She laughed. "I was talking about *this* woman, actually."

His hand rose from her thigh to her waist. "I like *every* part of this woman."

"No preference? No favorite feature?" she fished, shrugging so that her bra slipped even lower.

He swallowed. "Usually, it's your eyes."

"That's romantic," she said, pleased.

"But at this particular moment . . ."

"Mmmm?"

"Don't toy with me," he chided. "I'm injured, you know."

"It doesn't seem to be affecting your vital functions." She placed her hand on a strategic part of his anatomy and squeezed—not too hard, just enough.

"I think my heartbeat's just doubled." His voice was tight.

His breathing grew harsh. She leaned over and kissed him, caressing his tongue with her own, and stroked him rhythmically with her fingers. His arms came around her, and his impatient hands unhooked her bra, then smoothed up and down the length of her back. He murmured sweetly to her as he kissed her face, her neck, her shoulders, her arms. She closed her eyes and reveled in the husky incoherence of his voice, the loving touch of his knowing hands, the heat of his kisses, and the restless rocking of his hips beneath her questing hand.

She kissed his chest, brushing her open mouth across the smoothly curving muscle of his breast, the turgid warmth of his nipple, the rapid rise and fall of his belly, and the thin trickle of golden hair that led the way from his navel to his loins.

"Ohhh," she sighed, adoring him. She rested her cheek where her hand had been and kissed him intimately, inhaling his musky male scent.

He curled on his side and cradled her with his body, murmuring her name, touching her back, her hair, her arms, pushing down her panties so he could massage the smooth cheeks of her buttocks. Exploring further, he found the damp heat nestled between her thighs, and Ally's skin flushed with urgent desire.

She moved away from him long enough to sort through the pile of belongings he had left on the nightstand after emptying his pockets. She handed him one foil packet and started unwrapping the other herself.

"We only need one at a time," he whispered, pulling her closer. He massaged between her legs, making the ache there better and worse at the same time.

"Well, I read that . . ." She closed her eyes and inhaled sharply. *"Mmmm."*

"What?" His tongue was hot against her neck.

"That Dr. Ruth said that . . . *Oooh.*"

"What?" he whispered, slipping on the first condom.

"That if you use two . . . Oh, yes, *there* . . . Two condoms . . . Oh! Don't stop . . . You get . . ."

"Yes?" he asked silkily.

"Even more friction."

"Really?"

"Well, it's what I read." She pressed restlessly against him.

"Do you want to try it?" He grasped her buttocks and nestled intimately between her thighs.

"Do you?"

"I want to try *everything* with you." He stroked his hands up the sides of her torso. "But that's our last one until we get out of here. Maybe we should save it."

Their eyes locked. They kissed again. "Good idea," she murmured, unwilling to acknowledge the fears that his touch had temporarily banished.

"You feel good," he whispered. "So good."

She closed her eyes, drowning in the moment. "I want you."

"Now," he urged.

She straddled him, and with his hand supporting her hips, she lowered herself, sighing with relief when she felt him sink deeply inside her. "Ohhh. *More,*" she urged, pushing down, covering his hands with hers. He arched his hips toward her, pressing deep. Her head fell back, brown hair spilling around her shoulders in rumpled waves as she moved experimentally.

He groaned and guided her hips with his hands, watching her move above him like some love goddess from his most secret fantasies. They found the rhythm they wanted, and then their hands joined, holding on fiercely to each other as the whirlwind swept them away. They made it last a long time, writhing together in the ultimate erotic dance, letting their cries echo off the walls and ceiling, begging and praising each other without reserve. Ally was slick with sweat, panting with exhaustion, and trembling from her final, explosive climax when she finally collapsed against his chest, burying her face in his neck and hugging him tightly as he shuddered violently beneath her.

She lay limply atop him for some time, inhaling the scent of their union, knowing it would never be this way with anyone else. Despite the situation, she had never felt so happy in her life.

"Crazy," she murmured.

"Hmmm?" His hand stroked down her back.

"How do you feel?" She was worried about his head again.

"Great." His voice was rich with satisfaction. "You?"

"Mmmm. I feel like a Fourth of July sky."

"What?"

"We used to say that back home."

"It's a good expression." He kissed her brow. "That's *just* how I feel." After a brief pause, he added, "Only you make me feel that way, Ally."

"Oh, Chance." She rubbed her cheek against his chest. "You should get some rest."

"Mmmm."

"I wish I knew the best thing for a person to do after a blow to the head."

"Sex worked pretty well," he teased.

"A doctor would probably be horrified."

"Not Dr. Ruth."

She giggled. "Still, our only chance of escape is to get away from them after they open that door. So you should store up some strength."

"Now that you've depleted it."

"And I'll watch the door."

"No." He held her fast when she tried to move away. "Sleep with me."

"They might come back tonight. I should—"

"Sleep with me," he repeated. "Just for a bit."

Between her weariness and her desire to remain in his arms, she wasn't all that hard to convince. "Okay," she whispered. "Just for a bit."

The commotion in the hallway woke Ally. Chance had shut off the bedside light before falling asleep, so she fumbled in the windowless darkness, feeling clumsy and disoriented.

"What's going on?" Chance asked groggily, sitting up.

A shout and a scuffle were followed by a heavy thud, a grunt, and a few more heavy thuds.

"What *is* that?" Ally wondered, alternately trying to

find a light switch and her clothes. When she heard some-one fiddling with the lock on the door, she stopped wor-rying about the light and frantically felt around the bed for some clothing. The door swung open a moment later, catching both her and Chance in a ray of light from the hallway.

"Holy moly!"

"Harvey?" Ally was stunned into a temporary paralysis.

"They took your clothes?" Harvey asked.

"No, of course not."

There was a brief silence, followed by a snicker. *"Ohhh,* I see," Harvey said knowingly.

"Turn around," Chance snapped.

"Well, excuse *me.*" Harvey turned his back.

"Where's my dress?" Ally asked. "Where's the light? No, never mind the light. Where's my dress?"

"Here."

"I need my underwear," she added.

"Like, do you two have any idea that you're in a whole lot of danger?" Harvey sounded disgusted.

"What are you doing here?" Ally asked, slipping into her panties and bra. "No! Don't turn around! Just answer me."

"What time is it?" Chance asked. "Oh, God. My *head.*"

"Does it still hurt?"

"Where are *my* clothes?"

"What happened to the guard?" Ally asked. "How did you know we were locked in here?"

"Where's Wilson?" Chance asked, finding his clothes at last.

"Is there a light, Harvey? You can turn on the light now."

Harvey hit the light switch. Ally blinked and Chance swore. Harvey cast a glance at the bed, which they had fairly well torn apart. "I don't believe you guys," he said. Ally reddened.

"We've got to get out of here," Chance said, flushing.

A heavy thud made Ally jump a foot in the air. It sounded like someone in the next room had thrown a chair against the wall. It was followed by some muffled shouting.

"Hey! There's another prisoner!" Harvey said.

Ally gasped. "That's right! Just before we tried to escape, Chance, Wilson said something about putting us next door to the *other* guy. Remember?"

"Um . . ."

"Come on!"

They ran out into the hallway. Chance paused at Luther's recumbent form, found the guy's gun, checked the safety, and hid it in his baggy white trousers. Then he joined Harvey and Ally outside the door of the next room.

"The pass key should work on this one, too," Harvey said, fiddling with the lock.

"What did you hit that guard with?" Ally asked.

"A sockful of pennies. Didn't you ever see *Death Wish*?"

"Ouch." Chance winced in sympathy.

"That's a lot of pennies," Ally said. No wonder Harvey was jingling with every step.

"Yeah, well, a lot of people don't know how to tip," Harvey grumbled.

They flung open the door and rushed into the room.

"Dureau!" Chance stared at the man in disbelief. He certainly looked the worse for wear.

"What happened to you?" Ally asked. The whole left side of his face was bruised and puffy, his lip was split, and he looked like he hadn't shaved any more recently than Chance.

"The bellboys probably got sick of giving him receipts for his tips," Harvey guessed.

"My God! Was that you two in there?" Dureau demanded, looking at Chance and Ally. "I thought it was the guard and some bimbo."

Ally grew even redder. "Uh, no, it was us."

"Are you always that noisy? Don't your neighbors complain?"

"Never mind about that," Chance said irritably, his cheeks burning. "Did you and Wilson have a falling out? Is that why you're locked up in here?"

"A falling out?" Dureau winced and dabbed at his split lip. "No, my cover was blown. By *you*, I might add." He glared at Chance. "When you told him you'd caught me in his office, he figured out that I wasn't just an ordinary guest."

"Your *cover*?" Ally repeated.

"I'm with the Drug Enforcement Agency."

"DEA?"

"You're kidding me."

"Do you have some ID, mister?" Harvey asked skeptically.

"Of course not, you idiot. I'm undercover."

"I don't believe this." Chance sat down on the bed and held his head in his hands.

"What's this kid doing here?" Dureau demanded.

"Hey, this *kid* rescued us," Ally said, coming to Harvey's defense.

"I knew there'd be trouble," Harvey explained. "These guys attract it like honey draws flies."

"Now, wait a minute—" Chance began.

"So I tailed them."

"Even after Wilson caught us? Harvey! That was too dangerous! What did I tell you?" Ally chided.

"Yeah, yeah. Anyhow, I waited for the guard to nod off, then I crept up and—*wham*!" Chance winced again. "Only, he didn't keel over with the first blow. It took a few good whaps on the head to make him—"

"Please, no details," Chance pleaded, cradling his head.

"Who are you two?" Dureau asked. "FBI? IRS? Atlantic City Police?"

"No. I'm an actress, and he's a magician."

"That wasn't a cover?" Dureau sounded skeptical.

"What do you mean by that, buster?"

"Ally, please, not now," Chance said.

"But what are you doing here," Dureau demanded, "if you're just civilians?"

"You really don't know?"

"The last time I saw you," Dureau told Chance, "you had tailed Wilson to my suite. Then you disappeared. He couldn't pursue you without securing me first. I've been in here ever since then."

"Have they fed you?" Ally asked. "You know, they didn't feed us last night, and here it is, already after nine o'clock. Maybe they're trying to starve us all to death!"

"Miss Cannon, not now," Harvey chided.

"So were you operating undercover when I heard you talking about murder with Wilson?" Chance asked in confusion.

"No. I was already blown. We were talking about *my* murder."

"Rich people have the worst manners in the world," Ally said critically.

"But where does the necklace come in?" Chance asked. "That's really how we got involved in this mess." He briefly explained how Wilson had cast suspicion upon them, how they had escaped and hidden out, and why they had returned to the hotel. "We decided we had to discredit him ourselves."

"So where *does* the necklace come in?" Harvey repeated.

"Wilson's broke," Dureau began. "His enormous inheritance has been slipping through his fingers like water ever since his father died. We estimate that he's lost over seventy million dollars. Bad investments, stupid blunders, overindulgence, careless management."

"Wow." Ally couldn't even imagine that much money.

"So why did he spend a chunk of change to host this benefit weekend?" Chance asked.

"We suspect that the funds raised for homeless children this weekend will actually end up in Wilson's pocket."

"Oh, no." Ally felt sick. She sat down next to Chance.

"Why is the DEA interested in Wilson?" Chance asked.

"We have evidence that he has now added drug importation to his various activities."

"How does a blue blood get involved in that?"

"According to our informant, a high-ranking Mafia figure who's agreed to testify against his former associates, Wilson has been associated with the Corvino crime family—"

"Those guys in the news?" Harvey bleated.

"How did he even meet those people?" Ally wondered.

"When he decided to get involved in gambling," Chance guessed.

"They're his silent partners in the casino?" Harvey asked.

Dureau nodded. "And, apparently, rather than break every bone in his body when they found him pocketing some of their share—"

"Stupid," Ally muttered. "How stupid can you get?"

"—they made him a go-between in their drug trade."

"So if you nail him and get him to talk," Harvey said, "you can nail his contacts on both sides of the deal."

"Yes. And I get promoted," Dureau said reverently.

"Maybe then you could stop asking for receipts," Harvey suggested.

"The DEA requires a complete record of all of an agent's expenses while undercover."

"He's a government employee, all right," Chance said.

"We've got to get out of here," Dureau said.

"My thoughts exactly." Chance slid off the bed and took Ally's hand.

"But what's Wilson planning next? And how can we clear our names?" Ally asked.

"If I were Wilson," Dureau said, "and I had two fugitives and a DEA agent locked up, I know what I'd do." He paused dramatically before saying, "He'll want to make it look like you killed me. You're already a supposed dangerous criminal, after all."

Ally cleared her throat. "And what would happen to us?"

"Maybe he'll let you live and take the fall. But maybe he's afraid you'll talk and convince someone you've been

ʹframed. So, most likely, he'll have you gunned down after I'm dead."

"Could you use a hypothetical tense, please?" Ally requested.

"Let's get out of here," Chance said, dragging Ally out the door.

"Where are we?"

"The Blue Wing," Harvey said. "Over the casino. This whole part of the hotel has never been used. Couldn't pass inspection. Substandard wiring or something."

"And where's Wilson?" Ally asked.

"Cape May." Dureau brought up the rear as they followed Harvey back to the main section of the hotel.

"How do you know that?"

"His yacht party is today," Dureau said. "You asked how the diamonds are involved in all this. According to what I've pieced together by combining my discoveries with my informant's information, the Corvinos have instructed Wilson to pick up a small drug shipment, sort of a sample, from a potential new supplier. He's already spent the money he was supposed to use as payment, so he's going to trade the diamonds for the sample instead."

"Can this sample be worth as much as the diamonds?" Ally asked.

"I doubt it. I imagine that's why he's counting on the supplier being willing to accept them in place of cash," Dureau answered. "When Wilson realized he couldn't afford to keep the necklace, he insured it for its full value, which he hadn't been able to do when he originally acquired it; insurance companies don't take an IOU, no matter how blue your blood is."

"So he drugged Celine, who had no reason to suspect he'd do such a thing, and made it look like the necklace had been stolen," Chance murmured.

"Maybe Celine's in on it," Ally said.

"No, she's just another of his victims," Dureau replied.

"Oh."

"So, if his plan succeeds," Dureau continued, "he comes out okay; he can deliver the drug shipment to the

Corvinos, and he collects the insurance on the diamonds. Celine is the only one who really loses out, since the necklace was her birthday present, and he's not likely to buy her another one. Not the way his finances are crumbling.''

"So he might have killed you and pinned the blame on you for the theft," Chance guessed, "letting the diamonds remain forever unrecovered. But then Ally and I complicated things, and he wasn't sure who we were or how much we knew.''

"The deal's going down today. At the yacht party. That's where his contact will trade for the diamonds.''

"Who is his contact?''

"I don't know," Dureau admitted. "Half the people who were guests this weekend will be at the party.''

"Really?" said Harvey. "But that could be almost anybody.''

"Including my producer," Chance said bleakly.

"And my director," Ally added unhappily.

"Roland Houston is going?" Chance asked.

She nodded. "He told me at our meeting. Said he'd think things over there.''

"What things?" Dureau pounced.

"Whether or not I'm right for the part of Rainy in his next movie," she explained. "He's a hard man to win over. I just *know* I can play that part, Chance.''

"Of course you can.''

"I'm inside her head. I know what she—''

"Could we discuss your career plans at a more appropriate time?" Dureau suggested testily.

"So we're going to Cape May," Chance said.

"*You're* not going," Dureau said. "No civilians—''

"Forget it, Dureau. We're going," Chance said.

"No way.''

"Look, Miss Cannon and I can never have a normal life again unless Wilson is exposed. He has too much influence. And frankly, you've already screwed up once. I'm not going to bet all my chips on you.''

"Great minds think alike," Ally said.

"It's out of the question," Dureau said, as they finally emerged on one of the guest floors in the main section of the hotel. "You are remaining here if I have to lock you up myself. Meanwhile, *I* am going to call for backup. That is proper procedure."

"Bureaucrats," Harvey muttered.

"What floor are we on?" Ally asked Harvey.

"Twelfth. Don't worry about bumping into guests here. That Arab sheik rented the whole floor for himself and his wives."

Ally grunted. "That's probably why I couldn't get a separate room when we checked in."

"It didn't work out so badly," Chance reminded her.

"Shhh." Dureau motioned them all back against the wall as a door clicked open.

Sheik Nesib el Dheilan emerged from his suite, wearing a glorious white robe.

"Looks like Lawrence of Arabia," Harvey muttered.

The sheik crossed the hallway, and unlocked another door. Ally saw one of his wives greet him. Some sixth sense must have warned the man they were lurking nearby, for he whirled suddenly to confront them, hand on the hilt of his dagger.

When he recognized them, he relaxed. "You have come to offer me the woman at a reasonable price?" he guessed.

Chance hesitated for only a moment, then smiled beguilingly. "I think we can strike a bargain."

"What are you doing?" Ally growled.

"Bear with me. I think I've got a plan."

TWELVE

Twenty minutes later, Ally, Chance, Dureau, and Harvey slipped out of the hotel, confident that even their own mothers wouldn't have recognized them.

"I could be fired for letting civilians come along," Dureau complained. "In fact, that's the least of what could happen to me."

"Quit whining and straighten your veil," Ally chided. He had sulked about having to wear one of the women's costumes, but it was obvious that Chance was much too tall to pass for one of the sheik's wives.

"That sheik's got a pretty colorful vocabulary," Harvey said from beneath his heavy veil. He, too, was dressed as a wife, as was Ally.

Chance waved away the doorman outside the hotel and waited for Sheik Nesib el Dheilan's stretch limo to pull up. With some urging, the man had admitted that the chauffeur had been told he and his wives wanted to leave for Wilson's Cape May yacht party at precisely ten o'clock.

"This dagger is real," Ally said in amazement, examining the weapon attached to the belt Chance now wore, along with Sheik Nesib el Dheilan's robe and headgear.

"So's this gun." Chance examined the semiautomatic weapon he had taken off Luther's unconscious body. Harvey had really risked his life when he'd rescued them. They owed the kid a lot. That's why Chance hadn't had the heart to refuse to let him come along; Harvey wanted it so badly. Anyhow, he had promised to protect Ally with his life, and Chance was counting on him.

"You look very dashing, Chance," Ally said.

"Let's hope I also look unrecognizable."

"Between the stubble, the makeup, and the outfit, you don't look at all like yourself," she assured him. She had used the sheik's wives' impressive array of excellent cosmetics to make Chance look very unlike himself, if not precisely identical to the sheik. "We'll pass, if we're careful."

As Ally had said, great minds think alike. Once inside the sheik's suite, she had followed Chance's lead instinctively, taking the sheik and the two timid women by surprise. Harvey had readily assisted their efforts, while Dureau protested the whole time and kept demanding to know where Chance had gotten the gun. Chance had flatly refused to turn it over to him. Then Ally had herded the women into a dressing room, removed their clothing, and chosen an extra blanketlike outfit from their wardrobe. After delivering a brief feminist lecture to buoy their spirits and promising them they'd be released later that day, she had locked them inside the dressing room.

The sheik, despite his imaginative epithets and fierce expression, clearly considered a struggle beneath his dignity. Apologizing profusely, Harvey and Chance had locked him in the bathroom without much difficulty.

Chance didn't even want to think about how many more laws he had broken this morning.

"Here's the car," Ally murmured, seeing the opulent white limousine pull up before them. "Everyone remember what I told you. Stay in character."

Veiled and outwardly submissive, she, Dureau, and Harvey piled into the back of the car before the driver had a chance to assist them. Keeping his face hidden, Chance gestured to the chauffeur to forget the usual formalities and return to the driver's seat. Chance climbed into the car with his wives, closed the door behind him, and sat with his back to the driver. A moment later, they set off for Cape May. Chance glanced at the telephone and fervently hoped the chauffeur wouldn't want to speak to him about anything; the only Arabic he knew was words for food.

"Second part of the plan completed," Ally said with satisfaction. "I told you the driver wouldn't blink at the sudden appearance of another wife. *Men.*"

"Let's just hope your backup is in time, Dureau," Chance muttered.

"They'll be there. Now give me that gun."

"No. But I'll tell you what I will do." He unloaded it. "We'll scare them, but we're not going to hurt anybody."

"Don't be a fool. You can't go after them with an empty gun," Dureau snapped. "These people mean business."

"So do I," Chance said. "But Ally and I are in enough trouble without inadvertently shooting someone, even if a little thing like murder didn't bother us. And I'm no more inclined to put my fate in your hands, Dureau, than I was an hour ago."

"Give me the gun," Ally ordered. When Chance shook his head, she said, "Come on, you've got the dagger. Harvey's got his *Death Wish* thing. I need something."

"Dammit." He realized she was right. With a warning glare at Dureau, he handed her the gun and watched her conceal it within the voluminous folds of her robe.

They rode in silence for some time, Dureau clearly sulking while Harvey apparently snoozed a bit. Finally, unable to bear being confronted by three veiled figures who sat in total silence, Chance reached for Ally's hand. "You're awfully quiet," he said.

"I've just been thinking. After all my effort, if Roland Houston is Wilson's mysterious drug connection, I can forget about appearing in *Grass in Heaven.*"

"And if it's Ambrose Kettering, I can kiss my TV special good-bye."

She giggled after a moment.

"What?" he asked.

"Maybe we'll luck out. Maybe it'll turn out to be the Pollingsworth-Biddles."

He smiled. "Let's try not to drive ourselves crazy. It could be almost anyone, right?"

"Right." But there were two men who counted a little more than all the others.

When they arrived at the pier, Chance kept his face hidden and silently motioned for the chauffeur to go park the limo and hang out with the other chauffeurs. There was a bad moment when the driver spoke to him in Arabic, clearly asking a question. But apparently the poor fellow was accustomed to being ignored by his employer. An angry gesture and inarticulate growl from Chance had him scurrying back into the driver's seat, and he drove toward the parking area without a backward glance.

Dureau then left them to go find the Port Authority and, presumably, his backup assistance. Ally had feared that getting onto the yacht would be difficult, since Chance couldn't fool the sheik's friends up close. Luckily, however, Wilson's spaced-out son and one of his dippy stepdaughters had taken over greeting late arrivals of the party—which was already well under way—so Chance and his two veiled companions slipped past without arousing even a flutter of suspicion.

"You two stay here and keep out of trouble," Chance instructed in a whisper, guiding Harvey and Ally into a shadowy corner of the lower deck. "I'm going to track down Wilson. We don't know how soon this transaction is supposed to occur."

Ally reached for his arm, afraid of being overheard if she protested aloud, but he eluded her grasp and disappeared into the crowd. She stood silently with Harvey, shying away from any attempts to draw them into conversation. When a passing waiter offered them a selection of appetizers, Ally thought she would cry with hunger, but she had no idea how to eat without spilling food all over herself in this unwieldy costume. Anyhow, she could

hardly be ready to spring into action at any moment if her
hands were full of food. Wondering when she had last
eaten—Stinking Creek?—she reached discreetly inside her
robe and fingered the reassuring shape of the gun Chance
had given her. It rested inside the bodice of the baggy
white cleaning uniform she still wore.

"Yacht parties. Charity balls. Gala festivities. Don't the
rich ever have to work like the rest of us?" Harvey grumbled. "It's the middle of the week, for God's sake."

"Shhh." Ally was afraid they'd be overheard. The deck
beneath her feet jerked slightly. She gasped.

"What's that?" Harvey whispered.

"We're pulling away from the dock." She rolled her
eyes, disgusted that she hadn't foreseen this contingency.
It was a *yacht* party, after all. "Dammit, where are Dureau
and his people?"

"Bureaucrats," Harvey muttered.

"It's up to us now," Ally murmured.

Then, to her horror, Celine Wilson, looking wan and
sad from the loss of her beautiful necklace, espied them
and made a joyous exclamation. She rushed forward,
seized Ally's hands, and began speaking in French.

*"Mes amies! Vous etês bien arrivées! Je ne le savais
pas! Mais où est votre mari charmant?"*

After a terrible moment of blind fear, Ally did the only
thing she could think of. She doubled over coughing, as
if she had swallowed wrong upon attempting to respond.
This produced another unfortunate effect; it made Ally and
Harvey the center of everyone's attention. Ally had never
known anyone to be so concerned as Celine over a little
coughing fit, and she was forced to keep shaking her head
vehemently when Celine tried to guide her away, presumably to a private spot where she could remove her heavy
headdress and take a sip of water. Apparently hoping she
was finally recovered, Celine started questioning her in
French again, so she was forced to start coughing again.

Ally lost track of how much time passed while they
continued this farce. Finally she sat down in a little
wooden chair and pretended to be so embarrassed about

the whole incident that she couldn't even bear to look at
Celine. Harvey was forced to do the same thing when
Celine tried to speak to him. By the time they were left
alone and in peace, the shore seemed quite far away.

Where the devil was Chance?

It was damn hard to move around in those robes, and
attempting to be inconspicuous was absolutely hopeless.
Trying to avoid conversation and stay out of sight as much
as possible while simultaneously tailing Wilson was taking
all of Chance's concentration. He had a particularly bad
moment when Mrs. Pollingsworth-Biddle spotted him
from afar and called out loudly to him in twangy French.
He disappeared into the crowd and went onto the upper
deck, hoping to lose the woman and still keep his eye on
Wilson.

For once, Wilson wasn't acting the perfect host. Served
him right; he *should* look tense, nervous, and tired.
Chance thought sourly. No man had the right to frame
people, take them prisoner, plot their deaths, deal in
drugs, *and* look cheerful and well rested. When Chance
thought of how Ally had suffered during the past few
days, he wanted to throw Wilson overboard and let the
sharks have him.

He resisted the urge to abandon his vigil and go check
on Ally. As much as he instinctively wanted to guard her,
he knew that if anyone could handle herself in this situation, it was Alicia Cannon, actress, improviser, master of
disguise, and storyteller extraordinaire.

Chance smiled when random memories of the past few
days flashed through his mind: Ally flagging down a truck
on the road, juggling before the crowd in Dead Mare Hollow, wolfing down her food, making him hold still while
she altered his face with cheap makeup. Ally curled up
on a pile of damp straw in some old barn, dressed like a
cleaning lady, dressed in nothing at all. Ally slipping her
bra straps down her shoulders, leaning forward to kiss
him, sighing when he touched her intimately, sharing her-

self without reserve, making him feel he'd finally found what had been missing from his life.

"Ally," he whispered into the sea air, wishing they could just turn their backs on this mess and go away together. Well, maybe when it was all over. If it was what she wanted, too . . .

He forced himself to focus on the problem at hand again. When he saw Roland Houston, dressed like a refugee, conferring quietly with Wilson, his gut clenched. Please, he thought, for her sake, don't let it be Houston. For the first time, he felt more ambitious for someone else than for himself. He wanted Ally to have her film role. He wanted her to have it all.

Houston drifted casually away from Wilson—too casually? Chance frowned, wondering what had happened to Dureau. The yacht was getting farther from shore every minute, and no backup was in sight. Chance realized it was completely up to him and Ally now.

Mr. Pollingsworth-Biddle approached Wilson, shook his hand, and leaned over and said something in his ear. The two men laughed. Probably a dirty joke, Chance thought, kind of hoping Pollingsworth-Biddle was their man. He drifted away, too, and Wilson's smile grew more strained as other guests, most of them unfamiliar to Chance, surrounded him. When a crewman gave him a message some time later, he slipped away with obvious relief.

This must be it, Chance thought. Keeping his face lowered and avoiding people as much as possible, he followed Wilson below the main deck. However, forced to maintain a discreet distance, he quickly lost track of the man in the yacht's dark interior.

"This is no yacht," he muttered, looking at a dozen closed doors that lined the narrow passageway. "It's the bloody *QEII*."

Taking his chances, he eased open the first door on his left. Wilson was inside the small cabin, his back to the door. He was on the telephone, thanking someone for calling. He hung up a moment later and checked his watch. Chance closed the door and wondered where he should hide.

"Helmut! Helmut!" he heard Celine calling, then he heard her footsteps descending toward him. *"Tu es là-bas?"*

"Oui, chérie!" Helmut called wearily.

Chance whirled and slipped into the cabin directly across from Wilson's. The moment he closed the door behind him, his gaze locked with that of Ambrose Kettering.

Kettering backed up, so obviously trying to hide something behind him that he immediately drew attention to it. Chance's gaze went reflexively on an open briefcase containing a couple of hefty, plastic-wrapped bundles that, under the circumstances, could only be one thing.

"Oh, no." He felt utterly dejected.

Kettering blinked. "You're not the sheik." He frowned and peered more closely. "Chance?"

"Hi," Chance said weakly. He just had to use his head. Faced with this development, Ally would think of something. She was right; he should probably go to the movies more often, "I, uh . . ."

"Well, well! Pleasure to see you," Kettering boomed, closing the briefcase with a clumsy attempt as casualness. "Nice costume, kid, but I'm still leaning toward black leather."

"What's going on in here?" Wilson pushed the door open with such force that Chance, who was standing with his back to it, was flung straight into Kettering. By the time the two men had righted themselves, Wilson was pointing his gun right at Chance's belly.

"Helmut!" Ambrose clucked. "Is that really necessary? I can vouch for—"

"It's really necessary," Wilson answered. "He knows everything."

"Oh, I wouldn't say *everything*," Chance disclaimed.

"But far too much," Wilson said.

That took some of the hot air out of Kettering. "Dammit, Helmut, I've already spent money on this kid!"

"We've all had to cut our losses from time to time."

Kettering sighed and, to Chance's dismay, nodded. "Sorry, kid. Your act's not half-bad."

"Gee, thanks." He glared at Kettering while the man carefully took away the dagger that hung at his belt. "I really didn't want Wilson's contact to be you, but you know something? I've just realized that I'll be far better off with a different producer, anyhow."

"How optimistic you are," Wilson sneered.

"What are we gonna do with him?" Kettering asked Wilson.

"Our first concern is to find his partners."

"I'm alone," Chance said.

"Wrong again, Mr. Weal. I just received a phone call from Sheik Nesib el Dheilan, explaining that you and your friends have caused him to miss the party."

"How'd he get loose?" Chance asked. "And don't tell me that a maid found him when it was time to clean his room. I won't believe you."

Wilson's face contorted. "It's hard to get good help these days," he said defensively. "The sheik, who is known as a fearsome warrior in his own land, tore apart the bathroom door with his bare hands."

"Damn."

"And my wife has just informed me that one of *your* wives seems to be ill but won't accept any help. Miss Cannon, I presume. But who's with her?"

Deciding it was time to change the subject, Chance said, "Where are the diamonds, Wilson?"

"None of your business."

"What diamonds?" Kettering sounded confused.

"The one's he's going to try to pay you with," Chance said.

"Diamonds?" Kettering frowned. "No, no. I get paid in cash, kid."

"Not this time, Ambrose," Chance warned. "Just ask him."

"Well, Helmut?"

Wilson shifted uncomfortably. "I had intended to break

the news more gracefully than this, Ambrose, but . . . I'm having a little cash flow problem, so I thought you might accept Celine's necklace as payment.''

"No way. Do I look like a jeweler?"

"It's worth far more than the sum we agreed upon," Wilson insisted.

"We're *all* having cash flow problems," Kettering said without sympathy. "So don't piss me off, Helmut."

"Cash flow problems?" Chance said incredulously. "Is that what got you into this, Ambrose? You thought dealing in drugs was a reasonable solution to your *cash flow* problems? You thought *this*—" he gestured to the briefcase "—was a good way to recover from all the flops you produced, all those gambling debts you've been accruing, all the alimony and child support you're supposed to pay?"

"Can it, kid."

Chance shook his head in disgust. "Look at you jerks. Why don't you just sell off your assets?"

"I don't even *own* my assets anymore," Wilson snapped. "Now, Ambrose, just take a look." He pulled a velvet bundle out of the pocket of his blazer and unwrapped the necklace. It glittered brilliantly in the dim light, but Kettering was unmoved.

"I get cash or it's no deal. You think I get this stuff from Boy Scouts?" he snarled.

Chance interrupted them again, helping to escalate the argument. He was waiting for an opening, a chance to act. The most important thing now was to keep them away from Ally until help arrived.

Where was Dureau?

Having decided she couldn't bear to simply wait around any longer, Ally took Harvey by the hand and started looking for Chance. Her nerves were so raw that she nearly screamed when Roland Houston walked straight into her. He mumbled an apology and pressed a hand to his mouth, looking rather seasick.

"Okay, Mr. Weal is missing," Harvey said firmly when they failed to find him.

"Something's wrong," Ally was certain of it. Her belly clenched with fear. They had to find him. Deciding it was worth the risk, Ally started questioning the crew in heavily accented English. She finally found one lad who had seen the sheik go below about twenty minutes ago, Following his instructions, she and Harvey crept into a quiet, darkened passageway with a dozen closed doors. She heard angry voices coming from behind the first one.

"Why are they talking about Boy Scouts?" Harvey whispered.

"Get out of your robe," she ordered, realizing that Wilson and his contact must be in there. Where was Chance? The sound of his voice a moment later confirmed her worst fears. "We're going to have to move fast."

They quickly stripped down to their ordinary clothes—Harvey's bellboy uniform and Ally's cleaning dress. Then they checked their respective weapons. "I've got the gun. I'll go first," she whispered.

"Yeah, but my sock is loaded, and your gun isn't."

"They don't know that."

"Miss Cannon—"

The door cracked open. "We've got to find the others before they cause trouble," Wilson said from inside the cabin.

"Wait," Chance warned, stalling for time. "Don't you want to know about the bomb?"

"What bomb?" Wilson asked, hesitating.

It gave Ally the moment she needed. With a fierce war cry, which Harvey immediately emulated, she hurled through the door, knocking Wilson over. Everything seemed to happen at once then. There was a lot of shouting as four male bodies hurled wildly around Ally. Chance, hampered by his bulky costume, was struggling for Wilson's gun. Kettering—*Kettering!*—shot at Harvey, who dropped his sock. Pennies scattered all over the floor, causing Chance and Wilson to slip and fall.

"You should have tied that thing," Ally shouted.

"Not now, Miss Cannon," Harvey said, eyeing Kettering.

"Don't do it, Kettering," Ally warned, training her semiautomatic on him. "I'll blow you straight to hell."

Wilson lashed out a foot and, in the confines of the small cabin, tripped Harvey, who stumbled against Ally. "Yahh!" She fell against Kettering, and they both dropped their guns. Ally grabbed him by the hair—which, to her astonishment, turned out to be real after all. He grunted and gave her a hard shove, throwing her back into Harvey, then made a break for it while the rest of them flailed around on the floor.

"Get off me, Harvey!" Ally ordered. After a moment, she realized he was unconscious. That nasty cracking sound a moment ago must have been his skull hitting something. "Harvey!"

He gurgled when she shook him. Chance and Wilson scrambled after one of the three guns, which were all scattered across the floor now. "Go, go!" Chance shouted. "Get out of here, Ally!"

"Ow!" Harvey cried when she shook him again.

"Are you all right?"

"Get Kettering," Harvey rasped. "He never tips. . . ." His eyes rolled back in his head.

Ally picked up her gun. Spotting a glittering pile on the floor, she exclaimed, "The diamonds!" She scooped them up in her free hand and took off after Kettering.

"My diamonds!" Wilson screamed.

"*Arrgh!*" Chance turned green and collapsed when Wilson kicked him in the groin. He swiped at the man's leg and missed. Wilson grabbed his gun at last and followed Ally out the door. Struggling to his feet again, and trying not to trip on his robes, Chance went after them.

Up on deck, women swooned and men cried out when Kettering knocked them aside, closely pursued by Ally. She raised the gun and assumed the posture she had learned for her onetime role as a policewoman.

"Freeze, Kettering!"

He whirled to face her, but kept backing away. "You're

making a big mistake, Cannon. I'm a producer! You'll never work in this town again if you shoot me."

"Hold still or I'll turn you into Swiss cheese," she warned.

"Excellent," someone murmured. "That's excellent, Ally."

She risked a brief glance. *"Roland?"*

"That's Rainy to the core," he said admiringly. "But I thought you weren't coming to this party?"

"Put down the gun, Cannon, or you'll be sorry."

"Hands up, Kettering, or I'll shoot!"

A loud scream was her only warning. A moment later, Wilson barreled into her from behind. She squeezed the trigger when she lost her balance, and the gun went off. Ally screamed and dropped it.

"Ally!" Chance cried.

"You told me it wasn't loaded!" she screamed. "I've shot him!"

"You missed him by a mile. See?"

Pointing his gun at her, Wilson said, "Give me the diamonds, Miss Cannon."

Chance took them from her before she could comply. "Forget it, Wilson. It's all over now."

"Where *do* you get these clichés?" Wilson asked. "May I remind you who's the fugitive here? Give me the diamonds."

"Mes diamants! Mes bijoux!" Celine cried joyfully.

"That woman just doesn't have a clue, does she?" Ally muttered.

"Give them to me," Wilson ordered, raising his voice to be heard over the hysteria of the crowd.

"Forget it." Chance backed away.

"Aha!" There you are!" Harvey staggered through the crowd, holding the third gun. He trained it on Kettering. "Thought you could get away with it, didn't you?"

"I'm confused," Roland Houston bleated.

"I'm appalled," Mrs. Pollingsworth-Biddle sneered.

"Put down the gun and tell the truth, Wilson," Chance warned, "or I'll throw the diamonds overboard."

A horrified gasp passed through the enthralled crowd.

"Chance!" Ally was shocked.

"I'll shoot the woman," Wilson warned.

"No, you won't," Chance replied. Ally thought he sounded more confident than the circumstances warranted. "This is your last chance, Wilson. Put down the gun."

"Enough!" Wilson pulled the trigger. Nothing happened.

"That's *my* gun!" Ally cried.

Chance threw the diamonds overboard into a thousand feet of water. A dozen women screamed. Celine fainted. Ally looked up as helicopters flew overhead, drowning out the sound of Kettering's voice as he pleaded with Harvey, who looked demented. When Wilson made a dive for the loaded gun Ally had dropped on deck, Chance jumped him and finally, with great satisfaction, landed a knockout punch to his jaw.

Ally looked up at the helicopters. "The cavalry?"

"Dureau took his goddamn time about it, didn't he?"

Chance didn't care who was watching or what they thought. He swept Ally into his arms and kissed her as if there were no tomorrow.

THIRTEEN

Dureau's team apprehended Wilson and Kettering and took possession of the drugs in Kettering's briefcase. Dureau and several other men remained on board to take statements from the passengers. Chance, Ally, and Harvey were shown to another cabin belowdecks, where they could have a little privacy while Ally applied ice packs to the lump on Harvey's skull. He had refused to be evacuated to a hospital, afraid he might miss something. With her free hand, Ally held one of Chance's hands in a death grip, afraid to let him go for even a moment. She had come so close to losing him forever.

"How did you know Wilson had my gun?" she asked him.

He was still wearing the sheik's heavy white robes, although he had washed off the makeup and removed the headgear. He looked like himself, and Ally couldn't think of a better way to look. "It was a completely different make. Couldn't you tell?" She shook her head. He lovingly brushed a strand of hair away from her cheek. "Well, luckily it just didn't occur to him that we'd actually come on board with an unloaded gun. Not even after you screamed it at me right in front of him."

"I didn't mean to yell at you. I was a little distraught."

"It's all right." He kissed her. Again. It was at least the twentieth time he had kissed her in the last few minutes.

"Kiss me again," she sighed a moment later. "You haven't kissed me nearly enough yet."

"Ally, I want . . . I mean, do you feel the way—"

"Are you two at it again?" Dureau muttered, coming back into the cabin.

"I think it's love," Harvey said from beneath the ice pack covering most of his head.

"You're awake?" Chance flushed slightly.

"Go on," Harvey urged. "Kiss her again."

"Hold on a minute," Dureau ordered. "You've got a serious problem."

"You mean we're not cleared?" Ally asked weakly.

"Well, you'll be cleared of every charge except one."

"What's that?" Chance asked, his hand tightening over Ally's.

"Celine Wilson is having hysterics. She wants you locked up for the rest of your natural life."

"Because of Wilson?"

"No. Because you threw her necklace overboard."

"Oh, that." Chance waved a hand dismissively. "I can take care of that."

"You can?" Harvey, Dureau, and Ally all asked at once.

"Sure. I was just waiting for the TV crew to arrive. You *did* say that a news team was on its way, didn't you?"

"They just arrived, but—"

"Come on." He drew Ally to her feet, then helped Harvey rise.

"Chance, what are you up to?" Ally asked as he led them up to the main deck.

"I'm going to get the diamonds back."

"Uh, just one other thing, Miss Cannon," Dureau said.

"Yes?"

"I talked to O'Neal a few minutes ago. Did you really threaten a bouncer at the Wilson Palace Casino with a thirty-eight?"

"Oh, that. I can explain that."

"I certainly hope so."

Up on the main deck, it took nearly a half hour for Chance's scheme to unfold. Since the crew was accustomed to providing fresh seafood for Wilson whenever he relaxed on his yacht for a few days, it took them only fifteen minutes to catch a fish when Chance requested it. Titillated by his audacity under the circumstances, the television crew followed Chance's every move. Taking his fish and laying it out on a table, Chance asked the crowd for a large scarf or handkerchief. Ally was relieved when he accepted the first one proffered without employing his usual assortment of diverting tricks. He covered the fish with the scarf.

Ally recognized some of Chance's technique as he proceeded—the gestures that diverted everyone's attention, the casual conversation that distracted them—but she still didn't know what he intended. His promise to retrieve the diamonds, though, had everyone on board completely riveted, even Mrs. Pollingsworth-Biddle.

"Mrs. Wilson," Chance smiled charmingly at Celine, despite the woman's open hostility. "Would you care to assist me? They're your diamonds, after all."

"And probably all she'll have left by the time Wilson's trial is over," Harvey whispered to Ally.

"What do you need?" Celine asked sullenly.

"A knife."

"She's so lazy," Harvey muttered when Celine sent a servant to fetch a knife.

When it arrived, she handed it to Chance. *"Voici le couteau.* Now, where is my necklace?"

"Right inside of tonight's dinner. Do you like fish, Mrs. Wilson?"

"I . . ." She was left speechless a moment later, as were they all, when Chance revealed the missing necklace—which was inside the body of the fish he had just cut open.

"That's disgusting," Roland Houston said, looking green around the gills.

"Oh, I forgot. You're a strict vegetarian, aren't you?" Ally said. "Come away, Roland."

"Actually, I wanted to talk to you anyhow, Ally."

"Of course." She glanced over her shoulder at Chance and met his gaze briefly. He was practically being smothered by the spectators, who had all suddenly become ardent fans. Even Celine seemed to have forgiven him, for she clung to him like a burr now. Ally scowled at the woman and then asked Houston, "What did you want to discuss?"

Traveling back to Atlantic City in the backseat of Sheik Nesib el Dheilan's limousine, Chance remarked, "Dureau says the sheik has decided not to press charges."

"Good," Ally said, glad that they were alone for a change. Harvey had chosen to return to Atlantic City in Dureau's helicopter. The boy had already decided to drop out of college and become Chance's apprentice. Ally supposed it was inevitable. Growing tired of the chauffeur's nervous glances in the rearview mirror, she drew a curtain across the glass partition.

"The sheik has raised his offer for you, however," Chance teased. "Fifteen camels. I'm almost tempted."

"Hah!" She curled up against him. "I'm going to be worth much more than that soon. Houston has asked me to play Rainy in *Grass in Heaven*, and then he wants me to play the lead in his next film after that."

"Ally!"

"Seeing me chase people around with a gun apparently changed his mind about me."

"Whatever it takes," he murmured against her hair. "I'm so proud of you."

"I'm so proud of you," she responded. "And don't worry about losing the TV special. You're too good not to get another one."

"Dare I ask if you've revised your opinion about magicians?"

She kissed him warmly. "I've revised my opinion about *this* magician, anyhow. Chance, I love you."

"Ally," he whispered.

"Besides," she murmured a few minutes later, breathless and disheveled, "all that hocus-pocus did save my life."

"You were pretty amazing yourself." He started unbuttoning her baggy white dress.

"Not here." She cast a nervous glance at the curtain.

"He can't see or hear us," Chance assured her. She looked uncertain, so he said, "I guess I can wait till we get back to the Wilson Palace."

She blinked. "I thought we were just going to make a statement to O'Neal, get your car, and go home."

"Well . . . Celine has offered us use of the honeymoon suite, free of charge."

"But we just put her husband away!"

"I don't think she really minds, as long as she's got her necklace back."

"I'll never understand rich people." She nestled against him and said, "But I hate that hotel, Chance. I'll never feel safe there again. Not even after O'Neal arrests Luther and the other hired guns."

"Well, maybe we could check in at the hotel across the street. Lock the door, take a hot shower . . ."

"Together . . ." she murmured against his mouth.

"Order everything on the room-service menu . . ."

"Oh, yes."

"And spend the next few days in bed."

"I could handle that."

"Handle this." He drew her hand down to his body and sighed. "Hmmm, right there."

"We should call Monty and tell him the good news."

"About us?"

"That we're cleared."

"Maybe we could tell him more than that." She looked questioningly at him. "Could we tell him—" he shrugged "—that we're going to, you know . . ." He cleared his throat.

"What?"

"That we've decided to, um . . ."

"Chance?"

"Get married." His cheeks darkened slightly.

She smiled. "Are you proposing to me?"

"I'm trying," he admitted. "I haven't rehearsed, though."

"That's all right. You're doing very well."

"How well?"

She batted her lashes. "So well that I just don't see how I could say anything but yes." She hugged him. "Yes!"

He grinned; that slow, breath-stealing grin she loved so much. "I hope your father will be happy."

"He'll know I've chosen well this time," she assured him. "Besides, he . . . well, he really loves magic acts," she admitted.

"Aha!"

They kissed again. "Maybe we could put off seeing O'Neal till tomorrow," she suggested.

Chance stilled her questing hand when it slipped inside his robe. He glanced toward the shielding curtain. "I thought you said—"

"I just changed my mind."

"Oh. *Good.*"

"There is just one thing, Chance."

"What?" He finished unbuttoning her dress and stroked her warm skin.

"The diamonds. The ocean. The fish." She shook her head. "I just can't figure it out. How did you do it?"

"Misdirection. I made Wilson *think* I was throwing the diamonds into the water. So he panicked and lost control of himself long enough for—"

"But I *know* I saw you throw the necklace into the water!"

"Ahhh." He met her eyes, those extraordinary, expressive, blue-green eyes, which he would never get tired of looking into. "I'll explain it to you in detail after we're married. Fair enough?"

"But—" He kissed her, and a moment later she decided that explanations could indeed wait. The magic between them was more than enough for now.

SHARE THE FUN . . .
SHARE YOUR NEW-FOUND TREASURE!!

You don't want to let your new books out of your sight?
That's okay. Your friends can get their own. Order below.

No. 160 SLEIGHT OF HAND by Laura Resnick
Chance and Ally make sparks of the wrong kind—but the show must go on!

No. 67 CRYSTAL CLEAR by Cay David
Max could be the end of all Chrystal's dreams . . . or just the beginning!

No. 68 PROMISE OF PARADISE by Karen Lawton Barrett
Gabriel is surprised to find that Eden's beauty is not just skin deep.

No. 69 OCEAN OF DREAMS by Patricia Hagan
Is Jenny just another shipboard romance to Officer Kirk Moen?

No. 70 SUNDAY KIND OF LOVE by Lois Faye Dyer
Trace literally sweeps beautiful, ebony-haired Lily off her feet.

No. 71 ISLAND SECRETS by Darcy Rice
Chad has the power to take away Tucker's hard-earned independence.

No. 72 COMING HOME by Janis Reams Hudson
Clint always loved Lacey. Now Fate has given them another chance.

No. 73 KING'S RANSOM by Sharon Sala
Jesse was always like King's little sister. When did it all change?

No. 74 A MAN WORTH LOVING by Karen Rose Smith
Nate's middle name is 'freedom' . . . that is, until Shara comes along.

No. 75 RAINBOWS & LOVE SONGS by Catherine Sellers
Dan has more than one problem. One of them is named Kacy!

No. 76 ALWAYS ANNIE by Patty Copeland
Annie is down-to-earth and real . . . and Ted's never met anyone like her.

No. 78 TO LOVE A COWBOY by Laura Phillips
Dee is the dark-haired beauty that sends Nick reeling back to the past.

No. 79 SASSY LADY by Becky Barker
No matter how hard he tries, Curt can't seem to get away from Maggie.

No. 80 CRITIC'S CHOICE by Kathleen Yapp
Marlis can't do one thing right in front of her handsome houseguest.

No. 81 TUNE IN TOMORROW by Laura Michaels
Deke happily gave up life in the fast lane. Can Liz do the same?

No. 82 CALL BACK OUR YESTERDAYS by Phyllis Houseman
Michael comes to terms with his past with Laura by his side.

No. 83 ECHOES by Nancy Morse
Cathy comes home and finds love even better the second time around.

No. 84 FAIR WINDS by Helen Carras
Fate blows Eve into Vic's life and he finds he can't let her go.

No. 85 ONE SNOWY NIGHT by Ellen Moore
Randy catches Scarlett fever and he finds there's no cure.

No. 86 MAVERICK'S LADY by Linda Jenkins
Bentley considered herself worldly but she was not prepared for Reid.

No. 87 ALL THROUGH THE HOUSE by Janice Bartlett
Abigail is just doing her job but Nate blocks her every move.

No. 88 MORE THAN A MEMORY by Lois Faye Dyer
Cole and Melanie both still burn from the heat of that long ago summer.

No. 89 JUST ONE KISS by Carole Dean
Michael is Nikki's guardian angel and too handsome for his own good.

No. 90 HOLD BACK THE NIGHT by Sandra Steffen
Shane is a man with a mission and ready for anything . . . except Starr.

- -

Meteor Publishing Corporation
Dept. 793, P. O. Box 41820, Philadelphia, PA 19101-9828

Please send the books I've indicated below. Check or money order (U.S. Dollars only)—no cash, stamps or C.O.D.s (PA residents, add 6% sales tax). I am enclosing $2.95 plus 75¢ handling fee for *each* book ordered.

Total Amount Enclosed: $_____.

____ No. 160	____ No. 72	____ No. 79	____ No. 85
____ No. 67	____ No. 73	____ No. 80	____ No. 86
____ No. 68	____ No. 74	____ No. 81	____ No. 87
____ No. 69	____ No. 75	____ No. 82	____ No. 88
____ No. 70	____ No. 76	____ No. 83	____ No. 89
____ No. 71	____ No. 78	____ No. 84	____ No. 90

Please Print:

Name _____

Address _____ Apt. No. _____

City/State _____ Zip _____

Allow four to six weeks for delivery. Quantities limited.